The Pinnacle Club

by

Drew Thorn

Book 1 of The Sandy Powell Series

First Edition

THORNEBROOK LLC

THE PINNACLE CLUB

Copyright © 2019 Thornebrook, LLC

To request permissions, contact the publisher at awt@thornebrook.com

Paperback: 978-1-7352612-0-1
Ebook: 978-1-7352612-1-8

Library of Congress Control Number: 2020911379

First Paperback Edition June 2020
Cover Art by pro_ebookcovers

Thornebrook, LLC
827 W. Primrose Street
Springfield, MO 65807
www.thornebrook.com

THE PINNACLE CLUB

Many thanks to my partner in life, Judy for making this journey so amazing. Special thanks for your editing, smoothing and additions which made this a much much better novel.

To sign up for the Drew Thorn newsletter go to

https://www.thornebrook.com/sign-up-newsletter

To learn more about Drew Thorn go to

https://www.thornebrook.com/drew-thorn-1

THE PINNACLE CLUB

Special Thanks

I would like to offer special thanks to the restaurants I know and love for permission to use their names in this book. Please go and enjoy their incredible meals and mention the book.

L'Auberge Chez François
332 Springvale Rd, Great Falls, VA 22066

Charlie Gitto's
5226 Shaw Ave, St. Louis, MO 63110

Jimmy's Old Town Tavern
697 Spring St, Herndon, VA 20170

THE PINNACLE CLUB

Table of Contents

THE PINNACLE CLUB

THE PINNACLE CLUB

THE PINNACLE CLUB

Chapter 1   May 1916 – Beaumont, TX

For millions of years, the sun beat down upon the oceans and diatoms flourished grew and died. They drifted down to the seafloor like greasy snowflakes. Over the millennia they built up hundreds of feet deep. At some point, the oceans dried up and were covered with salt from the evaporating seawater. Time and pressure converted these decayed diatoms into oil representing millions of years of solar energy. The real power today in oil is in the people that control it and that power burns hotter than the sun.

It was a cool spring day in Beaumont, Texas, the weather almost as rare as the dinner about to be served. Malcolm Holden was a close personal friend of the McKinley's and while an unusual request, they were all too happy to oblige and vacate their home for the day. The McKinley's house was elegantly appointed in a distinctive Beaux-Arts Colonial style. The interior as stunning as the outside, with attention to every detail, ornate woodworking, Persian rugs, and graceful furnishings.

Holden had become a close friend with McKinley during the Spindletop oil discovery. McKinley and Holden both owned land at Spindletop and they had prospered drilling for oil in the salt dome. Malcolm Holden at 45, while wealthy beyond imagination, was everything people pictured of a wild cat oilman. At six foot one, he had broad shoulders and a narrow waist; his big hands could easily grab a four-foot wrench. His dark nearly black eyes gave the clear impression of a man who won the battles – not always fairly.

The planned dinner meeting was held in secret. Holden had brought his longtime butler, Cyrus and personal chef, Rene Petit as well as his sous chef. Petit a world-class French chef was busy in the kitchen pulling together another festive dinner. A constant stream of French expletives was emulating from the kitchen.

Holden, sipping a cup of strong rich coffee on the porch, was only mildly aware of the cool gentle breeze and the view of McKinley's gardens. While the flowers in bloom lent a wonderful fragrance to the air, Holden's thoughts were not on their aroma or, for that matter, the beautiful day, or the setting. His only thoughts were of propelling his company to even higher heights.

Over the past five years, the government had worked hard both through legislation and the courts to gut the monopoly he and a few others held over the oil business. Unfortunately, the government succeeded. The virtual monopoly

Holden and his business associates held had been gutted like a fish and their power to control prices was nearly gone.

Holden grimaced as he thought of the way oil prices used to swing before they were controlled, and he shook his head as he remembered the stories. In the 1860s Titusville, Pennsylvania oil had varied from fifty dollars to ten cents per barrel in part because there was no monopoly to control production. In 1900 with Spindletop pumping two million barrels a year the challenge was both price and creating new demand.

No doubt about it, Holden thought, a frown on his face, recreating the monopoly is key.

Holden expected Heinrick Schroder and Edward Walker to arrive shortly. He had confirmed that both had arrived in town, Heinrick earlier this week and Edward only yesterday. It had been a few years since they had seen each other, and today's meeting was risky due to the anti-trust lawsuits of the government.

Holden was immersed in his thoughts when he was interrupted by his butler, Cyrus, advising of Heinrick Schroder's arrival. Holden met Heinrick at the front door. Short and a bit stout Schroder always had a twinkle in his bright blue eyes. His eyes sparkled almost like blue opals. People often read him totally wrong, believing he was a really nice warm guy – he was not. Heinrick won his battles with his head, unlike Holden who often won them with his fists.

"Heinrick how was your trip?"

Heinrick looked Holden in the eye, "Great, I have a Pullman car so the journey while long was smooth and productive. I now have an office in Denver, so I stopped to see it and it was good to escape from Los Angles. It has been over a year since I visited my wells here at 'Swindletop' so your meeting was not only an interesting idea it was timely as well."

Malcolm thought how appropriate to use the nickname 'Swindletop' since so many deals, wells, and profits here were the result of honest men being swindled or fooled by men like themselves. Malcolm led Heinrick through the home, the ornate broad staircase prominent in the foyer and asked, "So you're sure no one followed you and no one but your driver knows of the meeting."

"Absolutely," said Schroder, "and Richard is not really my driver he is my personal bodyguard. No one else knows and I trust him with my life."

"Excellent, let's sit on the porch, the weather is delightful. Edward should be along shortly."

Heinrick and Malcolm had just settled into

comfortable caned high back chairs when Cyrus appeared, "May I prepare you a snack or perhaps something to drink."

Holden told Schroder, "My chef Rene is here preparing something for an early dinner so make certain you leave space."

Schroder thought for a moment and said to Cyrus, "I would like a muddled Bourbon old fashion with a touch of mint."

Holden thought a moment as well and said, "Cyrus make that two, the mint sounds like an interesting touch and will fit well with this bright weather."

Cyrus replied, "My pleasure sirs," and whisked off to the kitchen.

Holden and Schroder had first met here at the Spindletop dome over ten years ago. And today, they visited on the porch for over an hour, avoiding discussing business instead catching up as old friends do about travel, kids and in Heinrick's case grandkids.

The conversation moved on and Schroder mentioned the gift he brought for McKinney, a beautiful Quezal vase in a lily pattern. He described the deep iridescent finish and the pulled feather appearance in the finish on the vase. Holden nodded approvingly and described his gift, a large

Reed and Barton sterling silver punch bowl monogrammed for McKinley with matching monogrammed punch cups. At that moment, Cyrus appeared on the porch, "Excuse me, gentlemen, Mr. Walker has arrived."

Malcolm and Heinrick stood and moved through the house following Cyrus who opened the door just as Edward Walker was walking up the front steps. The three old friends greeted each other warmly, as Walker moved into the front foyer. Nearly six-foot-tall of slight build with piercing grey eyes, no one would guess he was only 58.

Edward said, "Malcolm I have a very large parcel in the coach for McKinley if you would be so kind as to ask your man to help my driver bring it up to the house."

"Of course," Malcolm replied. Just then Heinrick produced a whistle from his pocket and blew three short toots, his bodyguard Richard appeared nearly instantly from around the corner.

"Sir?"

"Richard if you would please assist Mr. Walker's driver in bringing up the package."

Walker added, "Please place it gently against the doorway to the parlor and use the greatest of care in handling it."

In a few moments, a beautiful wooden crate

about eight feet tall, five inches thick and nearly four feet wide was brought into the front entrance and carefully placed against the door jamb to the parlor. The crate was built of stunning mahogany wood and was a masterpiece in craftsmanship.

Holden and Schroder raised their eyebrows in surprise at the magnificent and large object as Holden asked, "Edward what have you brought?"

Edward replied, a slow smile coming over his face, "As you properly suggested, I brought a small gift for McKinley."

"The crate alone is gorgeous," remarked Schroder as he gazed at the mahogany box, "whatever it contains."

At that point Holden turned slightly and nodded to the driver and Richard, "Thank you, men," he said, "you may go now and join my men for a bite to eat. And see to it that we are not disturbed."

The two men nodded and left the foyer as Edward addressed his two friends.

"I recall being here a few years ago and thinking this home needs a front door to match the stunning interior. So," he grinned like a cat with a mouse, "I sent one of my trusted men to discretely obtain the dimensions of the door. Then I retained Louis Comfort Tiffany in New York to create the door with one of his stained-glass creations as the centerpiece. The challenge, of course, is the image must be stunning regardless of which way the light is shining unlike his masterpieces in churches where the light only shines in one direction. I am confident McKinley will love it."

"Well you have certainly topped our gifts, well done," said Heinrick, smiling and nodding in approval.

"Well done indeed Edward," Holden agreed, "I'm sure Mckinley will love it. And now, let's retire to the porch, shall we? Dinner will be served shortly."

Malcolm, Heinrick, and Edward moved through the house to the side porch and found that Cyrus had rearranged the chairs in a triangle. After the men had taken their seats, Cyrus took another drink order.

Holden said, "Gentlemen I have brought an absolutely stunning Scotch Whiskey I believe you will enjoy." Both agreed and Cyrus was off to prepare fresh drinks.

The men discussed Edward's trip from New York and gave brief family updates.

Cyrus returned with drinks and a box of cigars. He advised Holden that dinner would be ready in about 45 minutes and then left the men to their business.

Holden began, "Edward, Heinrick I want to thank you for each taking a long journey to meet. The past few years, ever since the breakup of our company by the Justice Department and Congress, I have felt we needed to find a way around the laws so we could work together again."

Heinrick injected, "I agree, I find it totally incredible that after all the money we paid those lousy politicians in Washington they still turned on us and ripped our industry apart."

Edward nodded, adding, "Those worthless bums, they're like leeches taking our money and not following through on their commitments to us. We need to find more trustworthy politicians to advance our agenda."

Malcolm continued, "The stark reality is you can never trust a politician and we will never get them to repeal the antitrust laws. I believe we have to focus on three things. First is supply, second is demand and lastly competition. If we control all three we can demand our price and reap the profits we deserve."

Edward thoughtfully added, "I think we also need to add transportation. Those railroads and teamsters are nothing but crooks. It's high time we take away their monopoly and the power to demand of us whatever price they see fit."

Heinrick injected, "That's a great idea Malcolm, but our hands are tied with the antitrust legislation. What's your plan to work around it?"

Malcolm had known this was the key question and had worked hard over the past several months on a plan of action.

"Heinrick, you're right this is key. I've thought about it a lot over the past several months and I think I've come up with the solution."

Henrick and Edward leaned in toward Malcolm as if to close ranks.

"Let's hear it," Henrick said.

"First, I have chosen the two of you because I trust you. We are all wealthy, ambitious and we have worked together in the past. We could all retire now but that's not who we are. I believe we need to create a new company, a joint company, equally divided, a private company outside the United States that can protect the interests of our public companies. This company will focus on the three things I mentioned and add transportation as Edward suggested. Together we control about forty percent of the oil business today and I believe we can once again dominate the business. However, if we truly compete with each other we will never dominate and never reap the profits that are possible."

Edward said, "Malcolm, I agree with your outcome, your goals, but we are prohibited by the new laws from working together. We know Justice and now the FTC is watching to see if we try to bypass the law. They have too many investigators and the power of the courts to take us down. How do you suggest we avoid the Justice Department?"

Malcolm replied, "Obviously this new company needs to be invisible, completely covert."

Heinrick interrupted, nodding slowly, "the new company has to be very small, too many tongues and one will leak. We can only hire people we can trust."

"Or ultimately control," added Edward, his eyes and tone making it clear what was meant by 'ultimately'.

Malcolm resumed his thoughts, "Let's discuss each area and what we can do to affect things to our benefit. First supply. I believe there is still a lot of oil here at Spindletop even though production has decreased the past few years."

Edward raised his eyebrows and questioned, "Malcolm there must be some basis for your thoughts?"

Malcolm nodded. "I have discretely pulled together information from many of the wells and asked one of my men to plot it for us." He pulled out several maps from his valise. "If you look at these maps you will see some patterns."

He spread the first map on the table between them. The map showed the extent of the Spindletop wells and who owned what. The three companies, controlled by them were highlighted with colors. "I added the color after my man drew the map."

Then he laid out a map showing production five years previous with graduation for production by well. "You can see it clearly shows the center of production and the shape of the core reservoir."

Next, he laid out a map of three years prior showing production had shifted south and the shape had changed. Many of their wells were on the fringe of the new core where they had been centered in the past.

Then he produced last year's map and again the shape changed and an old well out of the core showed high production.

Heinrick spotted the anomaly and asked, "Malcolm, what is this odd well?"

"Good catch, that is an old well they pushed deeper, down over 2,500 feet and they hit boundless quantities, almost another gusher. My thought is there is a lot more oil, but we have to drill deeper – much deeper. I think if we continue to pump our existing wells and, at the same time, drill new wells alongside our existing wells to this new depth, there is a whole new deposit sitting below. From what I have learned they drilled through shale before hitting this new deposit. I believe this could be a cap on the new deposit. I think we should move now to buy up the fading wells while the price is down. If we are patient and keep this quiet for say ten years, then we will own this new deposit. We can do it through shadow companies, so the wildcatters don't suspect anything."

Heinrick pointed out, "Once the wildcatters hear of this discovery, they will demand a fortune for their wells even though the wells are declining."

Malcolm frowned, nodded and said harshly, "I have seen to it this well almost ceased production. We drugged my men at the well one night several months ago; they thought it was bad beer. We inserted a restrictor down the well. They all believe they found a tiny pocket. The wildcatters can't afford to risk the cost to drill that deep. Remember they just want easy money."

Malcolm produced another map, like the first showing what they owned and suggesting where the three could purchase more property or mineral rights.

Edward had to ask, "Malcolm, this is all very

impressive but why share it with us? You could afford to buy it all on your own."

Malcolm sat back in this chair as did the other men. "You are correct, I could, but I firmly believe if we keep competing with each other it will be our downfall. As I said when we started this conversation, we can only win if we trust and share with each other in secret. Together we will truly become rich beyond our imaginations and we will control our destinies."

Edward added, "I agree, this is a good plan for Spindletop. We'll reap fortunes. But to really expand and keep things flowing we must find other even better sources.

Heinrick replied, "My friends, we are beginning to pull significant oil out of our wells near Los Angeles and I think we have discovered another Spindletop in Wyoming near Casper."

"Great news," said Edward, "let's buy up the property and capture the supply before we get a bunch of wildcatters sucking off the easy money and pushing the price down. Heinrick can you have your men draw up maps as Malcolm has done?"

"Of course," said Heinrick, "but there is a hitch in Wyoming. The government owns the land and the mineral rights. In fact, the Navy controls it and says it essential for national defense."

"When I am back east, I'll push the Secretary of the Interior to take control over the Navy, it is their land. I am sure some money spread around Interior will grease the skids because traditionally that's a very greasy organization."

Malcolm added a thought to the conversation, "Gentlemen we also must consider foreign opportunities for supply."

"Agreed," said Heinrick, "in fact, I have been pursuing a few ventures in Germany and Baku near the Caspian Sea. They have some interesting new developments we should pursue."

Edward piped in, "We have been having good fortune with wells in Persia, I will get both of you some information on those wells."

Malcolm put his hands up, "my friends I believe we have covered the big issues on supply, we will come back to all of this later but let's discuss demand."

Heinrick raised his hands. "As I was about to say, one of the interesting developments from Europe is the distillation of crude oil. We know the light sweet in Pennsylvania can be used almost out of the ground but the oil in Europe is not of the same quality. They call the process refining and essentially have built large stills similar to what is used for whiskey. They separate the oil into various components but with much more control then we have here. The result is they have many different products to sell, increasing the value of each barrel of crude.

Edward always patient but on-point said, "I stopped on my way here and met with Henry Ford. His model T and similar horseless carriages are beginning to sell, and they run on gasoline. I remember when we used to dump it in the river in Pennsylvania back when we made kerosene for lamps. We discussed his plans in some detail and he certainly has a passion for success. I invested $100,000 with Ford in exchange for stock to help prop up his growing company. If he can continue to build cars as cheap as he suggests they will all need gasoline."

Malcolm added, "I have been very pleased with my horseless carriage, simple, easy and at least as comfortable as a horse-drawn coach. I agree if he can build them as cheap as he says everyone will want one and will be able to afford it."

Edward thought for a moment, "There are several other fledgling companies trying to build autos. Why don't each of you support a company, you know how we believe in competition," they all laughed.

Malcolm said, "Cars are a potential demand, but

we also need to look at some large potential users today, such as the railroads, shipping, and the Navy.

"Railroads are switching rather quickly from coal to oil and we are seeing increased use of kerosene for city lights. I believe the key is to split the crude into a number of components and create markets for all of it. Done right we can increase the profit from each barrel through the roof," said Heinrick.

Cyrus approached the men on the porch, "My apologies gentlemen for the interruption but dinner is served, in the breakfast room."

The men arose and entered the house. Edward said, "Malcolm, it's odd that we are taking dinner in the breakfast room rather than the dining room."

Malcolm replied, "I understand your thought, however, I believe the breakfast room more elegant and more appropriate. It's a bit smaller than the dining room."

"I knew you had a good reason, as always," said Edward, nodding his approval and understanding.

The men took their seats and the first course of deviled quail's eggs was presented.

"Let's continue the discussion on autos," said Edward, "we will need establishments where people can purchase gasoline for their autos. I thought we could supply gasoline to the stores selling automobiles.

Malcolm interrupted, "I want to go back to supply issues for a moment. We have all seen the glut of oil from Spindletop push the price down; I believe we have to reduce production when the price drops too low."

Heinrick added, "Good point but we all know the wildcatters will just pump oil out of their wells and we lose."

"True enough but we can certainly disrupt some of their production, not ours," said Holden, "I think we need to knock some heads and maybe have a few fires. We all know how exciting it is to watch a derrick on fire – especially when it is not one of ours," the men all chuckled.

"Alright, we will let you organize it, Malcolm," said Heinrick.

"Now the most important leg of the table," Malcolm continued, "my biggest concern is competition. I see it in two ways. First is, of course, other oil companies and second is other forms of energy. I think we have a compelling case against coal for transport, such as rail, ships and of course autos. But electricity and city lights are still using coal and coal gas. There is talk about building more dams to create electricity. All of these threaten demand.

Heinrick said, "Some of this we can overcome with a steady supply and a solid business proposition. Oil is so much cleaner. We can assure our markets of supply and at the same time create problems in what others supply. In the end, we benefit."

Edward nodded and spoke thoughtfully, "Agreed, my concern is the unknown sources of energy. There are bound to be new inventions. If we can disrupt them early, it will be much less expensive than competing with them after they are established."

"Ok, I think we agree on the competitive nature," Malcolm began, "and we will disrupt where we can and be ever watchful. Now let's discuss transport. Edward's point earlier about the teamsters and railroads is exactly right. I have an idea for the railroads, but the teamsters are a growing problem. If we continue to switch the railroads from coal to oil, they will be in our control so I believe we do what we can to support their rapid conversion to oil. I suggest we focus on the railroads that haul our oil. The problem with their fees and cost will go away in a few years. Thoughts on the teamsters?"

Heinrick nodded. "Do you remember the pipeline we installed in Titusville? It certainly put the teamsters in their place. We pumped the oil down to the barges and bypassed them completely".

"Oh yes, right up until they busted the pipeline," said Edward, frowning. "I think we have to work with Congress to stop the teamsters."

"Those politicians won't help us," said Malcolm rather hotly, "I think Heinrick is right – build more pipelines and bring rail lines to the wells is the answer."

The conversation slowed a bit as the men enjoyed a delicious dinner of parsnip soup, duck a l 'orange, imported cheeses and classic vanilla crème brulee with a touch of mint. Fine wines were paired with each course.

After dinner, they continued their discussion with brandy and cigars on the porch. They talked at length about the division of tasks, funding and forming the new company. Just as they were planning how they would divide the country between their public companies for sales and marketing, they were interrupted by Richard, Edward's security guard.

"Excuse me, sir," said Richard, "we caught a reporter from the Beaumont Enterprise sneaking up on the house. We took him out and he is bound and gagged."

Edward asked, "How much does he know?"

"It would appear, nothing sir, he never got close enough to the house to see or hear anything."

Malcolm interrupted, "Edward, obviously he was on to something by the fact he was here." Then turning and looking straight into Richard's eyes he said sternly, "I suggest you gents dispose of him but make it look like an accident. We will all be ready to leave shortly so you can bring him and his horse and dump the body close to town – far away from here."

Edward added, "Tell the others we will be ready to leave shortly."

Richard nodded and disappeared as quickly as he had arrived.

"Well gents it has been wonderful, and I believe a very profitable afternoon and evening," said Malcolm, "again I want to thank you for traveling so far. What do you suggest we name our new venture?"

Edward replied, "How about the Pinnacle Club, we are at the top of the game, and it is a very private club."

"Perfect," said Heinrick. They all clicked their

brandy snifters and said: "To the Pinnacle Club."

The gentlemen stood up, shook hands and agreed to stay in touch through secret channels. A meeting in a year was agreed unless something more urgent required quicker attention.

Chapter 2   May 2015 – Fairfax, VA

Sandy Powell woke up a few minutes before 5:30 a.m. like every other morning. A crisp spring breeze was wafting through the open windows. He swung out of bed, though some might describe it as a lurch, only to almost step on Copper his golden retriever.

"Copper," he said in an exasperated tone, shaking his head but smiling at his faithful companion, "you have to find a better spot. What's wrong with your dog bed?"

He leaned his tall, handsome, strong 6' 1" frame over to rub Copper's ears. A former Navy SEAL turned high school biology teacher, Sandy loved his life. Great house and location, fun and interesting job that was stimulating, and of course his wonderful companion, Copper. He smiled at these thoughts and his blue eyes twinkled as he was off to the kitchen to make a strong pot of coffee and his routine morning call.

"Good morning mate," said Sandy over his Skype phone, "how are you tonight."

Sandy's best friend Jackson replied, "well you know just another fall day here in Australia, to translate to Fahrenheit for you Yanks, a cool 75 degrees, a bit of moon and sitting on the back deck by the pool."

"Nice here too, cool light breeze, almost fell over Copper when I got up."

"Any other exciting plans for today?" Jackson chuckled at his best friend's recanting of the familiar morning routine.

"Well, I am off to see Aunt Beth today. She called this week and asked me to stop by. I may go downtown tonight."

"From Aunt Beth to downtown in one day..." Jackson teased. "You know I'll expect a full report when you call tomorrow – especially about the downtown adventures."

"You got it," Sandy said smiling at his old buddy's interest in his social life – or maybe lack of... he thought a bit ruefully. "How about you?"

"Well today, I went into Sydney, down to the Rocks. You will remember that old small pub on George Street, the oldest Pub in Sydney? I met up there with some old mates from the service. Plan to do a bit of surfing tomorrow over at Merewether Beach. There's a nice right to left break and the swells have been good this week. Plenty of cute gals as well."

"I swear that is all you Aussie boys do is surf. Well, I have to get my morning run in and then off to Aunt Beth's. Have a great sleep, my friend."

"Thanks, mate, you have a great day too. Say hi to Aunt Beth for me," and Jackson signed off.

Sandy lived in a traditional split-level home in Fairfax, Virginia, a Washington, D.C. suburb. It was comfortable and in a great location. As normal, he and Copper started their day with a morning run in Mantua Park that was immediately behind his house. Then, after a shower for Sandy and breakfast for both, they were ready to hit the road.

"Copper are you ready for a road trip to see Aunt Beth?" asked Sandy, "Let's take the convertible." The 2014 Mazda RX-8 convertible technically did not exist, but Sandy had pulled a few strings through a friend in Hiroshima who acquired parts from a prototype. Last winter Sandy did the conversion and now he had a one of a kind. When he completed the conversion, he completely repainted the car a deep metallic blue with sporty yellow pinstriping. It was fast, sleek but not gaudy. He loved this car.

They jumped in the car and were soon off to Aunt Beth's home in Great Falls about 15 miles away. The Mazda purred down the road and snaked through the rolling corners on Trap Road. "Copper," Sandy sighed contentedly, "this car is so much fun to drive, it's like it's on rails." But Copper didn't reply, not even with his soft, 'woof' sound of agreement. Instead, he was standing on the seat with his head out the side window smelling a million scents and loving the rushing air. Sandy glanced at his dog, smiled and thought how lucky he was to have such a great life.

Aunt Beth's turn of the century farmhouse was on the right side of a long gravel lane. The white two-story house had black shutters and a full-size porch that ran the entire width of the front of the house. Several red barns and outbuildings were behind the house. Sandy pulled in the gravel drive and spotted Aunt Beth tending one of the flower beds alongside the house. As soon as the car slowed Copper leaped over the door and rushed over to Aunt Beth. Sandy ambled over while Copper, having already exchanged greetings, was off to discover rabbits and squirrels and any other potential playmates around the barns.

Sandy greeted Aunt Beth with a warm but gentle hug. Aunt Beth had the family blue-green eyes, a slight frame and at 72 was quite spry. "Aunt Beth you are looking well, and the yard is neat as a pin as always."

"Sandy, how about a cup of coffee while I enjoy a cup of tea? Let's go into the house and sit for a while, it feels a bit chilly."

Sandy thought this odd as the day was warming but he nodded and whistled as Copper joined them on their way to the back door. The kitchen had been remodeled several years ago so it was modern and airy with a small table.

"Sandy," Aunt Beth smiled a bit sadly as she looked into his face, "why don't you take a seat while I put on the kettle."

Sandy nodded and initially thought as much as he loved his Aunt, he had to prepare his mind for her instant coffee. It reminded him of his days in the service eating MREs. You did what you had to do.

As he looked down, Sandy saw Robert Frost's, 'The Road Not Taken' on the table. He picked it up and began to read.

Aunt Beth noticed and said, "That was Papa's absolute favorite poem. He used to read it to us at least once a week when we went to bed."

Sandy nodded as she put the mug of coffee down in front of him. "I always liked this piece too," he said, smiling a bit stiffly as he prepared to take his first sip of the brew.

Aunt Beth nodded, "how about some cookies? Homemade Snickerdoodles."

Copper rested on the floor close to Sandy's feet eagerly watching Aunt Beth prepare the plate of cookies.

Sandy laughed. "My favorites – and..."

"And if one happens to break up and fall on the floor for Copper," Aunt Beth grinned

"That would be just fine," Sandy completed the thought.

After that, Aunt Beth sat down with her tea Sandy started giving her updates about his students and activities at the school where he taught.

Aunt Beth, normally full of interest in her nephew's activities, seemed distant – with something else on her mind.

"Aunt Beth are you ok, you seem a bit tired."

"Well, to be honest," she looked him in the eye and said as calmly as possible, "my doctor discovered I have cancer and it seems to explain why I have been a bit tired and peeked of late."

"My goodness Aunt Beth, what did he say."

"Well you know me with doctors, I don't follow much of what they say and try to avoid them, but it is some kind of bone cancer. Unfortunately, it seems to have spread all throughout my body, and he felt it was untreatable. He said I have a few months."

Sandy was moved, almost to tears. It seemed hard to believe his Aunt Beth, with whom he had always been close, might not be around much longer. She had been there for him, had provided great advice when he was transferred to the Pentagon and then followed her footsteps into teaching. "How can I help?"

"You are too sweet," she smiled warmly, "if you could mow the lawn and do a few odd chores about the farm today, that would be a huge help."

Sandy spent the rest of the day working around the farm, mowing, trimming and pulling some weeds. Aunt Beth tired early but Sandy and Copper kept going and it was past five when they said good-bye to Aunt Beth, giving her a long hug and promising to come back very soon.

Sandy put the top up on the Mazda before he left as the day had turned a bit cooler.

He thought a bit about how he missed his dad who had died in an auto accident about five years ago, now Aunt Beth would be gone soon too. Then it would be just his mom left since he had no siblings. He sighed and decided he needed to get out to St. Louis more often to visit his mother – to spend more time with her while he could.

Over the next few months, Aunt Beth's health continued to deteriorate. True to his word, Sandy spent more and more time helping her. During their visits, she told him stories about when she and Sandy's dad grew up. Many of her stories focused on his grandfather and his inventions. She also told Sandy that Grandpa had secrets, but she never would say anything further.

Finally, the pain and the tiredness became too much, and Aunt Beth had to be put in a hospice in Reston. In the last few weeks, she mostly slept. One day in July, Sandy received the call he knew would come but dreaded the thought that Aunt Beth was gone.

The memorial was a beautiful service with so many friends and many of Aunt Beth's former students attending. Aunt Beth was interned with her parents in the Episcopal Cemetery in Great Falls. The one bright note in all of this was that Sandy got to spend some time with his mom who made the trip from St. Louis to honor and remember her sister-in-law. He also got to see many other relatives, some of whom he had not seen for years.

After everyone left, life settled back to a sense of normality for Sandy with a new regular routine. On the weekend he and Copper would drive to the farm, mow, weed and check on the house and barns generally keeping things up as Aunt Beth had for so many years. Then, about three weeks after the funeral Sandy got a call from an attorney informing him that Aunt Beth had included him in her will and asked if he would like to attend a reading of the will on Friday.

"Of course," Sandy responded, "Just give me the details."

Friday dawned and Sandy joined several people in the conference room of Waldon & Sutter's office in Reston. Aunt Beth's lawyer, Gary Sutter, entered the conference room and advised the others of their portion of the estate. She had left generous amounts to the Great Falls garden club, two close friends and the Great Falls high school where she had taught for forty years. He then informed them that those who already received the information on their bequests would have to leave as the balance of the will was intended only for Sandy. Thanks and condolences were offered to Sandy for Aunt Beth's life and generosity.

Gary and Sandy took their seats again. Gary advised Sandy that Aunt Beth had left the balance of the estate solely to him. Sandy was beginning to think of her old furnishings and things about the barn and realized that the extent of her holdings was unknown to him.

"Mr. Powell you will receive the farm, about 60 acres, house, and all the contents. There is no mortgage. After the distribution of the funds to the others, you will receive approximately $270,000 in cash, stock, and insurance benefits. Your Aunt Beth further instructed us to provide complete assistance to you with the transfers and any tax issues.

Sandy was floored; he could not believe what was happening.

"Sandy, Aunt Beth also left you an envelope with clear instructions that you are to read this in private; I can step out of the room if you wish."

"No, no I can read this when I get home." Sandy took the envelope and thanked Sutter for his assistance. He was still in a bit of a daze as he returned home.

Chapter 3   July 1933 – Troy, NY

Dick Powell was a natural inventor. His inquisitive mind was constantly getting him into trouble growing up on a small hill farm outside of Manchester, Vermont. Since he was 10 years old Dick had worked odd jobs on neighboring farms and at the sawmill in Shaftsbury a few miles from home. Despite being the height of the Great Depression, Dick always found an odd job to make a few dimes. People liked having Dick work for them; he was responsible, very bright and most of all he worked hard. Dick had always dreamed of going to college and saved every penny. He was very fortunate to submit a paper for a state-wide scholarship and won. It was a huge scholarship of four hundred dollars a year for all four years. Dick's Dad said he could scrape together $100 per year but Dick would have to fill in the difference.

Dick applied to Rensselaer Polytechnic Institute in Troy, New York and was accepted. RPI, an all men's engineering school, was one of the best in the world. The tuition at RPI was $600. Throw in books, fees, along with room and board and all it added up to about $1000 per year, an awfully large amount of money in 1933. Dick had saved enough so that with his scholarship and his Dad's help he could make it the first year. He knew he would need to find a job and really squeeze each penny and nickel – but he was off to college.

During Dick's first year at RPI, two amazing things happened. First, he met Mary Collins, and then he met Captain Scott, both would change his life forever.

Mary Collins was attending nearby Russell Sage College for women and they met at a dance, one of the co-ed activities sponsored jointly by their colleges. From his first glance, Dick was history. Mary was tall with reddish-blonde hair and green eyes. Just looking at her you knew there was some Irish blood in her veins even though she was from Cincinnati, Ohio. They dated regularly and the relationship blossomed.

The second significant event was when Dick was introduced to Captain Scott (retired) by one of his professors. Captain Scott was a career Navy officer who had recently retired and moved back home near Troy. Captain Scott had accepted a teaching position at RPI, teaching classes in the chemistry of munitions. At 62 years old, Scott had bright brown eyes, always had a pipe in hand and wore wire-rim glasses. His dirty blond hair was clipped short but he had a full head of hair. Scott always walked and sat erect – you knew he was military. Captain Scott became Dick Powell's informal mentor.

Scott was suitably impressed with Dick's brilliance and his Vermont farm work ethic. He also came to realize that Dick was financially stretched. In a meeting one afternoon Scott said, "Dick I would like to suggest an alternative career path for you."

"Captain, if you have a suggestion, I certainly welcome your advice."

"Dick the Navy is always seeking brilliant people. I have senior contacts, and, with your permission, I would like to put forward your name and see if the Navy might support your studies in exchange for a commitment."

"Captain that would be truly miraculous as I still don't know how I will raise the funds to pay for next year.

Before he knew it, Dick had joined the Navy and he spent his summers learning the Navy life. Although his school days and nights were full of study, Dick spent every free moment with Mary. They became inseparable and while Dick felt he spent four years convincing Mary, in her mind, he was her one and only. Mary, too, had known from the start that he was the only one for her and that she would spend the rest of her years as his biggest champion.

Chapter 4 September 1949 – Houston, TX

A warm very muggy evening in 1949, three old friends gathered for dinner in a small Italian restaurant in Houston, Texas. Other than the waitstaff and chefs they were the only patrons. Strategically placed around the perimeter were security guards dressed in plainclothes. Personal bodyguards were inside. This dinner like so many in the past was not happening.

John Whitney, Cordell Davidson, and Buck Weekes were now in control of the three largest oil companies in the world. Their reach was global, their power immense. Each company was a household name, and publicly appeared to be fierce competitors. While in secret, they continued to plan and operate as one large firm.

John Whitney, 5'9" with an average build, had brown eyes and a neat haircut. He looked every bit the corporate executive he was. Running the global operations of American Petroleum demanded his constant attention as the new property, mineral rights and companies were acquired by the company. The company had expanded operations by licensing dealers throughout the middle of the US and had subsidiaries beginning to form in the rubble of Europe. "Cordell and Buck, it is always too long since I saw you last. It's a shame we can't get together more often, more openly. Roughly 35 years ago our founders started what we have come to know as the Pinnacle Club and here we are again celebrating success, telling war stories and planning the future."

Buck Weekes, on the other hand, was every bit a Texas oilman as his father-in-law Heinrich Schroder was German. He was tall, lank with strong hands, and though living now in Los Angeles, his roots would always be Texan. Buck had met Heidrich's daughter, Heidi, at a party in Beaufort. While most would think Weeks should be working on an oil rig, he was actually a brilliant strategist, who had a nose for finding oil. Like American Petroleum, Sunco Power was global and very profitable for its stockholders. Sunco marketed gasoline and oil products both through franchises and company-owned stations. Weeks liked the fact that he controlled his retail chain. His operations ran on the West Coast from top to bottom from Mexico to Canada. He also had operations covering half of Canada. In some states, he and Whitney's company competed fiercely though, in reality, it was all a ruse to keep the Justice Department out of their hair. Buck leaned forward and said, "John you are right we have done very well."

Cordell Davidson ran TXO out of New York City.

Like the others, operations were global and TXO's marketing focused on the East Coast and South America. Cordell was a numbers guy like his predecessor Edward Walker. Everything about Cordell was average and he did not stand out in a crowd except his hawkish nose and his near coal-black eyes. "Buck, how's your father-in-law, Heinrich these days? "

"Thanks for asking, he's well, enjoying retirement. He spends a lot of time at the beach with his grandkids, but he still comes to the office once or twice a week and he is always thinking. I still think his most brilliant idea was the Hindenburg. Getting a dirigible to blow up was almost easy but getting the newspapers to focus on the hydrogen gas was what caused the explosion was absolutely brilliant."

"Well, my favorite is the Teapot Dome scandal. First, they got the control switched from the Navy to the Interior Department then they got President Harding and Albert Fall, Secretary of the Interior, to take the blame for the leases which ultimately, we won. The whole thing was so well planned from start to finish." said Cordell.

"Agreed, gentlemen, we have weathered the Great Depression, profited from the war and emerge controlling the oil business in the US and much of the world, but I am as concerned as ever that our business is threatened." said John. "Our business is selling energy to the world, to power industry and cars. The nuclear bombs dropped in Japan seem to represent almost unlimited energy and could threaten to take away our business."

"John, I concur with your assessment, but I have a strategy for this," said Buck. "Just like the Hindenburg scared people about hydrogen, we need to create the same panic about nuclear energy. I think we have several years before the scientists figure out how to harness the atom. We need to build our defenses now, so we are ready for this new competition."

Cordell said with a grin, "Buck, are you suggesting we influence people on nuclear? "

"I believe we create two lasting images in the public's mind. First is the nuclear blast, this huge ball of fire. In addition, the images of people near the blast that survived but were burned or poisoned by the bomb. We have to make this form of power very scary to people," said Buck. John and Cordell nodded their heads in agreement.

John said, "I have one other item of business we need to discuss. As our reach has extended globally it has become increasingly difficult to keep track of all that is going on around the world. I would like to recommend that we have our joint shell company retain the services of Paragon Research. Paragon has a global reach; it is a small tight company that does both investigative research and has a paramilitary arm that can be quite effective in foreign affairs. I discovered them when we had a dispute in Baku, Azerbaijan a few years ago. They pulled together information that pointed to several key politicians who were influencing against our interests. Based on this information, Paragon sent in a very small paramilitary group and eliminated the problem".

"John," Buck responded, "this sounds interesting, but two things jump out at me. One, how do we know they'll keep our joint interest quiet and two, how do you plan to use them?"

"First, they are a virtually invisible organization based in New York City. They use small offices around the world that they call cells. Only the top few people know about the cell details. Each cell is isolated and does not know about the assets of the other cells. So, any information breaches are contained. My plans are to have them keep an active watch on our mutual interests globally and watch for any competitive companies or energy sources."

Cordell nodded and replied, "If you feel this is a good investment, John, then I'll support it. We all know that we always need more information and occasionally we get issues that need elimination. In fact, I have someone in mind in the Middle East right now for whom It would be helpful if he had an accident. How much do they cost?"

The cost is manageable; they would work under our shell company of course. A $500,000 per year retainer gives us an exclusive. As they do work for us they bill us time and materials, so we just keep funding the retainer. They estimate about $1 million per year each unless we have a major action.

Buck said, "Let's do it." And Cordell nodded his head in agreement.

Over dinner, the men discussed at length developments in the Middle East, the British realignment of countries and opportunities to standup political leaders in the region.

Chapter 5   August 1952 – Washington, D.C.

J erry Weathering couldn't believe his luck. Weathering had worked at the Patent Office for almost 20 years. Shortly after joining the Patent Office, he had been transferred to a new division to examine energy patents. He still recalled the evening so many years ago when he had been approached by a man in a bar.

The man, whose first name was Paul, had offered to buy him a drink and one thing led to another. They had moved to a booth and ordered dinner. The conversation found its way to talking about life and money. Paul made it clear to Jerry he would pay well for information about any patent filings that posed a threat to current forms of energy. He explained that he would pay $300 for a copy of each patent filing Jerry discovered. If his boss determined a patent never needed to be issued, Jerry would be paid an additional $700. How Jerry derailed the patent was up to him.

Jerry couldn't believe his ears and repeated back to him, "Let me get this straight if I come across a patent related to a new form of energy and I derail it I get a total of $1,000."

Paul replied, "That's right".

"Paul, I see ten to twenty new patents a week all

related to energy. You don't want to see all of them, do you?"

"No obviously not," Paul frowned. "I only want to see patents that relate to new ways to create energy. You need to determine if you think it's of value and don't send me a lot of bullshit or this deal is off," he said in a firm tone.

"So how do we meet?"

Paul looked at Jerry and said, "we don't." Do you have an outside windowed office?"

"Yes."

"Well, when you have something, I want you to put a bright red coffee mug in your office window and then you can drop the document at an agreed location. I'll leave the money for you in the same spot. Where do you live Jerry?" Paul already knew the answer but needed to bring Jerry along.

"I live in Alexandria right across the river at 263 West Linden Street just off Russell Road."

"Jerry, check your mailbox on Friday and I will give you full details. Just to show you how sincere we are, here is a little something to get you along." Paul palmed $500 to Jerry as they shook hands. Paul slipped out of the booth and was gone.

Jerry shook his head in disbelief. He couldn't believe his luck but a part of him wondered what he just got himself into. "But, for the money," he thought... and he knew he was in.

Jerry had never saw Paul again -- in fact, he never even learned his full name and he guessed someone else did the drop because the handwriting changed from time to time.

Chapter 6   April 1957 – Great Falls, VA

After college, Dick and his wife Mary bought a small farm in Great Falls, Virginia. Having grown up on the farm in central Vermont, Dick wanted the farm life for his family. Dick, while he worked mostly at home, needed to be close to the Navy Yard and Annapolis and both were a reasonable drive.

Dick's inventive nature also meant he was a bit aloof and was more comfortable and creative on his own. The Navy made it possible for him to work, for the most part, from his home lab. Dick's latest challenge was to develop a new type of electroplating that prevented ordinary steel from rusting.

Dick, when he was 'at work' was in 'The Barn' as he called it, but in reality, it was a full working laboratory built by the Navy due to the classified nature of his experiments. While the ground level and loft looked like a barn, beneath was a full 12-foot-high basement with secret stairs behind a cupboard. Being the consummate engineer, Dick had his engineering notebook close at hand as he recorded his concoction of basic metal salts and catalysts. Dick had placed four steel plates in the water bath hung from a metal frame, each metal plate about 1 inch apart. At each end of the tank were large copper electrodes. Dick had added precisely measured quantities of various salts.

As Dick walked to another table to get more chemicals, he accidentally hit the power switch turning on the DC transformer. The transformer had been giving him fits for the past week and he had a new one on order. While he was at the other workbench measuring out more chemicals the transformer hummed away. Walking back to the tank with his chemicals he noticed the water boiling away and heard the distinct low hum of the transformer.

Dick always had a curved briar pipe hanging from his mouth, a habit acquired from his years with Captain Scott. Often unlit, it was an appendage of his face. Dick thought this is strange as he watched the water boil. He cautiously felt the side of the tank and it was cool to the touch. He pulled a wooden match from a box on the table and struck it to light his pipe. BOOM, a large flash of blue light erupted from the top of the tank and Dick was knocked ten feet across the barn floor, his head hitting the shelf on a bench anchored to the wall.

Several minutes later he came to. His head ached and it took him a moment to get his bearings. He noticed the ceiling above the tank had been scorched by the eruption and he felt a knot rising on the back of his head. Slowly he gathered himself together and approached the workbench. Everything was in disarray, but the water was still boiling away. Dick turned off the transformer and the boiling stopped.

He thought to himself; best not light another match here. He turned on the basement exhaust fan and air poured in from hidden vents in the ceiling. The fan pulled air out of the basement and it exhausted out through what appeared to be an old stone well about twenty feet from the barn.

Upstairs, he walked out the backdoor, his shoes crunched on the frosty grass and he approached the barnyard fence where three Guernsey cows were eating hay enjoying the warming morning sun. All three ambled over to the fence to see Dick.

Dick scratched Krista the oldest. She enjoyed being scratched behind her topknot right between her ears. Carol, the two-year-old, butted Krista out of the way, impatient to have the attention and her face rubbed. Robin, the third Guernsey and by far the most patient, stood alongside waiting until Dick rubbed her neck. A gesture that she enjoyed. "Well, girls I was just knocked ass over teacups." Dick rubbed the back of his head and felt the bump had grown to a significant egg. He lit his pipe and contemplated what had happened.

Dick recalled his college days and how they had burned various gases in the laboratory, gasoline, propane, butane, and hydrogen among others. Each had different characteristics. What was coming out of the tank? He lit his pipe and began to think. The cows realized they had received all the attention they were going to get and wandered back to the hay rack, except for Robin who stood close by watching Dick and patiently chewing her cud. Dick thought about the chemicals in the tank and his only conclusion was it had to be hydrogen. There were no carbon compounds in the tank and carbon was the basic building block for most burning gases like gasoline and propane.

Dick walked back to the barn and down to the shop. Once inside, he started straightening up the items that had been knocked about by the explosion. He made a few notes about what had just happened when his stomach told him it was lunchtime and the clock confirmed it.

Dick walked the 100 yards between the shop in the house. Having warmed up just enough, the grass was now damp, making a squishing sound beneath his feet. As he entered the house through the rear boot room, he removed his wet shoes and heavy coat before entering the kitchen.

Dick's wife Mary was at the stove warming up some homemade ham and split pea soup. Mary turned just in time to receive a warm peck on the cheek from her still very amorous husband of many years.

"Hi, honey. How was your morning?"

"Well interesting! I managed to set off a small unexpected explosion but only my noggin was seriously damaged."

"Are you okay?"

"Yes, fine. Just an ostrich egg on my head."

Mary said with a chuckle, "Well maybe that bump knocked some common sense into that hard Navy head of yours. Oh, Dick can you call the kids down to lunch?"

"Sure, dear. Josh and Beth, time for lunch" Dick blared out." Feet could be heard heading down the stairs.

Beth was the first to emerge in the kitchen. "Hi, Dad." Beth was a beautiful 17-year-old just beginning to discover the world and, Dick feared, perhaps boys too.

Shortly behind her was Josh, tall and lean he slid into his chair at the kitchen table. Josh was 12 years old with close-cropped light brown hair and an obvious bundle of energy.

Beth helped her mother by setting the table and getting milk out of the refrigerator. When everyone had sat down, Dick said a brief grace. The kids were home from school this week and enjoying the break.

Dick said, "Josh I want you to clean out the cow stalls, put fresh bedding down and clean out the empty calf pen." Josh just nodded.

Mary said, "Your Dad had a small explosion in the shop and bumped his head."

Dick kind of grumbled, "I want you kids to please stay out of the shop for the next few days while I work on this experiment."

Beth inquired, "Dad, what is it you're working on? "

Dick looked up from his soup, "Well I'm not really sure. This one has me guessing. I'll share it with you when I understand it better."

After that, the talk turned to activities involving the kids – school, 4-H activities and the like. And Dick realized he made the right decision bringing his family up in a farm lifestyle.

After lunch, Dick spent the afternoon documenting everything he could about what transpired that morning including information about the chemicals, the plates, and the transformer. It seemed pretty obvious that he was generating hydrogen gas out of the watery solution. When he replaced the solution with plain water no gas was generated. It is clearly a unique combination of electricity and the solution.

It was Friday afternoon and Dick had long ago promised Mary he would not work on the weekend, if possible. Being a bit anal, Dick spent the last hour cleaning up the shop. This always gave him a fresh start Monday morning.

He headed back to the house for a brief cup of afternoon tea before he went to the barn to milk and make certain all were bedded down for the evening. Beth was in the kitchen and put on the kettle as she saw her Dad walking to the house. When Dick entered the kitchen Beth asked, "Dad how are you feeling?"

"Oh, fine honey, just a nasty bump on my head when I got knocked across the floor."

Beth was always fascinated by her father's projects and eager to learn all she could. "So, what happened?"

Dick told his daughter about his experiment to create a new method of electroplating steel to reduce corrosion. He explained how the water started bubbling and he lit his pipe and then BOOM.

Beth went into the parlor where her mom was mending clothes and said, "mom, I'm going to go out and help dad with chores."

"Okay honey, just make sure you put your boots on and a warm coat it feels chilly out."

Beth and her dad headed off for the barn together. Beth always loved being with him. He was so smart, she always learned new and exciting things when they talked. Her dad's confidence also created an aura of security and Beth always felt so safe when she was near him.

When they were in the milk house, Dick turned to Beth and said, "While you feed the cows, I'll start the milking. Just remember their grain and that Carol gets three scoops while the other two get two scoops." With that, he grabbed the stainless-steel milk pail and the short three-legged stool.

When Beth returned from feeding the cows, her dad was milking Carol. The Surge milking machine was gently pulsing away. Dick knew about how long each cow took to milk out. He leaned his head forward against her side just in front of her rear leg and above the udder. This natural indent gave him advance warning if the cow decided to raise her leg, although they rarely kicked, and he knew they liked being milked. Knowing she was nearly done; he felt each quarter to make sure it had milked out. He turned off the suction and carried the milking machine out to the alley behind the cows where he removed the lid and poured the warm milk in the stainless-steel pail.

Krista knowing, she was next, she had leaned over tight to Carol. It was almost a game as Dick pushed her back over to create the opening where he could sit between the two. Dick was always fascinated at how cows knew just how to position themselves so that they could maximize contact with him. It was almost like a cat rubbing against your leg.

Beth sat on a bale of hay behind the cows and asked, "So dad, what happened in the shop today."

Dick explained to her about the experiment, how he was trying to develop a new way to protect the metal from rusting. "Beth," he said thoughtfully, "I think I may have come up with a new way to produce hydrogen gas."

Beth knew that hydrogen was the first element on the periodic table and that hydrogen and oxygen made up water and she shook her head, perplexed. "OK," she responded. "That sounds like a big deal, but I don't understand, why did it blow up?"

Dick was still sitting on a stool and leaned into Krista. Without looking up he smiled and nodded slowly, "You're correct. It is or could be, a very big deal. And, it blew up because Hydrogen is very flammable. It burns like gasoline but does not make any fumes. When it burns basically it creates water."

"So, then why don't we use hydrogen instead of gasoline?" Beth asked, a puzzled look on her face.

"Well I guess a couple of reasons; the first is that hydrogen is a gas and gasoline is a liquid which makes gasoline easier to handle. The other thing is it takes more energy to create hydrogen than you get from burning it."

"So, where did the hydrogen you created come from?"

"Well, the hydrogen had to come from the water in the tank."

"Do you think it took more energy to create it than you produced?"

"Well, Beth," this time Dick looked up and smiled at his daughter, "that is the million-dollar question I'll have to figure out next week, but my guess is perhaps not." And he chuckled, shook his head and said, "Beth, you do make me think and you ask great questions."

Beth just smiled as she carried the last pail full of the rich golden milk to the milk house. She poured the milk through a strainer and into glass bottles. A small old refrigerator in the milk house kept the bottles cold. When she returned to her bale, she said, "looks like enough for mom to make some butter and cheese tomorrow."

"Yes, dear. We will bring one bottle with us

tonight, so we have milk in the house for the morning."

As he walked back to the house, Dick thanked Beth for all her help and thought, did it take more energy – what a great question.

Chapter 7   April 1957 – Great Falls, VA

Dick couldn't help but think about his discovery all weekend. Monday morning right after chores and breakfast he eagerly went to the shop. Starting with a clean table he reassembled everything just as he had it on Friday. He poured the solution in the tank that he saved from Friday, positioned the plates and the transformer. When he turned on the switch, sure enough, the solution bubbled, and gas was produced.

Dick then replicated the entire setup on another table. He fabricated a sealed top to the tank that had a short pipe for attaching a hose. The hose looped down and attached to the bottom of another container half-full of water. Dick knew from his college days as the gas was produced it would go out through the hose and bubble up through the water. The water would prevent a flashback like what happened on Friday. Dick mixed a new batch of the solution, set up the system and borrowed the transformer from the original setup. Powered up, the solution bubbled away and generated copious amounts of gas.

Later that morning the new transformer arrived. Dick tried it out and could tell right away gas production was insignificant with a new transformer. He would have to figure out the difference quickly before the old transformer simply stopped working.

Over the next few days, Dick documented everything, and according to his calculations, he was generating substantially more energy in the form of hydrogen gas than the electricity required to run the system. If this held true it was a massive breakthrough.

Dick was now faced with a true dilemma, was this a Navy invention or his own? He could justify it in his mind as his own invention. First, he was trying to develop a means to improve corrosion resistance and this certainly had nothing to do with that. Second, if this really was a new form of energy production, then in the Navy's hands it might never see the light of day and could spend the rest of its useful life sitting on someone's desk.

Dick knew he had to talk to his superior, Admiral Keyes, about his discovery and get his blessing on how to proceed. Dick contacted the Admiral's office at the Navy Yard and got on his calendar.

Friday morning Dick sat stiffly in front of the admiral. He briefed him on his current project for a new steel coating and then briefed him on his discovery of the hydrogen gas production. After considerable thought and discussions, the Admiral agreed with Dick that he would keep his discovery. The Admiral asked Dick to keep him fully apprised of any new developments. The Admiral said he would send Dick a letter authorizing him to spend his free time on the gas experiment and that he was the inventor.

Several weeks later Dick completed writing the patent for his invention. He enjoyed visiting the Patent and Trademark Office in the Commerce Building on Constitution Avenue and E Street to check out and understand existing patents. In his research at the PTO's library on existing hydrogen gas generators, he was surprised to find only a handful. He completed the patent and hand-delivered it to the PTO, received a receipt for the filing, and watched as the clerk stamped it with the receipt date. The clerk took the patent and slipped it into a letter sorter in the slot marked Energy. Dick inwardly sighed knowing that he had his patent filed.

Arriving home, Dick packed up the experiment in several boxes and put them on a shelf in the lab. He continued his work on corrosion-resistant electroplating. Little did Dick know the tumultuous chain of events that were kicked off with his filing.

Chapter 8   August 1957 – Washington, DC

In August 1957 when Jerry finally read Dick Powell's patent for producing hydrogen, he recognized this was likely $2,000 in his pocket. Over the years the price had gone up, but one thing never changed - he could use the money.

Jerry once again placed the old red coffee mug in his office window and a copy of the patent in a plain brown envelope. Tonight, he would put the envelope in the drop spot and tomorrow he would pick up $1,000.

Unknown to Jerry his action would set a long string of dominos tumbling down.

Carla Sanner took her daily stroll up Fourteenth Street past the Patent Office in the Commerce building as she checked two windows with a quick glance. Each window was a different informer. Carla was a petite blond, her cropped hair and lack of flash made her look the part of a tourist or local housewife, perfect in her role. She immediately noticed the red coffee mug in the window on the third floor, second from the left of the last wing. She didn't know or want to know who the source was, but she immediately knew the drop spot for this source, an old fake fallen tree in the woods in Alexandria. This one was paid $1,000. The amounts varied depending on the person and, even though she had a coded note in her purse with the amounts, she knew them all by heart. Carla checked four more buildings in downtown DC, stopped at the bank for the cash and went home.

Carla left a note for her husband, Aaron, who was still at work patrolling his beat along Constitution Avenue. Aaron was a DC cop and had been a close friend of Ray Lewis, the president of Paragon Research when they were in the service together. When Ray took over Paragon, he arranged the job for Carla. She loved it, for the most part, because it was so easy. She walked around DC to see if various people had information for the firm and was well paid for her efforts.

Carla took the bus from their apartment near Capitol Hill across the Potomac. She changed buses in Rosslyn and went south to Alexandria. She knew she would be early and went to a favorite coffee shop to wait. Carla went to the drop a little after 7 P.M., reached under the fake log, and removed the envelope from the shelf in the log. She then replaced it with the envelope that held the cash. Putting the unopened envelope in her bag, she made a return bus trip home.

After reading Carla's note, Aaron had fixed a light dinner of ham sandwiches and canned peas. When Carla walked in the door Aaron got off the couch and gave her a warm embrace and a brief kiss on the lips. "How was your day?"

"Good," she replied. Carla was slipping out of her overcoat. "I had one pick up and all went smoothly. Let me change into something more comfortable," she said with a wink.

"You got it with pizzazz dear," the husky tone of anticipation in his voice. "Let's go to the range this weekend. With you carrying all that cash you need to practice."

The next morning Carla went to the Paragon office at 11th and F Street. She had become close friends with Max the latest district manager. Max Silverman was a small man who looked like a bookish accountant, but Max's cold grey eyes left little doubt he would cut your heart out if crossed. Max knew of Aaron and Carla's relationship with Ray and her many years with the firm. While he had only been with the firm a few years, he ran the office smoothly and it was an important office for Paragon. In the Paragon tradition, Max was compartmentalized and did not know the full nature of the firm's projects. Max took the envelope from Carla and added it to the short stack to review.

Even in his short period with the firm he had successfully led a number of assignments. Some were really easy, a word to the wise and many lobbyists would drop an idea or a legislative push. For the more difficult lobbyists, while truth be told, cash was generally all it took. In Max's mind, lobbyists had no morals, their only interest was in the almighty dollar.

The inventors were a bit different. Most of them seemed to be nervous ninnies. Pressure could come by threatening to tell their bosses or share photos of an indiscreet evening with significant people. Once you understood what made them tick, you could generally push them over. Some would take a bribe and walk away from an idea. Unfortunately, there were some, the truly hardcore inventors, that could never let go of an idea and required more direct persuasion.

Later that morning, Max reviewed the copy of the patent in the envelope that Carla had brought in. The patent looked very solid and well written, the process described certainly led the reader to believe it could create hydrogen gas in abundant amounts and that the net energy produced far exceeded the energy required to operate the system. Clearly, this patent required attention.

With the patent information in hand, Max called in Doris Adams. Doris, a bit overweight, middle-aged mother of four was his best researcher. Given a few days, Doris could find dirt on a heavenly angel. Max asked Doris to investigate Richard Powell of Great Falls. She began to dig.

A week later Doris had a slim report she presented to Max. "WOW! A whole week and that is all you got," Max exclaimed incredulously.

"Yup, the man is a real honest to goodness angel. Faithfully married, two kids in school, college-educated, small farm, a few cows and works for the Navy doing research. No mistress, no debt that I could find, and Episcopalian."

"What makes him tick?"

Doris replied, "As far as I can tell, family and his work. Based on some of his filed patents the guy is brilliant and works with explosives and metals for the Navy."

Max kind of huffed and said, "Ok, well I'll take it from here, thanks."

Wasting no time, he went straight to the phone, "Ray, this is Max in DC. I have a challenging inventor. Can you send one of your specialists?"

"No problem," the man on the other end of the phone replied. "I will have Tony meet with you at your office in a few days."

Several days later, Tony Ammasso knocked on Max's door.

"Hi, you must be Tony. Welcome to

Washington."

Tony, clearly Italian, was well built, at 5' 8" with short brown hair, sharp brown eyes, and a distinctive Roman nose.

He replied, "Glad to be here. How can I help?"

"Well," Max began, "I have an inventor that is as clean as a whistle and I think perhaps an unusual approach could get him to stop his new invention."

Max continued to brief Tony on what Doris had learned and provided him with individual photos of the Powell family.

Tony said, as he was leaving Max's office, "This sure is uncommon. I'll let you know how it goes down. See you in a few days."

Chapter 9   September 1957 – Washington, DC

Tony Ammasso slept in, which was easy to do in the comfortable and plush down comforter he was using. It was a misty rainy day in DC, and he was in no rush to drive out to Great Falls. After all, he didn't need to be there till 2 p.m.

When he finally did rise, Tony showered got dressed and put on a light raincoat and an old baseball cap. Over breakfast in a near-by coffee-shop, he reviewed the plan and was pleased with the weather for the day ahead. With the misty rain, his attire was appropriate and, even more importantly, non-descript.

Tony walked the mile from his hotel to the Key Bridge. Walking over the Potomac, he enjoyed watching the river lazily flowing through DC headed for the Chesapeake Bay. Looking upstream, he could see the Georgetown boathouse and the beginning of the Potomac Gorge. He finally arrived in Rosslyn at the Virginia end of the bridge where he was looking for a diner with a parking lot in the back.

People were starting to break for lunch and Tony leaned against a building watching the parking lot in the rear of Billy's Diner. After ten minutes the truck he had been hoping for pulled in and parked. Two men got out and walked around the side of the diner and entered from the front. Tony knew they would be in the diner at least for 30 minutes so he waited a few minutes to make sure one of them didn't return for a forgotten item. He walked over to the green 1950 F-series Ford Pickup truck. The truck with its classic snub nose had a six-and-a-half-foot bed. Tony easily popped the door lock and jumped into the bench seat reaching under the steering wheel. He easily started the truck and drove away.

Tony drove out George Washington Memorial Parkway towards Great Falls. The views from the ridge-top route over the Potomac gorge were beautiful and he even stopped at one of the scenic pull-offs to admire the view. Then, taking Georgetown Pike, he rolled out past magnificent horse farms and country houses. The countryside was a mixture of rural America and occasional opulence.

Tony continued his drive west and passed near the Nike missile battery. It was part of 13 Nike missile batteries that surrounded Washington to protect against Russian bombers during the cold war. It was the world's first surface to air missile system. He drove into Herndon, Virginia and parked on Locust Street a few blocks from the high school. It was 3 o'clock so he had a short wait until school let out at 3:30. He really appreciated all the research that Doris had completed, even knowing what bus the Powell Kids would take. He looked again at the photos of Beth and Joshua.

Fifteen minutes later he ambled down the street toward the high school. He would look like any other parent waiting for the kids to be released. A few minutes later he spotted Beth and Joshua.

Tony walked up to Beth and Josh well before they got to the bus. He reached into his breast pocket and pulled out a thick sealed letter-size envelope. Tony said to Beth, "Excuse me, Beth, would you give this to your father."

Beth was surprised, a look that registered on her face as she said "Sure," not knowing what else to say. Tony continued in the same direction walking away from them.

On the bus, Beth asked Josh, "Do you know who that was?"

"No idea. Must be a friend of Dad's".

They rode the bus home dropping them off on Georgetown Pike at the end of their road. Beth and Josh walked down the gravel road enjoying the now clear sky with abundant smell of the wildflowers enhanced by today's light rain. The envelope in Beth's book bag nearly forgotten as they entered the kitchen, and each grabbed a sandwich Mary had made for them. After eating and changing clothes they ran outside to see the cows.

After dinner, Beth started to work on her homework and came across the envelope. She went to her father and said, "Dad, a man gave me this when we left school today."

Taking the thick envelope Dick asked, "What man?"

"I don't know, he knew my name, so I guess it is some friend of yours."

"Ok, thanks."

Mary was in the kitchen as Dick opened the envelope in the parlor. He almost spit out his pipe as a pile of one-hundred-dollar bills and a letter fell out. He set the cash aside, unfolded the typed letter and began to read.

Dear Mr. Powell. We have come to understand that you have created a method to produce gas. We strongly demand that you stop your efforts. The enclosed cash is to offset any future potential gains. Please destroy all equipment, notes and stop pursuing this avenue. If you do not stop, you will be putting yourself and your family in extreme danger. This is your only warning.

Dick sat back in his old oak Morris chair, took a long pull on his pipe and then another and another.

He was thinking about what was going on. Dick counted the money. $5,000. This was his year's pay as a Lieutenant Commander.

Dick put the letter and cash back in the envelope. He went over to the walnut davenport desk and opened the top. Pulling out one of the inside drawers, he reached inside and flipped the hidden latch releasing the secret spring-loaded letter compartment. He added the envelope to the small pile in the compartment. He closed it and returned the top to its resting place. Dick walked into the kitchen and gave Mary a hug and said, "I am going out to check on the cows. I will be back in a bit."

Mary said, "Everything alright?"

To which he replied, "Oh fine, just need to think for a bit."

Dick walked over to the fence. The cows were laying down and chewing their cud. Carol the two-year-old rolled onto her front knees and then rocked forward and stood up with her rear legs and finally put her front feet under her. She arched her back getting a kink out and moseyed over to Dick at the fence.

Dick rubbed her head and neck while he pondered what was going on. His first thought was how did this person know about his hydrogen gas discovery? Only himself and Admiral Keyes knew, and he trusted the admiral implicitly. Maybe it was someone else like the admiral's assistant in the Navy office, but he didn't think that could be the source. As he thought more it occurred to him that the patent office also knew about his discovery.

The more important questions, he thought, were who and why. Who would threaten and pay that much money to stop his discovery?

And he realized it had to be someone who saw hydrogen either as a potential moneymaker or who felt it would be competition.

Of course, his patent filing did not provide enough detail on his solution for someone to replicate the discovery but perhaps they had already discovered the same thing and did not want the competition. Thinking back to his days at RPI, Dick could think of several multiple independent discoveries like Isaac Newton and others discovering calculus as well as Darwin and Wallace both postulating evolution independently.

The flip side was someone who saw his discovery as a competitive source of energy. Inexpensive creation of hydrogen gas would compete with nuclear, hydro, coal as well as oil and gas companies. He knew that inexpensive hydrogen would provide a pollution-free form of new energy at a low almost free cost.

There was a long list of potential people or companies that his discovery threatened. The list was far too long to solve this way. Being an engineer at heart, Dick flipped the equation in his head, he had to work backward to solve the problem.

The bottom line, he was not going to let someone threaten himself and his family and let this world-changing discovery disappear.

He began to formulate a plan to reverse the gears on this dilemma. First, tomorrow he had to eliminate the threat to his family.

Chapter 10   September 1957 – Great Falls, VA

Dick knew he could not make any drastic changes to his routine since someone might be watching him. He went about his normal routine and did his milking and a few chores before seeing the kids off to school. In the kitchen, he told Mary that something was going on and that he couldn't get into detail. But he wanted her and the kids to go to Grandpa's farm in Vermont for a few weeks.

Of course, she wanted to know why but he simply said, "I can't say but it is important for you and the kids to be safe. I am going to go over to the Schmidt farm to ask if we can borrow his spare car, so you can drive up to Vermont tonight. I want you to pack up some bags for you and the kids and stay in the house today."

"Dick, what is going on?"

Dick calmly replied, "Like I said, there is a potential threat I am aware of and I want you to go tonight. I will be fine."

Dick went through the barn and out the back door and then walked through the fields to the Schmidt farm. Kurt Schmidt was in the barnyard steering his dozen Holsteins out to pasture. Dick leaned up against the barnyard fence and patiently waited until Kurt closed the gate and walked over. Kurt was a full six foot two, lean with broad shoulders and thick callused strong farmer's hands. With his slight German accent, Kurt said, "Dick how are you, haven't seen you since the fair last month."

"I'm good, Kurt. But I'm here because I need a favor."

"Of course, anything, how can I help?"

Slowly Dick said, "Kurt I would like to rent your old Nash for a few weeks. Mary and the kids need to go visit my Grandfather in Vermont and I don't have a spare. I'll pay you $25 per week and of course, return it full of gas."

Kurt looked at him and said, "You don't need to pay me, it just sits in the shed. Just take it."

"No, I insist on paying and will be very grateful for letting me use it."

Kurt climbed over the fence and they began walking to the shed. He opened the car door and turned the key. The flathead straight 6-cylinder engine purred to life. The lime green Nash Rambler station wagon was not a huge car, but given the sleek lines of the car with its rounded nose, it was easy to see how it got great miles and was very dependable.

"There's a spare tire in the back along with the

jack and wrenches. We just changed the oil before putting it away this summer."

Kurt climbed out and said to Dick, "I hope she has a safe trip and says hello to the family for me. There's no rush to get it back."

Dick replied, "I can't thank you enough." He handed Kurt fifty dollars and said, "I insist".

Dick drove home, parked the car in the barn and closed the barn doors. Inside the barn, Dick went down to the basement and carried several boxes of stuff upstairs. He assembled the electroplating set up on a table. If someone came snooping around, he wanted them to think this was the discovery and not search for the hidden entrance to the basement. Confident that his first part of the plan was in place, Dick walked over to the house for lunch.

Mary had assembled the suitcases with clothes for herself and the kids. Dick told her that she and the kids would leave after dark and drive a few hours before stopping for the night. They had made the journey many times from Virginia to Vermont, so she knew the way. The 450-mile trip would take a few days, but it was all main roads until they got to Bennington, Vermont and then only another 30 miles on gravel roads to Manchester. They ate a quiet lunch with an undercurrent of tension in the air. After lunch, Dick drove to Great Falls and called his father from a payphone in town. He told his dad that something was going on here in Virginia and that Mary and the kids would be coming to visit for a few weeks. Dick's dad understood and knew not to ask the question why. He said he couldn't wait to see Mary and the kids.

After dinner and under the cover of darkness, Dick, Mary, and kids took the bags out to the Schmidt car. Everyone had big hugs and Dick reminded the kids to be good. Mary had a few tears when she kissed Dick and said, "You be careful and stay in touch."

Dick kissed her back, "Of course and I will be fine."

Mary drove down the road with the lights off till they reached Georgetown Pike and then headed east to cross the Potomac.

After they left, Dick went into the house and took his Winchester Model 70 wrapped in a blanket out to his truck and tucked it in behind the seat. Turning in for the night he took his prized Ithaca 'Colt Government' out of the bedside table drawer, pulled the slide back, put a shell in the chamber and laid it on top of the table.

Tony had spent the day comfortably nestled in the woods just north of the Powell farm. He had observed Dick walk off and return with the Nash but guessed incorrectly that he had gone to get one of Powell's cars back from a neighbor. He returned to the city at dusk and didn't see Mary and the kids drive off.

The next morning Dick was off to the barn a bit earlier than usual. He had slept well knowing Mary and the kids were safe and there was nothing he could do yet. Finishing chores, he turned the cows out and went in for breakfast. He tucked his pistol under the back of his trousers and walked over to the truck. Not knowing if his phone line was tapped, he drove to town and called Admiral Keyes to brief him on what he knew and what he did not.

"Admiral, I received a letter yesterday demanding I drop the gas project I briefed you on this spring. Somebody found out about it and clearly does not want me to proceed. I am unclear if it is a competitor with a similar concept or an energy company that wants it to go away. Any remote chance my discovery was disclosed by someone in your office?"

"Absolutely not from here. I did not share our discussion with anyone and filed my notes on our conversation in my personal office safe."

Dick sighed, "As I expected but had to ask. Then it had to come from the patent office. I'll check that out."

"Dick," the admiral's tone was somber and a bit worried, "would you like me to send a few marines out to watch over you and the family?"

"No sir, I am good. I sent Mary and the kids to my father's place in Vermont for a few weeks while I sort this out. I need to do a little reconnoitering so no need to send in the marines yet. But thank you and I will keep you in the loop. I don't expect to be in the office for the next few days."

Keyes replied, "Take the time you need but be safe and don't hesitate to call if you need support."

Dick drove back towards the farm but took a different approach so he could stop a mile from the farm on the north side. It was the only direction someone could hide since there was a pasture on the east, south, and west. Dick put the sidearm in his holster and slung the rifle on his back. He walked carefully towards the farm keeping his eyes open for someone hiding and watching the farm. A few hundred yards down the road he spotted the guy sitting with his back to a tree watching the farm from the woods. Dick knew if he kept watching, the guy would instinctively sense he was being watched. Dick knew what he needed for now and carefully returned to his truck. Circling back around he drove up to the farm from Georgetown

Pike and acted as if all was normal.

The next day, after chores, Dick dressed in his best suit and drove into DC. He parked, then walked in the side door of the U.S. Patent Office. In the Greek styled rotunda, he approached the same person who had received his patent many months ago.

"Hi, my name is Richard Powell and I registered a patent application with you in April regarding an invention for energy production. I would like to meet briefly with the Energy examiner."

The pleasant gal behind the counter replied, "This is unusual sir, but I will try to reach him to see if he is available for a brief chat. Please have a seat."

Dick sat on a nearby bench and patiently waited. About fifteen minutes later a short middle-aged bookish man with dark hair and thick coke-bottle glasses appeared from a door across the lobby.

Dick stood and walked toward the man. "Hello, are you Richard Powell?"

"I am and I wanted to inquire about the status of a patent I applied for regarding a new method for producing hydrogen gas."

"I am Jerry Weathering. I'm sorry Mr. Powell but we have no record of a recent patent filed by you. I have over 500 patents waiting for review and

I quickly reviewed our log of incoming patents and there is nothing in the log under your name for this year. Are you the inventor?"

Dick noticed the man was beginning to sweat and fidget like a child caught doing something wrong. "Yes, I am, and I registered it with the lady at the counter in April of this year."

"Well again I am sorry, but it must have been lost. Perhaps you could resubmit it."

Dick squared his shoulders and replied, "I will, but I have another issue. It would appear that someone, perhaps you Jerry, shared the patent information with someone else that has resulted in an unfortunate situation. Did you share my patent information with someone outside this office?"

Now sweating profusely Jerry replied, "Mr. Powell, I don't care for your tone or your accusation. I wish you would leave this office before I call security."

Dick looked down on him straight through his thick glasses and said, "I will go now but you have not heard the end of this from me and I have powerful resources at my disposal." Dick turned, with ingrained military precision and left the man shaking in his polished black shoes.

When Weathering returned to his office, he wiped his brow and immediately placed his red coffee cup in the window.

Dick reached his truck and sat in the cab. He now knew something he didn't know this morning. He knew who shared his discovery, but he still didn't know who he shared it with.

Chapter 11   September 1957 – Great Falls, VA

W hen Dick arrived home from his trip to DC he knew that things would likely escalate so he made plans.

Jerry Weathering's note was in Max's hand the next day. He called Ray in New York and updated him on the situation. What he knew was that Richard Powell's daughter had received the envelope, the next day Powell had sent the family away and yesterday he approached their source at the Patent Office. Tony was still keeping watch on Powell.

Ray Lewis leaned back in his chair at the Paragon Research office in Manhattan and thought about what brought him to this moment. Nearly twenty years ago his father, Bob, had been a cop and then became a private investigator. Through hard work, luck, and fortune he had grown and transformed Paragon into a global clandestine organization. Paragon Research had small offices around the world. These cells, each under a different corporate name, knew there were other offices but knew nothing of those offices. Some simply did research on individuals, companies or governments but others would provide 'wet' work when needed.

Bob had met John Whitney in 1939 and been retained to help him solve a problem in the oil fields in Baku. A few years later John again approached Bob with a project that transformed Paragon into the company it is now. Paragon was retained by a small company based in the Bahamas with virtually unlimited money to research competitive sources of energy and maintain information on competitive oil and energy companies. Paragon also influenced government officials and others to get lucrative arrangements for companies recommended by the office in the Bahamas. Bob knew nothing about the company in the Bahamas only that cash flowed freely.

Ray pondered the problem in DC and decided the cleanest thing was to see that Richard Powell had an accident. He put in a call to the Pinnacle Club to get approval to take this action. Several hours later he had the green light. His contact's final words, "It seems the best solution, just make sure it is an accident." He put a call into one of his best and Chris was on his way to DC to meet up with Tony.

****

Dick woke up very early and went out to the barn. He grabbed three halters off a hook and went to the pasture to awaken the cows. In the darkness, each slowly arose, and he put the halters on them.

Having been to the county fair since they were calves all were comfortable with the halters. Taking the three leads in hand he started to walk across the fields and through the gates leading the cows to the Schmidt farm.

Kurt was in the barn just beginning to start milking when Dick arrived. Knocking on the barn door Dick said good morning to Kurt.

"Kurt, I need another favor. I may also be gone for a few days, and I was hoping you could add my girls to your herd. I would be pleased if you would keep the milk in exchange for their care."

Kurt sat on his three-legged stool putting the milker on the first cow, "Absolutely, happy to add your cows but probably won't want to let them go. They always look terrific."

"Well once you taste that rich Golden Guernsey milk you probably will want more. Again, many thanks, Kurt. I will see you in a few days."

Dick walked back through the fields as dawn was beginning to brighten his walk. He jumped in the truck and drove to Herndon. It was still too early to make phone calls, so he enjoyed breakfast at a diner. After breakfast, he called Mary, "Good morning, dear. How was the drive?"

"Uneventful. The Nash was a pleasure to drive and we arrived yesterday afternoon. The kids were great and played in the backseat all the way. Your dad is a treasure, and all is well."

"Things remain complex here, but I am starting to sort things out and plan to meet with the Admiral later today. I left a note in the secret spot in the pantry and there is an envelope in the secret compartment in the davenport."

Mary asked, "Dick what is going on?"

"Some people want to steal my discovery, but I'm getting to the bottom of it. Don't worry. I'll have it all sorted out in a few days. I'll keep you posted."

Dick next called Admiral Keyes office to learn that he had to go to Norfolk and would return later that night. He made an appointment to meet the admiral at the Navy Yard the following day at 2 p.m. Dick then returned to the farm.

He went into the barn and discovered someone had torn apart his false setup on the table and left a note.

Mr. Powell this is your last and final warning. Cease and desist.

He went down in the secret basement carefully closing the entrance behind him. Dick worked in the basement straightening things up and making sure his hydrogen project was well packed away.

Carefully closing the secret door, Dick Powell exited the barn through the backdoor and circled around and walked to the house. He now was certain that his life was at risk, so he continued his plans. In the parlor he took his favorite poem from a shelf, 'The Road Not Taken' by Robert Frost and also took the book, 'The Autobiography of Benjamin Franklin' to the kitchen table. He wanted to create clues to help someone discover his secret, but he also wanted to make it difficult for someone to simply find it. First, he wrote a brief note.

Begin with my favorite. Remove all the spaces and punctuation.

1.6,1.1,1.22,1.3,2.10,4.19,1.10,1.18,1.7,

1.1,2.27,1.12,1.2,1.6,1.1,1.12,1.4,1.14,

1.6,1.8,2.24,1.20,1.4,1.10,2.10,2.27,1.6,

1.4,1.7,2.24,1.12,2.10,4.7,1.2,1.10,1.1,2.17

1.6,1.7,1.7,20

Then he took 'The Autobiography of Benjamin Franklin' and carefully covered the book with heavy white paper yielding a new white cover. He carefully labeled it 'The Water Gas' by Richard Beckwith. Having read the autobiography multiple times, he began to write on various pages in the book. He put the book in his bag that he took when going to the Navy Yard.

Dick then wrote a note to Mary. He opened the secret compartment in the pantry and left two envelopes. One simply addressed Mary, the other labeled For the Future. He added these to the other envelope already in the secret cupboard.

Dick went upstairs, using binoculars he was able to spot the watcher who was well camouflaged on the edge of the woods. He thought this guy was good. If he had not known where to look for him, he would not have seen him from the house or the barn.

Now for Phase Two of Dick's operation.

Chapter 12   September 1957 – Great Falls, VA

Dick walked out of the house straight to the truck without looking towards the woods. He jumped in the truck and spun the tires as he left the yard. He hoped this would give the watcher something to consider. As before, he drove back around and approached the farm from the north. Again, he crept up on the watcher. Taking his Winchester, he carefully sighted on the tree about a foot above the watcher's head and fired.

Bark flew everywhere, Dick pulled the bolt back ejecting the shell and fed another round in the chamber. The watcher hit the dirt and scrambled behind the tree. Dick yelled out, "This is MY last and final warning. Go away and leave me alone or next time I won't shoot the tree. Are we CLEAR!"

The watcher yelled back, "Crystal."

Dick walked backward the half-mile to his truck. He drove to Herndon to get an early dinner then returned to the farm. He hoped he was now safe but remained on guard. With the pistol back on the side table, he turned in.

Tony arrived back at the hotel in DC well after dark. There was an envelope waiting for him at the front desk. Tony read the note and called Chris's room. Together they walked quietly a few blocks and entered a steak house for dinner. In a quiet booth, Tony updated Chris on the events so far, finishing with today's details. It was agreed they would drive out near the farm and see how things unfolded and find an opportunity for an accident.

They drove past the farm and saw Dick's truck parked. Past the farm, they turned around and parked out of sight of the house. About an hour later they heard the truck start and drive out of the yard. At a discreet distance, they followed the truck to Georgetown Pike and saw it head toward DC. Still maintaining a safe distance, they followed the truck to downtown Washington. They speculated along the drive that Dick was headed for his office at the Navy Yard.

Dick had a feeling he was being followed but could not be certain. At this time of day, there were many cars driving into DC. He had an appointment with the Admiral at 2 p.m. but he had a stop to make before going to the Naval Yard. Dick drove east on Independence Avenue past the Tidal Basin and its famed Cherry Trees and the magnificent obelisk, the Washington Monument. Driving up the hill and past the Capitol, he turned left on First Street SE and was incredibly lucky to find someone pulling out creating an open parking spot right in front of the Library of Congress.

Tony and Chris were surprised by Powell's quick

turn but just made the turn themselves and drove past Powell as he exited the car. They circled around the Capitol and parked on Independence with a view of his truck.

Dick passed the beautiful Neptune Fountain and walked up the stairs to the right. He entered the building and walked through the Great Hall with its incredible marble floor and on through to the Main Reading Room. He walked up to the massive circular desk at the heart of the reading room. A librarian greeted him. Pulling his hand labeled book wrapped in simple string out of his satchel, "I would like to add this book to the permanent collection for future generations.

The librarian replied, "Of course, we would be honored, are you the author?"

"No, my grandfather created this modification of Benjamin Franklin's autobiography with his notes."

"Again, an honor. Is there anything else I may assist you with sir?"

"No, I have to keep going. I have a meeting at the Navy Yard, many thanks." Dick turned and walked back to the truck.

After climbing into the truck, he looked at his watch, it was nearing noon and his stomach told him he should grab a bite before what could be a long afternoon. Dick turned right on East Capitol and right again on 2nd Street and then took a quick left on Independence. After a block, he spotted a small restaurant on the left on the ground floor of a brownstone. With luck, he found a parking spot in a hundred feet. Dick crossed the street and entered the restaurant. While he ate lunch, he pondered the past few days determining what he would discuss with the Admiral to seek his advice.

Tony and Chris had to scramble to keep up with Powell but were lucky as they watched him enter the restaurant. Chris said to Tony, "I have an idea that could solve our challenge, clean and simple. Circle around the block." Before reaching the front of the restaurant they parked and waited.

Twenty minutes later, Dick walked out of the restaurant. What a delicious lunch, he thought and, confident in his plans for meeting with the Admiral, proceeded to walk back to his truck. He walked down the block and across the street to the truck. As he reached the vehicle and opened the door, a car shot down the street striking and killing him instantly. Tony and Chris drove off, a simple hit and run with a stolen car. They drove several miles away and parked the car in an alley, leaving the keys in the car. They simply walked away and back to the hotel.

The Admiral was surprised that Dick had not turned up for his meeting. Since it was completely out of character, he felt concerned. The next morning two DC policemen entered his office and he knew it was not good, he stood as they entered.

"Excuse us, Admiral, Commander Richard Powell was hit and killed by an apparent hit and run driver yesterday. We are still looking for the car. We sent someone to his home in Great Falls but there was no one home so we came here."

"Thank you, gentlemen, I know the family and will reach out to them from our office. Where is the body and who do I need to talk to about the next steps?"

"You can contact the DC morgue and they will work with you. We will inform them to expect your call."

Admiral Keyes had the emergency contact details for Dick's father, but he didn't want to deliver this news over the phone. He contacted the Naval Reserve office in Albany, New York and spoke with the commanding officer. He explained the situation and requested that a Chaplin, a senior officer, and two fully armed marines be sent to Dick's parent's house. He told them that they should escort Mary and the kids back to DC adding they should do whatever it took to keep them safe.

The entire family was shocked, and all returned to Washington. The Admiral made arrangements for Dick to be buried at Arlington if Mary wished. When they finally arrived in DC the Admiral met with Mary in his office at the Navy Yard. They shared what each knew which; was not a lot. The Admiral said he would have two marines stationed at their house 24-7 until they all felt safe. Mary decided she would prefer to have Dick buried at the Episcopal Church cemetery in Great Falls so his soul would be nearby. The following weekend a memorial service was held and over a hundred neighbors and naval personnel attended. Admiral Keyes was honored to provide the eulogy.

About a week later when things had settled down and the kids were back in school, Mary recalled what Dick had said on their last call. She went to the pantry and opened the hidden compartment and found the two letters. She opened the one addressed to her.

Dearest Mary, if you are reading this something terrible happened. I think it best you simply forget about my discovery and never discuss it again. I have left another note for someone in the future, someone strong and of good character to consider taking this forward but this is not for you or the kids.

I love you with all my heart and want you to know that I am looking down on you and the kids from heaven. Please move forward with your life

*and I look forward to seeing you in heaven, I pray
many years from now.*

Love Dick

Mary simply wept for an hour. She closed the
compartment and did not open the other envelope.
Later in the afternoon she opened the secret
drawer in the davenport and discovered the
envelope with the warning letter and the cash. She
burned the letter and put the cash back in the
hidden drawer.

Chapter 13   June 2015 – Westchester, NY

The Pinnacle Club formed in 1916 by three tycoons of the oil industry was now over ninety years old. The tiny office located in the Bahamas had a staff of five and two full-time security people. It was not on anyone's radar and planned to remain that way. Over many years, the leadership of the three parent companies had been passed down from one generation to another.

Jacob Holden, great-grandson of Malcolm Holden and CEO of Texas Oil and Gas, simply known as TXO was handing over the reins to Harold Watson or as everybody knew him HW. HW grew up in a tiny prairie town of Vega, Oklahoma on old Route 66, went to Baylor for business and entered Texas Oil straight out of college eventually transferring to headquarters in Westchester, NY. HW had worked his way up the ladder and grown the company both vertically and horizontally. Last evening the board had approved HW becoming CEO and asking Jacob Holden to stay on as Chairman, recognizing that he would be semi-retired.

In Jacob's former and now HW's new CEO's office, Jacob turned over the reins to HW. "Well HW welcome to the top, you earned it and I have every confidence you will grow and expand the company as the family has over the years. As you know, you are the first CEO of the company that is not a Holden which tells you how much respect we have for you. I am here for you and welcome your thoughts on how to continue to grow the company. And understand that I will only provide advice at your request. However, there are things you need to become aware of that only the CEO knows."

"Jacob, thank you for your support, over the years you have been a guiding light and I will work hard to do justice to the family and the company."

"I know you will, HW. And now, more importantly, you must continue to work smart, as you always have. So only a few people on the planet know what I am about to share with you. Nearly a hundred years ago, after the breakup of the oil barons by the politicians, a secret pact was created between my great-grandfather, Malcolm Holden, Heinrick Schroder, and Edward Walker. They created the Pinnacle Club, a secret organization to control the oil, gas and energy industries. You are now our company's representative on that exclusive board of three. Each of the companies secretly funds the Pinnacle Club which has a small office in the Bahamas. Currently the Club has about $300 million collectively in numbered accounts."

HW was surprised, to say the least about the revelation. "Jacob, what does the Club do?"

"The Club has stayed pretty much true to the vision of the founders. The three companies have worked together to control supply, demand, and transportation of our crude and products. To the public and politicians, we are fierce competitors, but in reality, we are working together. The other area that we address is competitive forms of energy. We have a global clandestine research and paramilitary group, Paragon Research, that we pay millions a year to watch for new forms of energy or to influence governments to support our efforts."

Jacob continued, "For example, many years ago an inventor discovered a method of inexpensively creating hydrogen gas from water. Fortunately, that inventor was killed by a hit and run driver and the discovery never made the light of day. Another example is the oil fields in Ukraine. Our three companies have shared in 30% of the oil and gas production for decades because we control the politicians in Ukraine and Russia. Totally off the books and we don't touch the politicians, our research group does it. The Hindenburg was our group effort to scare people about hydrogen. Three Mile Island was us; I could go on and on."

HW was stunned, "So the group kills people."

"Sometimes but not often, usually cash or a threat of a scandal does the job."

"Wow, where does all the money go?"

"You now completely control hundreds of millions of dollars growing in offshore numbered accounts that you can use anyway you see fit to invest in other growth areas and all off the books of Texas Oil. Today, you personally, now have complete control of all of that. There is much more I will share with you over the weeks to come. Right now, I need to show you something."

Jacob walked over to a large painting of an old oil rig hanging on the wall. He reached up and pressed hidden buttons on the top and bottom of the frame. Then he swung the frame away from the wall, but the wall looked like the rest of the wall. Pressing again on hidden buttons he swung the wall away revealing a large safe with a digital keypad. First, he scanned his fingerprint and then entered a ten-digit code opening the safe. Inside were stock certificates, bonds and a huge pile of cash. "HW there is a million in cash here in case for any reason you need it. In addition, tens of millions in stock certificates and bonds. All off the books. I will get your fingerprint and code registered next week. HW again, it is completely up to you how to use and invest these funds and securities."

HW sat in a chair near the desk and pressed his fingers together almost like he was praying. "Jacob this is all amazing, who would have thought a cowboy from Oklahoma would be in a position like this. I don't have the words to thank you enough for this windfall and opportunity. I give you my sacred honor to treat your trust with confidence and integrity."

Jacob looked HW straight in the eye, "I know, otherwise, you would not be in that seat. Let's go have a big steak dinner and celebrate."

Chapter 14   August 2015 – Fairfax, VA

Sandy arrived home after the reading of the will. He was amazed at his good fortune and at the same time missed wonderful Aunt Beth. He poured a generous glass of scotch on the rocks and sat in his favorite chair in the family room. Copper laid on his comfy rug near Sandy. He opened the letter from Aunt Beth.

My dearest nephew Sandy,

Knowing that you are reading this means I have moved on to a new and I know an exciting place. Having lost so many friends over the years I know your sense of loss. Please rest easy I am in a happy place.

Just before your grandmother died, she told me of a family secret and now I pass it on to you. Your grandfather was killed by a hit and run driver, but it was not an accident. It was murder. He had made a discovery and was killed by someone to keep that discovery a secret.

She told me never to open the hidden envelope or speak of it to anyone. She told me to leave it to someone in the next generation after I died. That person must be strong, smart, and capable and that you are. I was to warn you that the envelope could put you in danger and that you must be very cautious.

In the pantry next to my kitchen is a secret hiding spot. Go in the pantry and remove everything on the shelves in the cupboard on the right including the shelves. You will discover the back of the cupboard can be removed and will reveal the letter left by my father to a future generation. I believe you are that person to discover what he left.

Whatever you learn be careful and do not risk your life because neither my dad, your grandfather, nor I would wish that.

With all my love, Aunt Beth

"Well, Copper," Sandy said to his companion who looked up at him upon hearing his name. "This is an unexpected twist to the day. Let's have a nice dinner, turn in early and drive out to the farm in the morning. There's no telling what we're in for."

The next morning after breakfast Sandy and Copper jumped in the Mazda and were off to Great Falls. On the drive, Sandy thought about his good fortune. Great Falls, while appearing rural, was full of mansions. Football and basketball stars, lobbyists, and corporate executives lived in Great Falls. Sixty acres was worth millions of dollars, but he also loved the farm. Perhaps he should sell the house in Fairfax and move out here. A great idea he would have to consider. He rolled down the gravel road and turned into the yard, parking near the house.

Sandy unlocked the front door and turned off the alarm. Copper laid down on the floor in the kitchen and almost instantly was fast asleep. Sandy chuckled and thought "Oh a dog's life...I swear all you do is sleep."

He went into the pantry and began removing all the cans, jars and boxes from the cupboard moving them to the kitchen table. Then he removed the shelves. Behind the middle shelf were two half-inch holes. Using his fingers, he pulled the panel out of the back of the cupboard. There were two envelopes on a small shelf in the space behind the cupboard. Sandy took them and sat at the kitchen table.

One envelope had no markings and he opened it first. Inside he found three stock certificates. One was an old IBM stock certificate for 1,000 shares dated 1950, the second was 500 shares of John Deere dated 1953 and the third was 500 shares of Kellogg dated 1954. Well, this would take some work to figure out if there was much value, but very interesting.

The second envelope was addressed 'For the Future' he opened it to find a strange carefully handwritten letter.

Begin with my favorite. Remove all the spaces and punctuation.

1.6,1.1,1.22,1.3,2.10,4.19,1.10,1.18,1.7,

1.1,2.27,1.12,1.2,1.6,1.1,1.12,1.4,1.14,

1.6,1.8,2.24,1.20,1.4,1.10,2.10,2.27,1.6,

1.4,1.7,2.24,1.12,2.10,4.7,1.2,1.10,1.1,2.17

1.6,1.7,1.7,20

Well," he thought, I do have a puzzle of sorts to solve. This will require some serious thinking."

Sandy returned the back to the cupboard, restored the shelves and put everything back in place. Going outside he did some chores around the house and mowed the lawn. With everything put away in the barn he went back to the house, reset the alarm and locked up.

Driving home, he thought about the reading of the will and Aunt Beth's request that the following be engraved on her headstone, 'I took the one less traveled by'. It was from the Robert Frost poem and she had told him that it was Papa's favorite. Shaking his head in disbelief, he wondered "Could it be that simple?"

When he got home, Sandy went to the bookcase and pulled out a collection of Frost's poems. Turning to the most famous he read it through.

Remembering that Papa was an engineer, Sandy thought "Ok, just follow the steps." He turned on his laptop and got a copy of 'The Road Not Taken' from the web and pasted it into a blank word document. Using the replace function he removed all the spaces and punctuation. It looked kind of goofy.

tworoadsdivergedinayellowwood

andsorryicouldnottravelboth

andbeonetraveler,longistood

andlookeddownoneasfarasicould

towhereitbentintheundergrowth

thentooktheotherasjustasfair

andhavingperhapsthebetterclaim,

becauseitwasgrassyandwantedwear

thoughasforthatthepassingthere

hadwornthemreallyaboutthesame

andboththatmorningequallylay

inleavesnostephadtroddenblack

ohikeptthefirstforanotherday

yetknowinghowwayleadsontoway

idoubtedifishouldevercomeback

ishallbetellingthiswithasigh

somewhereagesandageshence

tworoadsdivergedinawoodandi

itooktheonelesstraveledby

andthathasmadeallthedifference

Sandy thought for a moment, "Ok next step, what do the numbers mean?"

He started with the first pair of numbers. Perhaps they were the line and position. 1.6 Line 1 sixth letter equals "a", 1.1 Line 1 first letter is "t". It was tedious. He decided a better way was to paste it into Excel and write a simple formula to find each letter. Soon he had decoded the note and it read 'atlocfindthewatergasbyrichardbeckwithadd20' by adding spaces he had.

at loc find the water gas by richard beckwith add 20

Sandy thought how much harder it must have been for his grandfather who didn't have a computer. He grabbed a short glass of scotch and went out on the deck with Copper. The weather was classic Washington, hot and muggy. So, what was 'loc'? He set the glass down and went back to his laptop and Googled 'books at loc' and the first answer was 'Book/Printed Material, Available

Online | Library of Congress'. Of course, the Library of Congress – cool. He wasn't sure about the 'add 20' part but figured it would reveal itself in time.

Chapter 15   August 2015 – Fairfax, VA

The next morning after a five-mile run and a light breakfast Sandy drove to the Vienna Metro station near Nutley Street and parked in the garage. At nine in the morning, he had to circle around and around up four floors to find a parking spot on the roof. Grabbing his backpack, he took the bridge over to the station which was situated between the inbound and outbound lanes of I-66. 66 inbound was the normal parking lot with all five lanes solid and crawling. He tapped his Metro card on the turnstile and took the escalator down to the tracks. Being the last stop on the Orange Line, a train was waiting to go into the city. He walked on and grabbed an open seat.

The ride in was uneventful and because he was going to the Capitol South Metro station, he just stayed on the Orange line. Riding the escalator up he came out on First Street. He walked up the hill on First and crossed Independence putting him in front of the Library of Congress. The day was already hot and sticky, but being in such great shape, he hardly drew a sweat.

He took a moment to admire the Neptune Fountain with its three massive bronze sculptures. A huge muscular Neptune in the center and two sea nymphs on either side. He loved the sound of the water splashing about the pool. Going up the stairs he passed through security and then entered the Italian Renaissance building's Great Hall. The mosaic floor of marble was stunning, but nothing compared the grand arches which supported the ceiling soaring 75 feet overhead. The ceiling was adorned with stained glass and aluminum relief decoration, it took your breath away. As he walked through the commemorative arch, he took note of an original Gutenberg Bible on display. A new technology, movable type, created about 1450, changed bookmaking forever.

Sandy entered the Main Reading Room and just paused to take it all in. He had come to the Library many times in the past but was always stunned by this room. The massive domed ceiling rose 165 feet above the floor, eight giant pillars stood tall taking the weight of the eight arches which supported the dome. The dome was capped by a stained-glass oculus. Sandy reverently walked slowly to the circular desk in the center of the reading room. He took note of the librarian's name tag and said, "Good morning Carol, I would like to request a book."

"Of course, sir do you have a Reader Identification Card?"

"I do," and he retrieved the card from his wallet.

"If you have the author and title please go over to one of those computer terminals and get the call number for the book. Fill out a request card and someone will retrieve it for you."

Sandy went to the computer and entered 'Water Gas' as the title and 'Richard Beckwith' as the author. The computer came back with the call number HD2763 .T67 19579. He filled out a card and returned to the desk. "Found it Carol, and here is the card. That was so easy."

"We will have someone retrieve it and I would suggest taking a seat and stop back here in an hour. Sometimes it takes longer but it is quiet today with Congress in recess."

Sandy took a seat at one of the long tables that circled around the central librarian's desk. Several chairs down was a very attractive young woman with a stack of books on the table, who appeared to be in her late twenties. Sandy retrieved a book from his backpack and began to read. The woman stood, which Sandy caught out of the corner of his eye and he turned to look at her. She smiled and began to move in his direction. Sandy smiled back and said, "Wow that is quite a stack of books you're working on."

She continued to smile and said, "Yup just another research project. Are you waiting for your books?"

"Yes, just one. It is kind of a mystery project for me."

"Well, I will be back in a few minutes, enjoy your wait."

About 5 minutes later the woman returned. She was athletic, tall, maybe 5'7" with beautiful long strawberry blonde hair in big long curls. Sandy stood and introduced himself, "Hi, I am Sandy Powell."

She replied as she shook his hand with a huge smile, "Morgan Dutton, a pleasure to meet you, Sandy."

"Morgan that is a beautiful name, reminds me of my favorite breed of horse."

"Wow! We just met, and you call me a horse," she said with a grin and a quiet chuckle.

"I did say beautiful."

"Yes, you did, so where did Sandy come from?"

"Well, actually it is short for Sandusky. My dad spent part of his summers in college in Upper Sandusky, Ohio and he had a special spot in his heart for those memories."

"Well, that is a great story. Mine is similar, my mother loved Morgan horses, so you hit it on the head. Well back to work. I hope your book turns up soon."

Sandy returned to the book he brought with him, but his thoughts were not on his reading. He was thinking about Morgan. Her green eyes were captivating, and she also had a great figure, narrow hips, and to die for smile that just radiated. Sandy also noted he didn't see a ring, possibilities.

Morgan likewise was thinking about Sandy. He was tall maybe 6'1" and in really great shape – broad shoulders, narrow hips and a tight butt, close-cropped light brown hair, huge smile, and the most amazing blue eyes. They really sparkled like dark blue sapphires. She too noticed no ring or even a tan line if he had removed it for the day.

After about twenty minutes Sandy approached the librarian and his book had just arrived. She said, "It is part of the permanent collection so please return it here if you step away or need it back tomorrow."

"Thank you so much I will do just that."

When he returned to his seat he looked over at Morgan and she smiled back saying, "Well it looks like your mystery is about to begin.

Sandy smiled back and said, "It started a few days ago and this seems to be the next chapter."

"Good luck, Sandy"

Sandy sat and looked at the book. A piece of kitchen string was wrapped around the book like a ribbon wrapping a package, tied in a simple bow like on a shoe, at the front center. Sandy gently pulled the two ends of the string releasing the bow. There sat the book, neatly handwritten.

The Water Gas

By Richard Beckwith

Sandy reflected for a moment that his grandfather had many years ago tied that bow. Then, he opened the book and could see how the cover had been wrapped around an existing book. Turning to the cover page, he saw the book was Benjamin Franklin's Autobiography.

Sandy thought, ok, I didn't see that one coming.

On the cover page was the number 12. Sandy turned to page 12 and there was nothing there. He started to flip through the pages and saw words underlined and numbers on each page that had words underlined. He flipped back to page 12 thinking he had missed something but there was nothing there.

Sandy leaned back in his chair and gazed at the magnificent arch on the opposite wall and ceiling and tried to think. Morgan quietly in her best library voice whispered, "You look perplexed, can I help?"

Sandy smiled and said, "Perhaps, but it's a long story." And then, in a moment of inspiration, he added, "Would you like to have lunch?"

She smiled back. Then nodding she answered, still in her library voice, "I like the plan. I enjoy a good mystery."

"Are you up for a walk, the place I am thinking about is about six blocks away."

"Sure," she said with a big smile, "Nothing like a nice long walk in August in DC, well that is if you're a horse."

"Do you like French food?"

To which she replied in perfect French, "Oui, mais bien sûr".

Sandy had this massive smile, "Ok, we're off."

Sandy and Morgan dropped their books off at the desk and walked out onto First Street. They headed east to Pennsylvania Avenue in no particular hurry. Morgan started, "So Sandusky tell me your history."

"Well, I was born and spent my youth near Manchester, Vermont near my great grandfather's farm. When I was about six, we moved to St. Louis where my father worked for what would become Boeing. He passed away several years ago and my Mom still lives there. No siblings. I went to VMI and majored in biology. After VMI I was in the Navy, got married, became a SEAL and did several tours in the middle east. While I was deployed, we got divorced, with no kids. After eight years in the Navy, I received a medical discharge and became a schoolteacher in Fairfax last year."

"Wow, Navy SEAL I can see that. Did you see any action?"

"Way too much, it never really leaves you. So, what about you?"

"Well, I grew up outside Ithaca in the Finger Lakes region of New York. My dad was a vet, mostly large animals, and now he teaches at Cornell. I went to Syracuse and majored in Political Science and then went to Cornell for law school. I took a year off in between and lived with a friend in France. I took a job with a big firm here in DC doing intellectual property law and struck out on my own two years ago."

Sandy shook his head and replied smiling broadly, "So bottom-line you're brilliant as well as pretty."

"Ahhhh shucks," in a mock southern drawl, "you just know how to say all the rights things to a bell."

They walked on, commenting on each other's lives and soon arrived at a French Bistro on Pennsylvania Avenue in the Eastern Market neighborhood. The airy light-filled space was known for their scrumptious lunch and dinner menu. Stepping inside the air conditioning was refreshing coming from the humid tropical steam bath outside.

They choose a table near the expansive widows and Sandy ordered a bottle of Perrier and Brie de Meaux with baguette to start. Morgan started, "So tell me about your mystery."

"Well, about a month ago my aunt passed away."

"Oh, I am so sorry, were you close?"

"Yes, she lived in Great Falls and I saw her often. My grandfather, her Dad, died many years ago in a hit and run accident. I never knew him, we all believed it was an accident. She left a letter for me which I received last week at the reading of the will. Apparently, my aunt learned from my grandmother, just before she passed, that my grandfather's accident was really murder. Further in the letter, I learned there were secrets left by my grandfather before his murder. Based on her note, I uncovered another note that he left which led me to a book at the Library of Congress and pleasantly to you."

"So, do you know why he was killed?"

Sandy stared into her bright green emerald eyes, "Not yet, but hopefully I will discover it, perhaps it is in the book."

They ordered lunch. She got a bistro salad and seared octopus, while Sandy ordered the French Onion soup and two dozen Mussels Mariniere. They shared the mussels. The conversation drifted back and forth on their lives and related stories. Time slipped away and at last, somewhat reluctantly, they headed back to the library.

After retrieving their books, they return to their table except this time Morgan sat next to Sandy. Morgan said, "So you looked perplexed before we left for lunch, can I help?"

Sandy retrieved from his bag the deciphered note and shared it with Morgan.

As she looked down at it she frowned slightly and asked, "So what does the 'Add 20' mean?"

Sandy replied, "That one has got me, plus it was separated a bit from the rest."

Morgan opened the book again to the cover page and said, "What if you add 20 to the 12 and turn to page 32."

Together they turned to page 32 and the word 'Go' was underlined. At the top of the page was 17. They then turned to page 37 and the word 'to' was underlined. They turned and looked at each and in harmony said, "WOW" and chuckled.

Several people shushed them for being so loud. They just beamed at each other.

Sandy began the tedious work of flipping through the pages and writing down each word or in some cases a single letter. The last number sent him to page 131 where he found a folded slip of paper inserted in the book with the blank side facing out. Sandy gently removed the paper and read it.

Hello, the fact that you are reading this letter means I must have been killed.

If you were not intended to receive this letter, I strongly advise you to stop reading now and simply return the book as it will place you in grave danger.

To the future person who is reading this now, the fact that you were chosen means that you are trusted. Please know if you continue on this quest you may place yourself in harm's way.

With best wishes, God's grace, Be Safe, Richard Powell

Sandy looked at Morgan, "Well another clue."

Morgan read the sentences he had written and then the note, "Wow! Looks like an adventure! Want some help?"

Sandy looked thoughtful and said slowly, "Morgan, the note says grave danger. I don't want you to get hurt."

"Me, I have my knight in shining armor plus you're a SEAL, what can possibly go wrong."

"Well," Sandy grinned, "In that case, would you grace me with dinner tonight, fair Princess."

"Ahhhh," Morgan smiled, "a very gracious offer, but sorry I have plans. You see I spent so much time today with this captivating knight that now I am behind on my work for my client and I will be up half the night catching up."

"Oh, I am sorry to have kept you from your duty, my lady."

Morgan beamed, "It was worth every moment. How about tomorrow night?"

"Perfect, can I pick you up about six? What ethnicity would you treasure?"

"Well like you, how about hot and spicy", she said in a sultry tone. "Let's do Indian."

It was Sandy's turn to beam, "I know the place, you will love it."

They exchanged phone numbers and addresses and Sandy was on his way to the metro while Morgan plunged back into her pile of books.

Chapter 16   August 2015 – Fairfax, VA

Sandy was up a bit later than normal, knowing it might be a late night. Copper was ready to go, and they were off on his perfunctory five-mile run. Light rain made it cooler but just as humid and they were both soaking wet when they returned.

He was busy all morning around the house and by midafternoon he dressed in grey slacks, white shirt and navy sport coat, no tie. Knowing that traffic was horrendous on a Friday night he left at 3:30 for the 20-mile drive to downtown. 66 was not yet a parking lot so he made it with plenty of time to spare. Shortly before six he parked on Olive Street in Georgetown and found Morgan's home - a recently built Federal style brownstone townhouse. The architecture was classic, and she had a middle unit. He rang the bell next to the bright red front door.

In less than a minute she opened the door. She simply glowed, wearing a soft blue dress with a slight plunge on top and a matching pleated bottom which stopped just above the knee. Her white open-toed shoes accented her beautiful legs.

Sandy caught his breath and took her hand as she stepped down from the threshold. "Wow, you look stunning."

"Well my knight, you dress up pretty good too." She tucked her arm in his as they walked together to his car. It felt natural. He opened the door and she slipped comfortably into the Mazda. After he slid into the driver's seat, she said, "This is pure sport. I have never seen one like this, sweet."

"One of a kind, it's a prototype. I had shipped over from Japan in pieces, a friend is an executive at Mazda. I built it last winter."

They drove across downtown and parked in a garage across the street from the Indian restaurant. After starters, Morgan had the shrimp moilee and Sandy had the adraki lamb chops. Dinner was amazing and they enjoyed the small talk and getting to know each other. After dessert Sandy with a totally serious face said, "If you are free tomorrow, I was hoping you could join us at the farm for the next clue."

Morgan looked shocked, "US?"

"Oh yea, I always have my companion with me when I go to the farm."

"Your companion, I thought you were single."

"Oh I am, it's my Golden Retriever, Copper."

Morgan hit him hard in the shoulder, "You have a warped sense of humor."

"Ahhhh, just having a bit of fun," Sandy said with a big grin, "you should have seen your face."

"Love to join you and Copper. He is probably better mannered than you are."

Then she added, with a smile, "Ok, we're not done yet. Let's go to a club I know. It's not far, so we can walk."

"Sounds great - the night is young."

Ten minutes later after walking north on Connecticut Avenue, they arrived at the pub. The place was full of people and they got drinks and found a comfortable place to enjoy the music and chat. Morgan texted her best friend Vicky and soon they had a whole group of people. Vicky and Morgan headed off to the ladies' room and once inside Vicky said, "Oh my God, he is amazing! Not only is he a dish to stare at but smart, witty and fun to be with. He is a catch and don't let him get away."

"I know I know! I only met him yesterday but already I am head over heels for him and I feel like I have known him forever."

"Well hang on tight! He is such a catch."

From time to time Sandy and Morgan would get up and dance and the next thing they knew it was midnight and time to call it a night. When they walked out Sandy said, "Better hurry before garage closes."

"No worries, we will grab an Uber and go to the garage first. That will get you there faster." And she laughed seeing the concerned look on Sandy's face, "Ahh, my knight, never fear. I'll be fine. I have done this Uber routine once or twice before going home...if you haven't noticed Georgetown isn't exactly on the metro line."

Sandy nodded. "Ok. But be ready for Copper and me to pick you up first thing in the morning."

"I can't wait..."

Saturday morning Sandy woke early with Copper crossways on the bed. He groaned as he stroked the dog, rubbing Copper's ears.

"What's wrong with the dog bed?" he sighed. "You're too used to it being just the two of us, huh? BUT..." he said dreamily, thinking of Morgan, "with a little luck, we might have someone else to make our twosome a threesome – sooner rather than later."

Then he jumped up quickly, startling Copper. "No run this morning, buddy." And Copper cocked his head, his ears pulled out inquiringly.

"We're sure to get plenty of exercise at Aunt Beth's farm." And with that, Sandy started for the shower to get moving on the day ahead.

Sandy and Copper made good time and they enjoyed a traffic-less weekend morning drive in on 66 from Fairfax to Georgetown. They, surprisingly, found a parking space on the street close to Morgan's house, walked up and rang the bell.

Morgan came to the door, smiling widely. She was dressed in skinny jeans and a teal polo shirt with stylish boots. "Come in," and looking down at Copper she added, "both of you. I hope you're hungry. I have breakfast in the oven, almost ready to come out."

Copper greeted Morgan wagging his whole body as happy as could be and Morgan smiled leaned over to stroke his back.

Walking into her house Sandy was blown away. It was like it was out of Architecture Digest. A brick wall ran from front to back, hardwood floors in the open concept and it was tastefully full of stainless and glass furnishings. They walked to the back where the kitchen had a wall of cabinets, marble countertops, and a large marble island.

As they entered the kitchen Morgan pulled something from the wall oven and said questioningly, "I hope you like quiche?" She set it down on two potholders strategically set out on the counter.

"It smells amazing," Sandy exclaimed, as he

ambled over and pulled her tight. Giving her a generous kiss he murmured in her ear, "You smell amazing too."

She laughed lightly, then pulled away and gestured to the island in the center of the kitchen. "Why don't you pour the coffee, while I cut the quiche," she told Sandy, "And," with a grin at Copper she said, "there might be a breakfast style treat of some ham for you too...that is," she raised her eyebrows and looked at Sandy, "if you dad says it's ok?"

Sandy laughed. "You got him at 'treat' and 'ham'. He knows those words – now you have to deliver."

Copper gave a guttural 'woof' in agreement and Morgan laughed.

"No problem...let's eat."

They ate slowly, enjoying the sumptuous quiche Lorraine along with a delicious espresso blend coffee and fresh orange juice while sitting at the breakfast bar on the large center island. Copper sat at their feet enjoying the scraps of ham that Morgan had saved for him. When they finished, they made light work picking up the kitchen and went out into the already warm and humid summer day to Sandy's car to make the journey up to Great Falls.

Chapter 17   August 2015, Great Falls, VA

S andy, Morgan, and Copper pulled up to Aunt Beth's house. As soon as they got out of the car, Copper was off like a shot sniffing and running around the barn and the outbuildings. Sandy unlocked the door and turned off the alarm. He asked Morgan if she wanted anything to drink and she said she was fine.

"Well, what do you think of my new spread."

Morgan looked about, "A few updates and this could be a sweet home."

Sandy beamed, "That plus 60 acres in Great Falls, it could be whatever we want. Let's go see where the next clue leads us."

Morgan's heart skipped a beat, and she smiled from the inside out. She had clearly heard the 'we' and liked how it felt. They were certainly going at warp speed in the relationship, but she had never felt safer or more comfortable with anyone. It felt great. "Lead on Sherlock."

The clue they deciphered yesterday read:

"Go to the NE corner of the barn. Tilt up the middle shelf in the cupboard and pull the right side of the cupboard out."

Sandy unlocked the hasp and opened both big

sliding doors. Inside was a collection of machinery and on the right stalls for horses or cows. They walked to the far end of the barn and in the corner stood a roughly eight-foot-high, four-foot-wide cabinet. Sandy cleared off the items on the middle shelf and put them on a nearby table. He then lifted the middle shelf and could hear a click. He pulled on the right side and the cabinet rotated out revealing stairs going down.

Sandy looked at Morgan, "Ok, I never imagined this was here. I'm going to go get a flashlight or two out of the car. Copper you stay with Morgan."

Copper sat and was happy to be with Morgan. When Sandy returned, he put a paint can in front of the cabinet to make sure it didn't close behind them. Then he entered the space and flicked a light switch on. Light shown up the stairs from below.

"Looks good so far. Morgan you and Copper stay here while I check it out." Sandy carefully went down the wooden stairs and could not believe what he saw. It was a full laboratory. He looked around and could see no snakes or mice and the place looked safe. He yelled up, "you got to come down and see this."

Morgan felt a rush of adrenaline and took a deep breath. "A real mystery," she thought. "And what a Holmes to my Watson," she grinned, and she and

Copper descended into the basement lab.

Down the center between the posts that supported the ceiling were black stone-topped tables covered with flasks, beakers, and assorted chemistry equipment. One wall had shelves with cardboard boxes and jars full of various chemicals. An antique desk and more workbenches lined the opposing wall. An exhaust fan was mounted on one wall and Sandy guessed its exhaust came out in the stone well twenty feet from the barn. Sandy said to Morgan, "time for the next clue."

"SE corner, middle shelf, in the bottom of a box of papers are the details."

Sandy and Morgan walked to the far corner and pulled a box out and placed it on a blacktopped table noticing that there was surprisingly little dust anywhere. Slowly removing the papers in the box, they came to an upside-down laboratory notebook. They took it and all the papers below and set it aside. Together they opened and began to read Sandy's grandfather's lab notebook.

"This is it. This is why he was murdered. Let's take this to the house where it will be easier to read."

The threesome went back up the stairs, turned off the lights, closed the cupboard, and put a few things back on the middle shelf. A few minutes later they were back at the house, sitting at the kitchen table.

"Sandy, the Navy must have built that for him. Remember, it was the height of the cold war and he was doing top-secret work for the Navy. Do you think the Russians had him killed?"

"It is certainly possible, but I would think the Navy would have removed everything from the lab."

She thought, "Good point, but it is a possibility."

"Let's look through his notes and try to figure out what his discovery was and that may give us a clue to who wanted it."

After an hour Sandy said he was hungry, they put the notes and lab book in a kitchen drawer and locked up the house. Sandy told Copper to stay in the kitchen as he and Morgan drove to Great Falls for lunch. The Irish Pub in the heart of Great Falls looked like a great spot. They ordered the Warm Crab & Avocado Crostini to start – a treat they both loved and remarked how the avocado was a great twist to the blue crab. For the main part of their meal, Sandy had an Angus burger and Morgan a grilled Rueben. Both were amazing. To accompany the feast, they each enjoyed a draft of Smithwick's Ale.

Sitting in a back-corner booth, they quietly

compared notes on what they had learned so far. Sandy remarked, "It looks like he discovered a way to produce hydrogen gas using a solution and electroplating."

Morgan replied, "Yes, and even more interesting he had written a patent on it, so we can see if that patent was filed. That's pretty easy to do."

Sandy thought for a moment, "you know I am supposed to start teaching in about ten days. But I'm thinking I will take a sabbatical for the fall semester. This is going to take a bunch of research and we also need to test to see if it really works. I don't need the money. I just inherited a small pile and I may just sell the house in Fairfax and move out to the farm. What do you think?"

Morgan thought a moment, her heartstrings pulled again, thinking he used "we" and values her opinion about his life moving forward, "It's an interesting idea but pretty major. I'd sleep on that one for a couple of days. There's nothing you can do till Monday anyway."

"Great point"

"I have an idea, let's go back to the farm, gather up all the papers, then go back downtown. You can read through the pile I can get some work done and we could order in some Chinese or something...we can pick up something for Copper."

"I love the idea, but are you sure about bringing Copper?"

"Sure, I have a feeling he is going to be spending a lot of time at my place we might as well get him adjusted."

Sandy turned on that million-dollar smile, "Well I am not worried about Copper adjusting. I am worried about you seeing all the clumps of dog hair and you throw us both out."

"You don't have to worry about that, remember I am the daughter of a vet. I love dogs and grew up with them," Morgan replied with her own million-dollar smile.

"Well then, it's a deal. But don't worry about Copper. I'm sure Aunt Beth has dog supplies. We'll pack up some from here."

And they walked out, two people falling in love on a beautiful Saturday afternoon.

Chapter 18   August 2015, Georgetown, DC

They arrived late afternoon back at her house in Georgetown. Morgan directed Sandy to a parking area behind her house and they entered through her small fenced yard leading to the back door.

"This is convenient," Sandy remarked about the parking. Copper was on his leash looking all about as Sandy carried in a small gym bag with dog food and bowls for Copper that they snagged from Aunt Beth's house.

The backyard was compact but lovely. Flowers and a small hedge were against the fence. A bluestone walkway gently curved from the gate to the rear door and patio. Comfortable patio furniture and a grill completed the area. In the far corner, a small pool provided a babbling sound of water running down over a pile of round rocks. Sandy, taking it all in, said, "this is like an oasis in the city, absolutely beautiful."

Morgan smiled, "I am really lucky a friend of mine from Syracuse is a landscape architect and she designed it. And I have a great gardener who keeps it so lovely. Let's go in first. We can come back out once we are settled."

Morgan entered the key code and the door

unlocked. They entered the mudroom off the kitchen. A washer and dryer also occupied the space as well as a coat closet.

Copper was sniffing everything as they entered and Sandy unhooked the leash and said, "Copper you behave." Copper was off exploring the downstairs smelling everything and then returned to the kitchen. Sandy set the bag in a corner and pulled out a water bowl to give Copper some water.

"How about some cheese and crackers on the patio? The heat seems to have broken and there's a light breeze. Would you like wine, beer or something else?"

Sandy smiled, "White wine sounds great. Can I help?"

Morgan directed him to the wine glasses and the wine frig under the counter while she got plates, cheese, and crackers. Sandy choose a New Zealand Oyster Bay Chardonnay which he loved for being both vibrant and creamy.

As he watched, Morgan made quick work pulling out a creamy blue cheese, smoked gouda, and a sharp Vermont cheddar along with water crackers and some baguette slices. She arranged it all on a tray and they were off to the patio. Copper was right on their heels and rushed out the door to explore the yard.

They sat and chatted about the day, their discoveries and talked about Sandy taking a sabbatical and selling his house. Copper, having explored every corner of the yard, returned to the patio and laid down next to Morgan.

After a bit, Morgan said, "I really have to get some work done."

They returned inside and she said, "I will be upstairs in my office, please make yourself at home."

"I will, I already feel at home," Sandy grinned, "I am going to dive into the papers my grandfather left. Take your time."

Sandy sat at the dining room table and began to read from his grandfather's notes and papers. Morgan headed upstairs with Copper following closely behind. Several hours later Morgan came downstairs and Sandy smiled at her return. Copper was in tow and was the happiest dog on the planet.

He looked at her, "I think Copper has fallen for you. Looks like I'll have some big competition on that front."

Morgan felt her muscles deep down in that special place clench. "Oh, I think you are safe mister. Any interesting discoveries?"

"Actually, yes. His notes and papers go into extensive detail so we should be able to recreate his setup. There are a lot of details on the transformer he used that was acting differently. He was actually in the process of replacing it. And then there's this piece," he looked up at her, "You may find this interesting; I found a receipt from the Patent Office saying he filed it."

"Wow, that is helpful. I'll check Monday to see if it was issued or what the status is for the patent. Would you like Chinese or something else?"

"Chinese sounds great. We can munch, relax, watch a bit of TV before Copper and I take our leave."

Morgan laughed, "Well, I certainly can't resist those puppy dog eyes...yours or Copper's. I'll get the menu...and maybe some kind of a doggie treat." She winked as she left the room.

They relaxed, enjoyed their Chinese food feast, and watched a bit of a pre-season football game. Then the three of them walked slowly to Morgan's back door where she and Sandy had a very amorous good night.

Sandy sighed as they broke apart. "Until tomorrow then..."

"Mmmm," Morgan murmured. "Plan on breakfast again."

"You got it," Sandy said as he and Copper disappeared into the gently lit backyard and slipped out the back gate to the car.

Sunday dawned bright and early. "First things first," Sandy said to Copper and they went for a five-mile run, the refreshing day made it a pleasure.

After giving Copper his favorite Blue Buffalo breakfast, and taking a quick shower, the two were ready for the drive to Morgan's for breakfast. Over delicious scones and croissants, they discussed the plan for the day. Morgan decided she really needed to get more work done.

Sandy nodded and said, "I think I am going to sell the Fairfax house and take that sabbatical. So, I might as well start moving into the farm. What do you think?"

Morgan nodded thoughtfully, "I think it makes a lot of sense, you don't need two places to live and I think it will take a lot of time to research and see about your grandfather's discovery."

Sandy grinned at that thought. "My house in the suburbs and my country home...It does sound like a bit much, doesn't it?"

Morgan laughed. "And," she smiled wickedly at Sandy, "if you play your cards right you could be looking at a great little place in Georgetown too..."

Sandy's eyebrows shot up. "Really..." he said as a grin spread across his face. "Well, by all means, let's explore this issue later. Would you be up to driving to the farm after you finish working? I'll go home and get some things packed so Copper and I can stay up there. I'll fix dinner – sunset on the farm..."

"Sounds romantic..." Morgan teased. "And, what a catch! Not only a SEAL but also a chef. I love the plan. I should be up there between 5 and 6."

Soon after Sandy and Copper were on their way, driving over the Key bridge and out the GW Parkway to 495 then jumped off in Tysons and took 123 through Vienna to Fairfax. The day was a pleasant 70 and sunny with a breeze out of the north a nice change from the heat and humidity of last week.

Sandy called Jackson and gave him a full update on Morgan, plans to sell the house and his grandfather's discovery.

Jackson said, "Well mate it looks like you are over the moon in love and clearly off the eligible bachelors list."

"Well, I think you just might be right, old friend. I don't think I have ever been so happy. I will keep you updated."

Sandy could hear Jackson's smile. "You'd better, mate!" And the two signed off, promising to stay in touch.

"Ok," Sandy thought to himself. "Let's get organized and work the plan."

He made a to-do list:

- Contact School about a sabbatical
- Find an agent
- Line up movers
- Pack essentials for the week
- Move critical stuff to the farm
- Get cash from attorney

Going down his list, Sandy first called Lezlie Anderson his high school principal and told her about his plan to take a sabbatical for the fall semester. She totally understood and instructed him on what he needed to write. He should send it to her and the administrator for the county school system immediately. He got off the phone and wrote the letter while it was fresh in his mind.

I'll be able to mail it tomorrow, Monday, he thought.

Next, he called three well known real estate agents and made appointments, also for tomorrow to have them look at the house.

He then packed two suitcases of clothes to bring to the farm. In the back of the closet, he pulled out his footlocker and carried it out to the car. Next in his closet he removed the false panel in the back and extracted his small arsenal of guns; pistols, shotguns, and several rifles and put them in cases. He packed a bag with shells and spare clips. All of this went out to the car as well.

Finally, he put in a call to his attorney, Gary Sutter and updated him on his plan and discovery. He instructed him to transfer twenty thousand into his account at a local bank. Then he and Copper headed over to the farm to unload the car. He did not trust leaving the weapons in the house, so he decided to hide the weapons in the lab. He knew I would need to get a heated weapons safe soon if he kept them in the lab.

"We're on our way to our new home, boy," Sandy said to Copper. "I think you will be very happy there!"

Copper gave his series of "woofs" that meant he liked what he heard...or at least that's what Sandy took it as.

On their way out, Sandy stopped at a great butcher shop in Reston and picked out two huge dry-aged tomahawk ribeye steaks. He went to another shop and got a bottle of cabernet sauvignon, several russet potatoes, asparagus, and a peach pie. Back in the car, he took Fairfax County Parkway north towards Great Falls.

Arriving about 5:30 Sandy had just finished unloading his car – when Morgan pulled in. After a warm and affectionate greeting, they sipped some wine while Sandy prepared the luscious steak dinner – happy that Aunt Beth still had a full tank of propane for her grill.

After dinner, Morgan brought in a bag and cleared space in the guest bedroom closet and dresser for some of her clothes. "You don't mind..." she asked Sandy slyly.

"Not at all," he beamed. "It is a bit of a drive...and there's plenty of room."

And the two sat snuggled on the back deck, watching as the stars came out, content to sit in each other's arms and talk.

Chapter 19   August 2015, Lagos, Nigeria

Bob and Sally Lancaster had planned a weekend get-away from the US Embassy in Abuja to celebrate 20 wonderful years together. It would also give them time to catch up with friends at the Consulate in Lagos. While Bob's State Department salary was modest, the cost of living in Lagos was so cheap. The Oceanview Restaurant on Victoria Island had a reputation as the classiest and best seafood restaurant in town, so it was well worth it. They were seated off to the side of the restaurant in a quiet corner.

After they were seated Bob glanced around and then whispered to Sally, "I can't believe who is seated next to us. Don't stare but that is three of the richest people on the planet."

At the table right next to Bob were Harold Watson, Bryce Carrington, and Reginald Clark. They were the respective CEOs of Texas Oil, American Petroleum, and Sunco the three largest oil and gas companies in the world. With the US anti-trust laws Bob was thinking these guys should not be in the same city, let alone having dinner together. Bob focused on Sally but was also listening to their conversation, beyond curious.

HW began, "We should have gotten a private

dining room I hope we don't get seen together."

Bryce replied, "Nobody in this corner of the world knows who we are, I am sure we're safe. We need to talk about what we should do with Ali Mohammed. We've paid him nearly half a million BUT he's demanding more."

Reggie piped in, "I don't mind paying the money, but he is not delivering. Actually, it's his vice minister who is aligned with our thinking about control of the various oil fields and tariffs. I think we have to take him out."

HW was very uncomfortable with the direction this conversation was going. As the newest member of the Pinnacle Club, he was surprised at how they matter-of-factly they discussed killing someone.

"Gentlemen, I'm not sure I can go along with this solution. Perhaps there is a better way to turn him in our direction."

Reggie looked disgusted, "You know HW this is a tough business and we've grown our companies to what they are by working together and secretly controlling the world's energy supplies. Sometimes, we are forced to make hard decisions in order to maintain our control. This is not the first time and I am sure this won't be the last where the best solution is permanent."

Bryce looked HW in the eyes, "You will see in

good time that Reggie is right. It is never easy, but it must be done. With Ali out of the picture, Arsalan Aziz will be in power and we will have our oil at our price. Further, I believe we will find new oil fields and will be pumping here for decades."

Reggie asked, "Everyone in favor of putting Arsalan in power."

All three nodded their heads but HW remained uncomfortable with the development.

"I will reach out to Paragon and have them fix things," he said somewhat reluctantly.

Bryce looked around the table, "With that problem solved, we need to talk about the situation in Saudi and Indonesia while we are together. Aren't these prawns amazing."

Bob was shocked at what he had overheard. It was unbelievable. He excused himself from Sally and went to the men's room. On the way back to the table he discreetly took a picture with his phone of the three men together.

The following day, Bob went to the airport and with his diplomatic credentials was able to drive around the private jets. He took pictures of all the jets' tail numbers. That afternoon he called a former college roommate who worked at the Justice Department to share what he had overheard and securely emailed him the pictures of the men and the jets.

Bryan Park thought he had heard everything until the call from Bob Lancaster. Bryan had been at the Justice Department for over 15 years, and while he was a prosecutor, he did have friends across the department. He reached out to Mark Taylor a good friend who was in the anti-trust division at Justice and they agreed to meet in Mark's office the next day.

In Mark's office, Bryan shared what he learned from his former roommate about the meeting between Harold Watson, Bryce Carrington, and Reginald Clark. He shared a thumb drive with the pictures Bob had sent over.

Mark shook his head in disbelief. "If this is true," he began slowly, "and I have absolutely no reason to believe it is not true, this has massive implications. I'll talk to my boss, Melissa Pearson, and see if we can get a go-ahead to start an investigation. We will take it from here. I really appreciate you and Bob putting this together. I will reach out to Bob and remind him to keep this classified."

Shortly after the meeting Mark called Bob Lancaster at the US Embassy in Nigeria and told him he appreciated his information and emphasized that the matter was highly classified.

He asked Bob to memorialize everything he saw and heard in as much detail as possible. He also advised Bob that they would be sending a DOJ agent down to interview him on the event.

A week later Bob reached out to both Bryan and Mark to let them know that Ali Mohammed the Nigerian Minister for Oil and Gas had died of apparent food poisoning. Mark immediately contacted Sarah Hughes, the US Ambassador to Nigeria, and asked her to have someone discreetly contact the person performing the autopsy on Ali and request they wait until someone from the US could attend the autopsy. He suggested that they tell the coroner that the US had seen recent attacks by Al Qaeda against leaders in other countries and we would like to confirm it was food poisoning.

Still moving quickly, Mark then reached out to a colleague at the FBI and requested a forensic pathologist be sent immediately to Lagos. He shared the storyline with his associate.

Matthew French was unaware of the details but knew it was important when an FBI jet was standing by at Joint Base Andrews to fly him directly to Lagos, Nigeria. Normally the dead can wait for his arrival. His instructions were to assist in the autopsy, collect specimens and confirm the food poisoning assumption even if it was not.

After the 12-hour flight with a brief refueling stop in Puerto Rico, Matt was ready to go, and arrangements were made to meet with the coroner, Dr. Habib at 3 p.m. He reviewed Habib's notes and saw that Ali had died approximately 12 hours after eating at a local restaurant. Ali had told his wife he was suffering from a headache, severe abdominal pain, and nausea. He died in bed. Within a few hours, he was transported to the coroner's morgue and fluid samples were collected and the body was placed in cold storage. Fortunately, the busy coroner had not yet performed the autopsy.

Ali's body was moved from the cooler drawer and placed on the examination table. Habib and Matt did a routine examination of the body and there was no indication of any external trauma, as expected. They then propped the head and neck up and exposed the brain and took several samples. Next they did the classic 'Y' incision, cutting across near the shoulders and then cutting down from the top to the groin. The Striker saw was used to cut through the ribs. Pulling the skin and ribs back all the major organs were revealed.

Matt immediately took note of the pulmonary edema of both lungs and congestion of the liver, since this was common in food poisoning, he told Habib. Matt suggested they open the stomach to see if any food was still present and several samples were taken. They also opened portions of the small and large intestines to take samples. Finally, they took fecal samples.

Matt said, "Looks like you called it right Habib. It certainly looks like acute food poisoning. I'll take my samples back to our lab and let you know our results in a week or so."

"Thank you so much and it is good to know that it was not a result of terrorism. I hope you have a safe trip home."

"Very happy to help. Would you like me to assist in closing up the body?"

Habib replied, "No I will have one of my staff close and prepare the body for the family. Again, have a safe trip home and thanks for your assistance."

After Matt boarded the plane, he used a secure phone to reach his boss at the FBI. "It certainly appears to be arsenic poisoning, but we will have to run some tests when I get back to confirm. I left the coroner with the impression it was my opinion that it was food poisoning and he concurred."

Chapter 20   September 2015, Georgetown, DC

It had been a busy week for both Sandy and Morgan. Sandy was able to select an agent who recommended a few changes and suggested what should be moved out and what should stay for staging the house. Sandy lined up movers and in two days he packed and moved things the fifteen miles to the farm in Great Falls. Some of it went in the barn or one of the sheds since he did not need it right away, the rest in the living room for now. By Friday the house was ready for the staging company to come in and get it ready for the market. The photographer came in the afternoon and by Friday night the house was on the market with an open house on Saturday and Sunday.

Morgan had been equally busy supporting several clients' patent applications and revisions to get their product through the tangled weave of USPTO. She also had several clients that were foreign companies, supporting their efforts for US patent protection. Particularly challenging was taking the translated patents and making them acceptable English for the application.

They decided to go out for Italian at a nearby restaurant on M street, a short walk from Morgan's house. Over dinner, Sandy said, "I have an idea, not sure if we can pull it off, but what if we went out to the Eastern Shore tomorrow morning. I know a place near St. Michaels right on the bay, we can rent a sailboat and go sailing tomorrow."

"Sandy," Morgan smiled, "have I told you how much I love you? That sounds amazing, we both could use a break and it would be nice to get out of town."

Sandy smiled, feeling very good inside. "Consider it done!"

Sandy made a few calls from the restaurant and soon they were all set for a weekend of sailing on the Eastern Shore. Both were up early and two hours later they were in St. Michaels picking up the boat. Sandy walked up to neat shack in front of the boatyard, carrying their bags poking his head in the open door, "Master Chief, how are you sir?"

"Commander Powell you are looking great and who is this beautiful woman?"

"Chief meet Morgan Dutton, she is the answer to many prayers."

"I can believe that, and you were in luck when you called that I had a cancellation and was able to get you a Catalina 30 that will give you a great weekend. I don't need it back till mid-week so enjoy. It is fully equipped with charts, fishing poles and all the gear you need."

"Thanks so much, Master Chief, we plan to be

back Sunday night or early Monday morning."

While Sandy got the boat ready, Morgan bought some food to eat on the boat and by ten in the morning they were underway. Copper enjoyed the boat but mostly stayed in the cabin and slept.

They motored out of the harbor and were under full sail after 15 minutes. With a gentle breeze out of the south Sandy had to tack back and forth so they could sail south on the Chesapeake Bay. After a few hours, they found a quiet cove where they dropped anchor, ate some lunch and took a dip in the warm water of the bay. Sandy and Copper swam a hundred yards to shore and ran around a bit and Copper relieved himself. They had a quiet afternoon sailing about the bay and then across to the western shore and they docked at Chesapeake Beach. There they had a wonderful meal in a local crab house restaurant then. The next day they sailed south past Tangier Island almost to the ocean before turning about and heading north to St. Michaels. It was very late by the time they returned to the dock so they crashed in the cabin of the boat one more night and left very early Monday morning when the traffic was still very light over the Bay Bridge. They arrived back at Morgan's house in great time.

As they unloaded their gear, Sandy watched Morgan, Copper following closely behind her into the house. He sighed contentedly.

We are definitely an item, he thought, a warm feeling inside. One of these days we should discuss next steps...

Monday evening while they ate a quiet dinner the real estate agent called to say she had received three offers all above asking. Sandy chose one and they celebrated.

What they didn't realize was that Sandy's exploration into hydrogen gas was only just beginning. While there had been a lot unearthed since his grandfather's discovery, on first reading, it did not appear that any method produced the volume of gas with so little energy input. The puzzle intrigued him, and he pushed hard all week at the Library of Congress learning more and more about hydrogen and its production. Little did he know how this would totally change their lives.

Chapter 21   September 2015, Menlo Park, CA

Brooke Tate was working at her station when an alert came through. Paragon with nearly limitless resources was like a mini version of the NSA. They had installed backdoors in major systems around the world and were constantly monitoring traffic for keywords to determine if competitors to the Pinnacle Group had emerged.

Brooke's alert was that someone at the Library of Congress was doing a deep dive into hydrogen. The system was smart enough not to send up a flag if someone pinged one of the keywords once or twice but only when it was more constant. Brooke started her analysis. Pretty quickly she was able to determine that the person had pulled up over 40 papers and articles on hydrogen gas and its production over the past three days. She had the IP address as the Library of Congress wireless network. She installed a tiny virus that would signal them whenever the device connected to the internet. So far, she had been unable to break through the firewall on the device to pull down data off its hard drive. Brooke sent an alert to her boss, Lynn Nash, with the information she had.

Ten minutes later Lynn sat down at Brooke's station and looked on with her at the three monitors with data on the suspect. Lynn asked if there was any new information or progress. Brooke said, "I am still trying to break through his firewall, but it seems pretty strong. I should be able to get through in the next thirty minutes. Lynn looked at the clock on one of the displays and realized at most they had an hour before it was 5 p.m. eastern time.

Lynn said, "I am going to have Van come over and work with you. He is a black hat extraordinaire if anyone can break it, he can. Heck, he probably designed the firewall."

"Thanks so much."

Van arrived shortly and slid in beside Brooke. Van was a pure techie, overweight, zooming on the caffeine from his non-stop energy drinks and clearly needed a trip to the corporate shower. He quickly assessed the data on the three screens and then asked to use her keyboard. He rapidly typed some commands and sent them through the ether to the device they were tracking. Before long, he cracked the firewall and slipped a different virus into the device. Through the crack, he also harvested some key data including the device's digital fingerprint.

Van said to Brooke, "I am going to leave the hole open so you can capture some files but don't copy too much or they may notice. I will be back in five minutes to close it, so move quickly."

Brooke quickly scanned through the directories and found some key files and grabbed them. She activated the camera and took a picture of the guy using it and thought he was kind of cute. A few minutes later Van returned and closed their opening. Brooke began her more in-depth analysis. An hour later she had a pretty extensive background on the person using the device. She created her report and let Lynn know she was ready to review.

Lynn sat with Brooke as she reviewed the report. The user appeared to be Sandy Powell. He lived in Fairfax, Virginia and had several bank accounts. He was doing research on hydrogen gas production for the past week. The intent was unknown. Lynn looked at all they had and said, "Ok let's keep a track on him 24/7 for a week and see if this leads to something or if it is just another flash in the pan."

Brooke agreed with the assessment and began tracking. Unless something big happened, this was often was the end of an assignment.

Chapter 22 September 2015, Washington, DC

At the Robert F. Kennedy Department of Justice Building, things were spinning up fast. With the confirmation that Ali Mohammed the Nigerian Minister for Oil and Gas had been murdered, this case became very real. Add to this the apparent involvement of three of the global leaders in the oil and gas business, and this situation became much more than an ordinary antitrust matter.

Melissa Pearson entered the office of the Attorney General. It looked very much like a judge's chambers, dark wood paneling, a simple marble fireplace, a large desk covered with papers and a whole bunch of photos and curios on the mantel and scattered about the room. A United States flag stood in a corner by a glass-paneled curio closet. The room felt very personal. Meredith Drake, Attorney General rose to greet her. Drake was of medium height with brown hair just past her shoulders, a rich smile, and with her mixed-race background a beautiful light brown olive tone to her skin. "Welcome to my office, I appreciate you jumping over the chain of command and sending this matter to me directly. I will personally smooth any feathers that may have been ruffled. The potential political nature of this means we need to keep it very tight. I have invited Assistant Deputy AG Rodney Holloway to join us and he should be here momentarily. Have a seat."

Just then there was a light knock on the door and Rod stepped into the room. Meredith continued, "Rod thanks for joining us. As I mentioned to Melissa, I want to keep the circle on this tight. Rod, I want you to personally take the point on this investigation. Based on the sworn statements from Bob and Sally Lancaster I believe we have probable cause. We can skip doing an assessment and begin a preliminary investigation. Due to the nature of this investigation, I can imagine we could have several other agencies involved including the CIA, State, and NSA. I would like you to request warrants from a magistrate judge to get phone and other records for these three individuals and their companies. We should probably go back five years and see if we can find any correlation in their records. Additionally, I want a team assembled at the FBI to do a deep dive into the financial records to see if there is anything there."

At this point, Meredith paused, and with a grim smile on her face turned to her Assistant Deputy AG and asked, "Rod your thoughts?"

Rod was 5'10", a former Air Force prosecuting attorney, his hair high and tight and the gray was beginning to show. "As I see it there are two additional points that require immediate investigation. One is to determine, if possible, who poisoned Ali. I will reach out to the CIA to see if we have resources in-country. Second, in Bob Lancaster's notes, he mentioned Paragon. So, I want a group at the FBI to try to determine who that is. I will coordinate with Lester Hodges at the FBI to get it started on their end."

"Excellent. I have a meeting with the Director tomorrow and will bring him in the loop. Obviously, loop me in if we reach out to other agencies. Melissa, I want you to report directly to Rod on this and Rod I want you to talk to her supervisor to smooth over the chain of command issue." Meredith stood and it was clear the meeting was over.

After exiting the AG's office Rod said to Melissa, "Walk with me, we will discuss the next steps in my office." They walked down the long corridor, turned the corner and entered Rod's suite. Walking past his admin he called out, "hold my calls, please, Doris. Melissa do you want anything to drink?"

"Yes, thank you, coffee black would be great."

They entered his office and sat at a table adjacent to his desk. A moment later, Doris entered with a large mug of steaming coffee. "Anything else

Mr. Holloway?"

"No, I am good thanks, Doris." Turning to Melissa, "I know your background is in antitrust so I would like you to chase that rabbit. Let's start with the following assumption. First, let's assume they are working together. Next, make a list of the evidence we need to convict them on antitrust violations say under the Sherman Act or similar. Next figure out who in the department, the FBI or other agencies could collect that evidence and get back to me. I will help you assemble that team and then we can collect the information."

"Excellent, I'll start on it straight away. And Rod," she said sincerely, "thank you for your support in this investigation."

He nodded and smiled at Melissa as she stood and headed out of the office. "Let's hope we get to the bottom of this...quickly," he said.

And with the door still open, he called out, "Doris, do you have a second?" Doris stepped into Rod's office. "Can you ask Lester Hodges to meet with me at his earliest opportunity. Thanks."

"Absolutely. Is there anything else?"

"No, I am good. I need about 30 minutes uninterrupted to pull some thoughts together. Thank you." Doris stepped out and closed his door. Rod went to his desk and pulled out a yellow legal pad and started making some notes.

What do we know? There was a meeting between the CEOs of the three largest oil companies in the world in Nigeria. They are all US companies. They discussed joint problems with Ali Mohammed the Minister for Oil and Gas. They also discussed paying him, but he wanted more. They talked about problems in Saudi and Indonesia. A week later Ali was murdered. They mentioned Paragon would fix things.

What are our next steps? Rod started a list.

- Who is Paragon – FBI to investigate
- Who killed Ali – FBI, State, CIA and Nigerian government – can we trust the Nigerian government at this point? No, we have no idea how high the infiltration goes, so we need to do this without their help at this point. Nigeria does not know that Ali was murdered. He crossed them out. Have to use the CIA to investigate – follow the money.
- Need in-depth profiles on Harold Watson, Bryce Carrington, and Reginald Clark – three separate FBI analysts so the investigators don't see the correlation. - FBI
- Need briefing on their companies and subsidiaries. – FBI
- Need warrants - Dean Mclaughlin to draw

up a request

- Need five years telephone records to see if there are matches – NSA & FBI
- Follow the money – can we backtrack from Nigeria to find out where the money tree came from – FBI analyst
- How did Watson, Carrington, and Clark arrange their travel and where did they stay, who coordinated the meeting. Clearly not the first meeting can we see if travel plans align on other dates – FBI and FAA
- Political implications – make sure that is included in the profiles

That afternoon Rod met with Lester Hodges, Deputy Director of the FBI in his office. "Lester, how are you?"

"Good, what's up that you need to meet rather urgently."

Rod said, "We have an interesting investigation and I am going to need a bunch of your resources. My gut feel is this could be huge, and it could have some serious political implications."

Rod spent the next thirty minutes reviewing his notes and requests for the Bureau to investigate. They discussed the involvement of other agencies and agreed they needed a bit more evidence, even if it was circumstantial, before getting this too far out of their control.

Lester agreed to get a small team and multiple independent analysts working on various aspects. They both agreed at this point they did not want too much coordination so that people could see where it was leading. The more people in the dark at this point, the better.

Chapter 23 October 2015, Georgetown, DC

Sandy and Morgan were now nearly inseparable. And they had finally taken their relationship to the next level spending most weekdays in Georgetown with weekends at the farm keeping up with the outside work and starting to think about what changes they wanted to make to the interior.

Weekday mornings they would go for a run through Glover Archbold Park and if they ran the whole length it was a good six-mile run. Sandy adjusted his pace, so Morgan was comfortable with the run.

Most days Sandy and often Morgan would take the bus from Georgetown to Union Station and then climb the hill up to the Library of Congress, somedays they would work from her house. Generally, every other day they would touch base with Sandy's best friend Jackson in Australia. Morgan's best friend Vicky met them for dinner several times and overall life was good.

Sandy had discovered a great deal about hydrogen. Besides being the most abundant chemical substance in the universe it is also a highly combustible gas. The fusion of hydrogen into helium had powered the sun for billions of years. Since hydrogen easily bonds with oxygen and carbon it creates water, natural gas, and many other compounds.

Sandy was telling Morgan some of what he learned over breakfast, "Industrial production is mainly from steam reforming natural gas. What they do at a chemical plant is combine methane with steam, aka water, at high temperatures with a catalyst creating carbon monoxide and hydrogen. The problem is it is very inefficient, so the resulting hydrogen is expensive."

"Wow you are really getting into this aren't you. I thought you were a biologist," she said with a smile.

"Oh, I am, but you know there is a lot of chemistry that goes along with a biology degree. I had to take organic chem in college. That was an intense class. So, this really is fascinating to me. The cool thing is if my grandfather's process really works as efficiently as I hope it does, it changes the whole economic picture."

"So, do they create hydrogen using electrolysis?"

"Oh, yea. But that is even less efficient than steam reforming."

Morgan looked a little perplexed, "So what would they use the hydrogen for?"

"They use hydrogen today to split long-chain

petrochemicals into more usable products. They also use a lot of it to produce fertilizer. If we had a cheap source of hydrogen we could switch from gasoline and diesel engines to hydrogen fuel cells to power cars, trucks and lots of things. Even to produce electricity with the only output being water. No pollution.

"Wow!" Morgan shook her head. "That is big...it could,"

"It could totally change the way we work and create energy on a global scale," Sandy cut in. And he sighed, shaking his head slightly, "That's probably why my grandfather was killed. Someone found out about what he was doing."

"But," Morgan started to say, frowning...

"So, how is your work going?" Sandy cut in abruptly as if to cut off her questions.

Morgan smiled slightly and said, "I see what you're doing, and I'll let it go for now...but remember, we are a team you know."

She held up her hand, as Sandy was starting to protest and said quickly, "My work is great. I'm actually a bit ahead so I thought I would take some time this week to begin researching your grandfather's patent."

"What do you mean research? We have his patent; can't we just file it?"

"Well, over the years others may have invented something similar so I will look at existing patents and literature to see what is out there. Then I need to craft the claims to weave through the existing information, so they are unique. It is more or less what I do every day."

"You know sweetheart you are pretty amazing. I am truly a lucky guy."

"Yes, you are, and it seems to me you been getting lucky a lot lately."

"For sure and no complaints from me," Sandy just giggled.

At breakfast on Friday Sandy said, "when we go out to the farm tomorrow, I think I feel comfortable testing Grandpa's invention. You know, see if it works."

"Sounds good. Plus, we have the swatches and samples to look at for our remodel."

Saturday morning, they were off and Copper loved riding along with the top down. The farm looked great but, as usual, the lawn grew, to what Sandy thought, exponentially. Something about the Northern Virginia weather...and he made a mental note that he needed to mow the yard this afternoon.

He and Morgan left Copper on the porch and went to the barn, opened the cupboard and descended into the basement. Sandy turned on the fan and cool air was replaced with fresh air from outside.

From Grandpa's notes, Sandy knew to look on the shelves under the staircase to find the box with the ingredients to build the electrolysis setup. "This is pretty cool to think this has sat here for about fifty years hidden away."

"Even if it doesn't work it's incredible."

Sandy and Morgan carried the boxes over to the table in the middle of the room. They took notes Sandy had written from his Grandfather's directions and began to assemble the electrolysis tank. Pretty soon they had it assembled, water and chemicals in the tank and the transformer hooked up. "Why don't we just turn it on for a minute and see if anything happens."

"Ok, sounds good to me, but remember your Grandfather mentioned getting blown across the room when he put a match near it, so just keep it quick. Then we can set up the cover and put the hose into the pail of water.".

"Great idea." Sandy turned on the transformer and immediately bubbles were created near one of the plates in the tank. He immediately turned off the transformer. He and Morgan did a high five.

"Alright, time to get the lid on the tank and set

up the hose and try that."

After making sure the lid was on tight and the hose secured, Sandy turned on the transformer and it began bubbling away. Sandy held a lighter near the end of the hose and they had a powerful flame shooting out from the hose.

"We did it. We are making hydrogen; this is too cool."

"Very cool! Ok, I'll turn off the transformer. I remember from his notes that he could not get it to work with another transformer and he felt that was part of the equation. Let's see if we can find the other transformer."

After fifteen minutes of searching, they found another transformer that looked like the first one. According to the plate on the bottom, it was the same model number, so this had to be it. They hooked it up and turned it on, and they only saw a few bubbles.

Morgan said, "Let's check to see that it's working."

They found a meter and hooked it to the transformer wires and sure enough it was working. Then they hooked the other transformer up and it had the same reading on the meter.

"This is strange. It must be something we are not seeing," Morgan said, shaking her head and frowning.

Sandy sighed. "Well, you're right. I'm going to have to do some digging on this situation. How about we close this up and go back to the house." He smiled, "I feel a nice evening of barbeque ribs, roasted potatoes, and a wedge salad coming on..."

Morgan pecked his cheek. "Any moonlight and star gazing with that meal?"

"I'm counting on that."

Sandy and Morgan cleaned up a little bit, turned off the fan and headed upstairs. They carefully closed the cupboard.

Sandy thought for a moment, "I want to see if I close the cupboard behind me if I can reopen it. Just wait here in case I can't get out."

He stepped in at the rear of the cupboard and pulled it closed. He heard the click and noticed a small latch on the back of the cupboard. When he turned the latch, he heard the click and was able to open it again.

"Ok, now I want you to lower the shelf and see if it still works."

Again, he pulled the closet closed, "Ok, please lower the shelf." He heard Morgan lower the shelf and noticed there was a mechanism that moved when she lowered it. He turned the latch again -

click. The door was unlocked.

Stepping out he said, "This is good to know that we won't get locked in the basement." He showed her how the latch worked on the backside of the cupboard.

They walked over to the house and Copper was wagging his whole body so happy to see them back. They went into the house and got some more water for Copper. As always, he was glued to Morgan.

As they walked through the house Morgan said, "beyond a few minor things this is a great house. Your Aunt had great taste with the kitchen remodel, so it is really up to date and with the layout and four bedrooms and two baths upstairs it really is lovely. I think some bathroom updates" she pointed to the box with paint and flooring samples on the kitchen island, "is all it really needs."

"I agree, so we just have to figure out what to do down the road," he said. "You know it is kind of remote. I am going to find out if we can improve the internet, and also have the security system upgraded next week to add some cameras so we can keep a better eye on things when we are downtown."

"I think that is a really good idea, especially with what we know is in the basement of the barn!"

Sandy thought for a moment. "I need to mow the yard it should not take me more than an hour. Are you ok just hanging around?"

"Of course. Copper and I will check to see if there are any rabbits and may do a little gardening in the flower beds. You take your time and we will see you soon."

Sandy headed off to the barn to get the John Deere rider out and Morgan and Copper went around to the front of the house. An hour or so later they all met up on the front porch. Somehow it was already five o'clock.

"Well," Sandy looked down at his watch, "I'm afraid it's too late for our delicious barbeque – we won't be eating for hours!"

"We can have it tomorrow," Morgan said. "Go out tonight?"

A knowing look came over Sandy's face. "Yeesss," he said slowly. "And, if you'll excuse me for a minute, I'll make a quick call for a reservation."

"Sounds fancy," Morgan raised her eyebrows, "I'll just go upstairs to freshen up a bit."

Sandy nodded and walked out onto the deck while Morgan went upstairs into the master bath to freshen up.

After Sandy cleaned up he and Morgan settled Copper in until they returned. A few miles away tucked off a local road they pulled into the gravel parking lot of L'Auberge Chez François. Sandy parked and put the roof up on the car and they walked in.

Sandy remarked, "You won't believe this but this a very coveted restaurant and consistently ranked in the top 100 in the DC metro and even top 100 in America."

"Wow, out here off the beaten trail!"

"Yup, fortunately, I know the owner and was able to get us a table on short notice." Just then the hostess returned to her stand.

With a very French accent said "Sandy!!! How are you and who is this lovely woman?"

"Marie, allow me to introduce you to the love of my life, Morgan Dutton. I am surprised to see you, seating guests."

"A pleasure to meet you. You are a very lucky gal to capture this guy. Our wonderful hostess came ill today, so I am stepping in."

Morgan replied with a grin, "Le plaisir est pour moi et oui j'ai beaucoup de chance. Je ne vais pas le laisser partir." *(The pleasure is for me and yes, I am very lucky. I will not let him go.)*

Marie smiled, "Bien pour vous. C'est un hic."
("Good for you. He's a catch.")

"Ok, you two enough talking behind my back."

Marie led them back to a quiet table on the side of the restaurant.

"I will let Jacques know you are here with your love."

"So now I am the love of your life, that is a huge upgrade."

Sandy glowed and he grinned from ear to ear, "Well you are, and I am very lucky."

After dinner but before dessert Jacques and Marie came to the table. Greetings were shared and hugs around. Jacques expressed his sadness for the loss of Sandy's aunt, and he insisted that they come back again soon on a Monday for lunch when the restaurant was closed so they could relax and catch up. Sandy and Morgan happily agreed.

Chapter 24   October 2015, Lagos, Nigeria

anjuma and Ismail were police detectives in Lagos, but they were also undercover CIA agents. They enjoyed double-dipping and their day jobs gave them both cover and a great deal of latitude to gather information. Their CIA station chief had advised them that he had it on good authority that Ali Mohammed, Nigerian Minister for Oil and Gas had been murdered by poisoning. They needed to find out who at the restaurant the evening before his death had delivered the poison and more importantly who paid to have it done.

After a few days of observation, it became obvious that Faruq Eze had been paid off. While he still worked at the restaurant, he just purchased a new TV and furniture. He was also seen haggling over the price of a car. Danjuma and Ismail entered Faruq's shack on Odunnukan Street at three a.m. The shack had two rooms, one for sleeping the other for cooking and relaxing. Faruq's wife shrieked when the two men entered their bedroom. Danjuma told her to be quiet, while Ismail pulled a sleepy Faruq from his bed. Together they cuffed and dragged him out of the house and pushed him into the back of their unmarked police car.

They took him five kilometers away to a deserted

dark road bordering the Lagos Lagoon. Dragged from the car, Ismail punched him as hard as he could in the stomach, doubling Faruq over and he fell to the ground. They stood him up against the car. "We know you poisoned Ali Mohammed and got paid for it. Who paid you to do it?" asked Ismail.

Faruq gasping for breath, "I don't know." Ismail hit him again and they stood him back up against the car.

"We need to know who paid you or this doesn't end well for you."

"He was English, he comes to the restaurant from time to time. He was about one and a half meters tall, slight build, strong English accent, brown hair, and eyes."

"Where did he meet you and what did he tell you to do?" asked Danjuma.

"He met me behind the restaurant in the afternoon and gave me a large sugar packet and told me to put it on his food and make certain he got that plate. Then he handed me a thick bundle of One Thousand Naira notes. About three and half million Naira. He said if I didn't put the powder on his food my family would die a terrible death. Then he walked away. That is all I know."

"If you see this man again call me, immediately."

Danjuma handed him his police card. They removed the cuffs and put him back in the back seat of the car. They drove him back and dropped him off a block from his home. "Do not speak to anyone, even your wife, about tonight. Ever."

A week later Danjuma's cell phone rang. It was Faruq, "The man is in the restaurant eating lunch."

"Don't do anything, don't even look at him. We will be there in a few minutes."

Danjuma and Ismail pulled up to the restaurant and parked in front. They walked in and up to the obviously Englishman.

Ismail said, "Please stand up, you are under arrest."

The man stood and started to speak when Ismail shook his head said, "not here, not now".

With his hands handcuffed behind his back, they walked him out of the restaurant and placed him in the back of their car. They drove across town to Tin Can Island and pulled into a sea of shipping containers and parked.

It was a hot 90-degree sunny day when they got out of the car. Danjuma opened the door to a 20-foot shipping container. The heat rolled out the open door. Danjuma and Ismail pulled the Englishman from the back seat and walked him to the container. They pulled out his wallet and a roll of bills from his front pocket. The man was yelling, "What are you doing? What are you doing?"

Neither one said anything. They pushed him into the container, closed and locked the door. Returning to their car they drove off. The man in the container heard the lock being put on the door and heard the car drive off. He sat up in the darkness and slid his butt across the floor and leaned against the container wall. It was getting really hot and he thought this is a shitty way to die.

About midnight they returned to the container. Leaving the car running and the lights on they unlocked the container and opened both doors. "Oh my God, it really stinks in here," said Ismail.

The Englishman was on the floor in a fetal position. They both walked back to the car and got three folding chairs from the trunk. They set up the chairs inside the container. One chair facing the car and the other two facing the single chair far enough apart that they would not block the glare from the headlights.

Together they pulled the man erect and led him to the chair facing the car. As they walked over to their chairs Ismail pulled a roll of bills from his front pocket and peeled off the top one and handed it to Danjuma, "You were right, he soiled himself." They both chuckled.

Danjuma said, "Ok, what's your name and who do you work for?"

"Who are you? Why am I here?"

Ismail said, "I told you he was not going to cooperate."

He walked over and pulled the chair out from under the Englishman, who collapsed to the floor. Danjuma stood and folded up the other chairs and they started to leave the container.

"Wait, wait, I will tell you everything you want to know."

Ismail looked at Danjuma, "I don't think he has had enough time to think about this. I think he will be more trustworthy tomorrow night. Let's just go."

The man was curled up on the floor and sobbing, "Please, I will tell you all you want to know."

They calmly walked back, set up the chairs again. They lifted him off the floor and put him back in his chair.

Danjuma started again, "What's your name and who do you work for?"

"My name is Harry Atkinson and I work for Global Research here in Lagos."

Ismail was writing notes and Danjuma asked, "Where is your office located?"

"39 Obafemi Awolowo Way, Agidingbi"

"What does your company do?"

"We do background research on mostly the oil and gas industry."

Ismail stood up, "See I told you he would just feed us a line of bullshit. Let's go."

Danjuma said, "Let's see if he gets a bit smarter and if not, I am with you and we can come back tomorrow night. So, Harry, this is your chance to be brilliant or not. Totally up to you."

"That is what we do and then other projects."

Danjuma continued, "So, why did you have the Minister for Oil and Gas murdered?"

"Murdered?"

"I told you, he is having that credibility problem, let's go."

"Ok, it was a project ordered by headquarters. I don't know why."

Taking a different tack, Danjuma said, "So how many people work in your office on Awolowo Way and what are their names."

"Five including myself," and he told them their names.

"Do you have any other offices in Nigeria?"

"Not that I know of."

"Are you the boss of this office?"

"No, Bob Jones heads the office."

"Where is headquarters?"

"I don't know. I just work there, and my only contact is with my coworkers."

"Ok, Harry this is all good. We are going to take you downtown, so we can talk further then we will book you for murder."

"Wait you can't charge me with murder. I didn't kill him"

"Right Harry, that is like the guy with the smoking gun saying, I didn't kill him the gun did."

Danjuma and Ismail dragged him out to the car and put him in the back seat, then pulled a black hood over his head. They went back and got the folding chairs and drove not to police headquarters but rather to a CIA safe house. Another CIA operative dressed as a local cop began questioning Harry.

The next day about 10 a.m. a CIA team went to the office dressed as Lagos police. They entered the office and arrested the four people including Bob Jones. They were led out of the building in handcuffs and placed in separate cars. As soon as they left the office another team of three entered the office and removed all the file cabinets, computers, and any loose papers. It was like the office had been vacuum cleaned. All the material was transported to the CIA office at the embassy.

Bob Jones and his three staffers were all placed in separate rooms at the safe house and one by one they were questioned.

Danjuma and Ismail started the interrogation of Bob Jones, who was handcuffed to the desk, by informing him he was being charged with conspiracy to commit murder and they already had a confession from Harry Atkinson.

Ismail turned his laptop so Bob could see it and hit play. The screen showed a man with a noose around his neck drop from a platform and struggle for five minutes while he was slowly and clearly painfully asphyxiated.

Bob was visibly shaking from what he watched.

"See here in Nigeria we hang people for murder. We have compassionate hangings that are swift, or we have less compassionate hangings. Kind of depends on how helpful you are. It is even possible if you are really helpful that we could get your charges reduced. So, we would like to know who you report to at headquarters?"

"I don't know his name or where headquarters is even located."

"Bob see you're not being helpful and that does not have a good ending for you."

Danjuma now playing bad cop said, "Let's just send him to the general population and let them soften him up for a few days. He can be a bitch to a whole bunch of those thugs and see if his memory comes back."

"Works for me," said Ismail. They stood and started to head for the door.

"Wait, I can tell you some things."

"Ok, tell us about headquarters," said Ismail.

"I don't know much, we are pretty isolated, my boss's name is Todd and he has an American accent."

"Ok, how do you contact him?"

"It is all through encrypted email, I never call him, and he rarely calls me."

Ismail asked, "How do you get funds?"

"We have a numbered account; I don't know where and we transfer funds to a local Nigerian bank which we use for payroll, expenses and other things."

"Do you bribe officials with those funds?"

"Sometimes, it depends on the person. For example, we paid Ali Mohammed nearly half a million US over the past two years. We also paid Arsalan Aziz, the Vice Minister, about $250,000 US and others."

"We'll need a list. So, if you were paying Ali why have him murdered?" asked Ismail.

"He was not doing what we told him to do."

"And what did you want him to do?"

"We wanted certain companies to win the leasing rights in various oil fields, but he was awarding contracts to other companies."

"Bob, here is where we are at. I appreciate you are beginning to cooperate. I am going to get a pad of paper and pen and I want you to write down everything from when you first met these guys through to today. Every single detail, account numbers, passwords, names, everything you can think of. We will arrange for you to have a comfortable safe cell and we will come back tomorrow and review your notes."

Chapter 25   October 2015, Washington, DC

Rod Holloway had Dean Mclaughlin prepared the applications and affidavits and received warrants against Watson, Carrington, and Clark and their companies and affiliates. Since the individuals and companies were located in different states the warrants were obtained in different District Courts. All the warrants were sealed due to the nature of the alleged crimes. Rod passed this information over to Lester Hodges at the FBI.

****

Melissa Pearson summarized the elements to build an antitrust case in a brief memo to Rod Holloway.

Core to any antitrust action are three laws; The Sherman Act (1890), Federal Trade Commission Act (1914), and the Clayton Act (1914). There have been minor revisions, but these are the basis for antitrust action. Separately and together they prohibit;

- Price fixing, for example, predatory and discriminatory pricing
- Conspiracy to monopolize
- Restraint of trade
- Anti-competitive mergers

- Limitation of competition

Should the department prove that the companies' leadership endeavored to work together to achieve one or more of the above acts we would have a strong case to bring against these companies. Settlements in a case like this could be substantial as shown by the recent class action settlement against Enron of over $7 billion.

I believe one avenue to pursue would be to determine the price-fixing of finished products such as gasoline, jet fuel, and diesel fuel. This would include coordinated price reduction allowing one or more of these companies to acquire competitors.

Another avenue would be to demonstrate their conspiracy to monopolize the industry. It would require DOJ to find documents or testimony clearly showing their joint efforts to control the industry.

Should you need further information or clarification please contact me. Melissa

****

Dylan Harrison got the call early on a Wednesday afternoon from Lester Hodges' office to come to his office at 4 p.m. for a short meeting. Hodges was Deputy Director of the FBI and Harrison was multiple levels below. Dylan had no idea what was going on but was understandably nervous. Arriving ten minutes early he waited in the reception area.

Precisely at 4 p.m. Lester walked into the office area and greeted Harrison. "Dylan, come to my office."

"Yes, sir."

"Have a seat, we have a small project I want three of your analysts to work on. I have secured access to the FAA plane registration records and the flight log database, while much is public information with this access you may get more and certainly easier analysis. The usernames and passwords are on this sheet of paper as well as specific instructions for what we are seeking. It is critical that the three people assigned to this project not know what the other person is working on. This is a highly classified project. The people you select must have a TS-SCI clearance"

"Ok"

"Dylan, I want five years flight records of dates, times and airports for all planes owned or used by American Petroleum, Sunco Power and TXO anywhere on the planet. Each analyst will work up the data for one company independent of the other two. When the data is assembled, I want you to take that information and determine where there is overlap for two or all three companies. You will report directly to me. If you have any issues come directly to me. Are we clear?"

"Crystal, Sir."

"This project is your only priority. I want a comprehensive job, but time is of the essence. I have already spoken to Jodie Harper and she knows you are working on a classified project for me directly. Good luck." Lester stood, shook hands with Dylan and sat back down.

Meeting over, Dylan turned and left the office.

Thank God I was not called on the carpet for something, he thought. And, I'm sure glad he cleared it with Jodie, so she is not looking over my shoulder on this.

Back at his cubicle, Dylan thought of who would do the best job and keep it quiet. He picked Leo Gibson, Hannah Cox, and Erin Palmer. He sent out individual emails for meetings tomorrow morning and afternoon.

****

Lester Hodges asked Amber Dean to meet him in his office at 9 a.m. tomorrow. Amber was a 35-year-old senior agent, Caribbean black mother of two middle school kids who enjoyed binge-watching boxed sets, and yoga. She was known in her department for delivering on challenging cases.

"Amber thanks for coming up. I have an interesting case and I know how you especially enjoy those. We have reason to believe that Harold Watson, Bryce Carrington, and Reginald Clark are conspiring together. Their names may not ring a bell, but they are the CEOs of the three largest oil and gas companies in the world. You do not need to know the details, but here is what I need your analysts to do. I want you to drill into their phone records; office and cell and see if you can find them talking to each other over the past five years. These guys travel internationally, and we know of one international meeting recently, so if you need assistance from NSA just let me know. This is a highly classified project so make sure the people you assign are cleared and understand this is not to be discussed. While we don't need it, we do have a search warrant for each of the individuals and their companies. Contact Dean Mclaughlin at DOJ if you have any questions on the warrants."

"Sounds like fun, love a challenge like this."

****

Lester also had teams assembling a brief on the individuals and the companies as well as looking at their financial records.

Chapter 26   October 2015, Georgetown, DC

Morgan asked, "would you like some coffee?" as she, Sandy and Copper walked into the kitchen from the backyard in Georgetown.

"That would be awesome, thanks!" Sandy smiled and looked up as he was taking off Copper's halter and leash. "We had a great run this morning...how do you feel?"

"Really good. You're getting me in great shape. Now I can eat anything I want, and I don't have to worry about putting on a single pound. Oh," Morgan looked over from the sink where she was filling the drip coffee pot with water, "I forgot to tell you I finished the research on your Grandfather's patent, and I am ready to file it."

"Awesome, do we file it in his name?"

"Nope, it has to be in your name since your grandfather passed away many years ago and if we used him it would be invalid due to the elapsed time. But we'll always know it was his invention. Have you had any luck with the transformer issue?"

Sandy nodded, "I think so. I contacted a friend of mine and he recommended a guy who is a genius at electronics. I set up a meeting for tomorrow and I am going to bring both transformers and we can figure out the difference and see if we can buy or build a transformer like the one that is producing the hydrogen. So, I am going to run out to the farm today and pick them up. Would you like to ride along?"

"Sorry. Wish I could. I have a couple of things I must do at the patent office, and I will drop off your patent today. If the electronic guy discovers something novel, we can amend the patent after it is filed but still maintain the filing date." Then, with a huge grin she added, "So, you're going to get help? I thought you would be an electronics wizard as well as a hydrogen expert."

Sandy just smiled and didn't bite. The coffee was ready, and they relaxed at the kitchen table and watched the morning local news. Being DC, the bulk of the news was on the political diatribe that DC thrived on.

Morgan reflected, "This drives me nuts how they can all carry on about things and act like they are actually doing something."

"Its politics, if they weren't politicians, they would be actors, which is really what most of them are. Overpaid actors."

After that, they each headed off in different directions.

Copper, as always, loved riding up front in the

car with Sandy and soon the twosome was at the farm.

"A bit like old times," Sandy said as he rubbed Copper's ears. Copper looked up into Sandy's face and gave his happy "woof" and Sandy laughed. "Ok," he said to Copper as they disembarked from the car. I'll take off your leash and let you run around but don't go too far. We're not here for an overnight this time!"

Copper gave several excited barks and started running around, sniffing out whatever small game had been nearby.

Sandy shook his head and smiled. Then went to work. Start with the basement in the barn, he thought. And he headed over to the barn and went down into the basement, happy he had checked the locking system. Not that I plan on getting locked in down there, he mused, but it is a lonely place to get stuck if something did happen that way.

Once down in the barn basement, he labeled and collected both of the transformers his grandfather had been working with. It didn't take long and before he knew it, he was walking back to the house where he noted that the new internet line was installed on the side.

I have to thank Ben, he thought, another thing off the list... and he went inside to check out the connection.

Ben Schmidt was the son of Kurt Schmidt Aunt Beth's closest neighbor. The two had grown up together – their families very close and the Schmidt family stepping up to help the Powell family after the death of Dick. Sandy enlisted Ben's help to look after the place when he was in DC. That included being at the house during the install of the new internet system.

As he went inside, he thought about all the happy memories in this house that had been in his family for generations.

He smiled. I wonder if Morgan and I will make some new memories – new Powell generations in this house. He certainly hoped so.

He went into Aunt Beth's office and read Ben's notes about the system – the password was Copper13 – too easy. He would have to change that no matter how much he liked it.

Well, he thought positively, it will be easier for Morgan and me to come out here and work, even this far out, now that we have high-speed internet. Next, he continued ticking off the list in his mind, I need to schedule the new security system installation for next week. Maybe I'll come and take Ben and Kathy out to lunch to thank them. Kathy was Ben's wife of 40 years and a wonderful, down to earth woman. A good friend to Aunt Beth. He went out to the car through the back door off the kitchen and was happy to see Copper just standing by the front door waiting to go in.

"Copper!" The dog raced toward him and, with perfect timing, jumped into the front passenger seat.

"Don't get too used to this," Sandy said to his canine companion, "You know that's normally reserved for Morgan."

Copper just ignored him and settled comfortably into the seat.

They got back around three just before the rush hour, when traffic went crazy. A moment later Morgan walked in the door and, upon seeing him, a mysterious smile came over her face. "I have an idea for dinner, I want to celebrate."

"Ok, I am game, in fact, I am always game."

"I want to take you out tonight. Let's say six."

"I am all yours," and he remembered his daydreaming at the farm earlier and thought, you have no idea how much I am yours.

Later at the Indian restaurant, Morgan said, "Do you know what tonight is?"

"I am guessing, another wonderful dinner with the most beautiful woman on the planet."

With that wicked grin of hers, Morgan said, "Yes, well there is that. Silly, tonight is our anniversary. It has been three of the most wonderful months of my life. Thank you, Sandy, for making my life so amazing."

"Well dittos to that, but it is you that completes me. I love you, Morgan."

Her heart raced and she felt warm, "I love you too."

The next morning, Sandy drove out 66 and took the cut-off to the Dulles Toll Road. Exiting at Reston he quickly found the convenient parking garage at Fountain and Freedom and walked the short distance past the fountain to the building. Riding the elevator to the fourth floor he knocked on the unlabeled door to 4138. A moment later the door opened.

"Hi, you must be Sandy," said Jake Nicholson.

Nicholson was built. He looked like he lifted daily. High and tight brown hair accented his chiseled face. "You got me, a pleasure to meet you. You come well regarded."

"Come on in. Hope I can help."

"Thanks, were you in the service?" asked Sandy.

"Oh, yea. Rangers 75th and you?"

"SEALs."

"You guys get all the press, we just get the fun," Jake said with a cheeky grin.

After a quick coffee, they went to the back. Jake had an insane lab with instruments, devices and all sorts of things in the large room.

"Wow, this is quite the setup."

"This is my toy land. I am really lucky I don't go to work. I just have fun every day. Companies pay a ton of money to figure out how to reduce the amount of current drawn by their device, battery life is everything."

Sandy began, "Too cool. My challenge is a bit unusual... I need to understand why these transformers are different."

"No problem. I'm happy to help, plus Rich told me you were a friend and that means a lot. On top of that, you are a fellow comrade in arms. Glad you're here."

After an hour with incredibly complex oscilloscopes hooked side by side to each transformer, Jake said, "The difference is this transformer has an underlying, call it a buzz, on the line. This means when you look at the signal on the scope, this one," he pointed to one of the transformers, "has one clean line while the other has a fuzzy line. When we zoom into the fuzz you can see the harmonics on the line. This is caused by one of the components going bad."

"If I got a brand-new transformer could you make it create that 'buzz' consistently?"

Jake replied pointing inside the transformer, "Yes I need to modify this Zener diode, see the barrel-shaped piece. And this other barrel-shaped element."

"Ok, what is a Zener diode and what is the other barrel-shaped piece?"

"Simply the other barrel-shaped piece is a rectifier diode which only allows current to pass in one direction. It essentially converts AC to DC current. The Zener diode allows current to flow in the opposite direction at a specific threshold. Do you want me to go into detail?"

Looking a bit misty-eyed, Sandy said sheepishly, "Oh no, you lost me at the diode."

"Bottom line, this old transformer has kind of failed. That said I can build one for you that will deliver the same 'buzz' as the old one."

Sandy was ecstatic, "Ok, order whatever you need and build me three of them that perform like the old one."

"No problem, give me two weeks and I'll have them ready for you."

Sandy beamed, "Just let me know how much and

I will send over the funds for the parts and of course your time as well."

"Will do, it won't be much these things are pretty inexpensive these days. I'll give you a call when they are ready. Can you leave the transformers so I can test against them?"

"Absolutely, see you in a few weeks," Sandy headed to the door and looked back, a thought just occurring to him. "Jake," he said, "let's keep this on the qt. I don't want anyone else finding out what we're doing."

"My lips are sealed for the SEAL." Jake gave him a grin while Sandy groaned.

"Yah, well, thanks, so much – see you in a couple of weeks."

Chapter 27   November 2015, Menlo Park, CA

Paragon's tracking of Powell's laptop led them to realize he operated in five different locations: three in DC and two in Virginia. Lynn authorized an in-depth digital research project on Powell and assigned another person to work with Brooke. They knew his locations, where he grew up, that he was an only child, that he recently sold a house in Fairfax and had inherited his aunt's farm in Great Falls, that he was a former Navy SEAL, and that he taught biology in the Fairfax County school system and most importantly, that he was continuing his research at the Library of Congress and online.

Brooke Tate got another alert. She picked up the phone and call her boss Lynn Nash. "Lynn, do you remember the guy we have been tracking on the hydrogen?"

"Sure, the guy in Virginia?"

"Yes, that's him. Well, he just filed for a patent on hydrogen gas production."

Lynn thought a moment, "Well that changes things. Clearly, he is not working on a thesis. Ok, send me the link to his file and I will take a fresh look at it. Great work."

Lynn sent a secure email to headquarters with

her assessment of the situation. Todd Peterson read through the profile on Powell and the current status. He sent an email to Harriet Campos in the Washington office.

Harriet, please begin a 24/7 agent coverage of Sandy Powell, details attached, and give me a brief in a week. Todd

Harriet assigned three of her agents to discretely follow and collect on the ground info on Powell.

Leon Davies, former DC detective, began his surveillance of Powell. He had a pretty complete dossier on Powell supplied by the research team in California. Using freeware and knowing Powell's cell phone number he quickly got the GPS location of his phone. Driving around the neighborhood he finally spotted Powell's car on the back alley behind Morgan's townhouse. Sitting a discrete distance away he watched the car through his shift and was lucky to see him, a woman and a dog leave through the back gate at seven in the morning. They were headed west through Georgetown towards the river. Leon got out of the car and did his best to keep a hundred yards behind as they began their run. Middle-aged and seriously out of shape, Leon very soon tired of trying to keep up. He decided to return to the car and watch for their return.

About half an hour later he watched them return from the run, enter the backyard and he assumed entered the back of the townhouse. He could not see for certain because of the high fence surrounding the backyard. An hour later, Karen Young called Leon to confirm his location and to relieve him from the watch. She arrived within 15 minutes, and Leon drove off. She sat all morning and saw nothing. As a former CIA operative, she was used to sitting and watching for hours. Generally, the most boring part of this job, still it was a good-paying job.

Karen called Harriet about noontime and gave her an update, "I haven't seen anything all morning. I wonder if they went out the front of the townhouse?"

Harriet agreed with Karen's assessment and said, "You're probably right. I'm going to assign another person to watch the front during the morning and afternoon. You might as well take a short break and come back and watch the back for the afternoon just in case they are inside and decide to leave in a car."

Karen walked a couple of blocks to M Street in Georgetown and caught lunch at a Vietnamese restaurant. One of the great things about this job is no one cared about expenses unlike her former government job where everything had to be documented and within guidelines. She loved the job. It paid well, had a company car and she was almost always home for her kids. She handed off the watch to Verna Elliott about 6 p.m. Fortunately, this assignment was close to her home in Falls Church, Virginia.

Verna had an uneventful evening watching the rear of the house. She did note lights going on and off upstairs, nothing unusual. The next morning while Leon watched the rear, Ivan Hammond watched the front. About the same time as the previous day Leon watched Sandy, the woman and dog go for their morning run.

Sandy noticed the shiny black Escalade parked down the street and it seemed out of place. Also odd was someone sitting in it. Maybe it was his sixth sense polished in Afghanistan kicking in. When they returned the car and driver were in the same spot.

Leon updated Ivan that they had returned. About an hour later Ivan watched as they left out the front door and advised Leon. Knowing the specific address in Georgetown, Paragon had begun assembling information on Morgan and they now knew with certainty which cars on the alley belonged to Sandy and Morgan.

The next day Leon and Ivan switched places, so

Leon was watching the front. Despite being a cold blustery November day, the three went for their run at the normal time. Sandy took note of the blue Chevy truck sitting almost in the same spot as the Escalade yesterday. On the run, Sandy said to Morgan, "Someone on the street is being watched."

"Really how do you know that?"

"I noticed an SUV with a guy sitting just down the street yesterday and today there is another truck sitting in almost the same spot with a guy just sitting in it."

Morgan said, "I guess it could be anybody on our block. Do you think it is a security detail for someone? We do have some wealthy, important people in the neighborhood."

"I don't think so. They didn't look like security detail type vehicles. My guess some private eye is watching somebody." When they arrived back to the house the truck was in the same spot with some guy sitting and watching. After freshening up and a light breakfast they headed off in opposite directions. Morgan had meetings downtown and went out the front, easier to catch a bus than drive and park. Sandy went out the back to his car.

Leon saw Morgan leave the house out the front door. She was walking east and turned right heading down the hill to M Street. Leon pulled out of the parking spot and drove slowly down to the corner and watched her cross M street and wait at the bus stop. He pulled down the street and was able to stop in front of someone's garage entrance. Not a legal parking spot but he would only be there for a few minutes. Leon saw her get on a city bus and head for downtown. He followed the bus which was a bit tricky with all the morning traffic. He was able to see her get off the bus and enter an office building on K street. There was no way he could stay parked in downtown DC and wait for her return. He updated the team and went home to rest before his next shift.

Meanwhile as Sandy backed out of his parking spot, he noticed the truck start up and as he headed west down the alley, he took note that the truck pulled out and began to follow at a distance. When Sandy got to 33rd he turned right, not the way he needed to go, and sped north up the street. He was almost two blocks away when he saw the truck turn to follow in his rearview mirror. He sped up the next two blocks and turned left continuing north on Wisconsin Ave. Several blocks up Sandy pulled into a small parking lot and backed into an open spot with a car blocking him from the view on Wisconsin. As he suspected the truck drove by him a few minutes later. Sandy waited a minute and pulled out of the parking lot and headed south on

Wisconsin back in the direction he needed to go.

Ivan updated Leon and Karen that Powell had given him the slip for the moment. It was time for Karen to take over the watch. So, she used the cell phone GPS locator software to discover that Powell was now headed west on the GW Parkway.

Chapter 28   November 2015, Washington, DC

Rod Holloway had scheduled a meeting of the various people working on the oil executives' case. He had named the investigation Valdez after the huge oil spill that occurred ten years earlier in Prince William Sound, Alaska. The team assembled in an executive conference room.

Rod kicked off the meeting by thanking everyone for attending, reminded them of the secret classification and then asked Lester Hodges, Deputy Director at the FBI to have his person provide a brief on the three CEOs and their companies. Lester looked at Tiffany Flores and nodded. Tiffany walked to the front of the room and delivered a PowerPoint briefing on the men, Harold Watson, Bryce Carrington, and Reginald Clark. Then she went through the highlights on the companies; TXO, American Petroleum, and Sunco. An interesting fact is that the three companies emerged about 1915 from the breakup of Touchstone Oil due to antitrust legislation.

Rod then asked Diana Scott from the CIA to provide an update on the situation in Nigeria. Diana now moved to the front of the room and opened her PowerPoint on what they had learned. She began with a summary of the sworn statement from Bob Lancaster and his wife. She then reviewed Matthew French's autopsy results which clearly showed that Ali Mohammed had been poisoned by a massive amount of arsenic. She then put up a photo of Faruq Eze. She told them that Faruq had been paid to poison Ali's food, subsequently, he had been interviewed and arrested.

Diana then briefed the room on what they learned from Harry Atkinson, the man who paid Faruq and gave him the arsenic. The interview of Atkinson led them to his office in Lagos and the interviews of four other people who worked with Atkinson. The CIA was able to access the staff computers and email. Jones so far had not given them his password. Beyond the name, Todd, they had been unable to determine who the parent company was. They did know that funding for the office came from a numbered bank account in the Cayman Islands. She closed by saying the five people from the company were being held at the CIA safe house and thought they were being held by the Nigerian police.

Rod remarked to Diana, "Please reach out to your counterpart at Treasury who is active with the Financial Action Task Force. FATF monitors progress to stop money laundering and the UK is also a member. Leverage that to get the detailed ownership and transaction records for that numbered account in the Caymans."

"Yes, sir will do."

"If you have a problem call me directly."

Rod asked Amber Dean to review what they had found in the analysis of the phone records. Amber had lived for decades in the US but her colorful Caribbean accent was a delightful undertone to her presentation.

"We gathered the past five years' cell phone records for the men and looked for numbers they had dialed in common as well as if they had called each other," Amber explained. "Over the past five years, we found only a few numbers in common and the majority of those were other wealthy people or politicians that they appeared to know independently. We are still investigating the other phones. The overlaps occurred with Bryce Carrington and Reginald Clark. There was only one overlap with Harold Watson and that happened about a month ago. That call was a three-way conference call."

Rod thought a moment, "Wait a minute, Tiffany when did Watson become CEO of TXO?"

"Sir, he was elected by the Board of Directors to become CEO in June of this year."

"Who was the CEO prior to Watson?"

"That was Jacob Holden, great-grandson of Malcolm Holden the founder of Texas Oil and Gas."

Rod announced, "I'll get a warrant for Jacob Holden's information with regards to this conspiracy later today. Each of you will do a deep dive into Holden for your respective areas. Lester," he turned toward his colleague, "can we now cover the information on the executives' flights?"

"Absolutely, Dylan would you be so kind as to brief us on what your team discovered."

Dylan Harrison stood and moved to the laptop at the front of the room and opened his PowerPoint. "We were quite lucky in that all three companies primarily use the jets they own and on a limited basis use rentals. Each CEO has a preferred jet which made it easier. We looked at five years of data on these jets and were able to find common airports. Since corporate jets can often land in smaller fields, we used a 50-mile radius to account for the jets landing at different but adjacent airports. For example, one might land at National while another landed at the Manassas airport."

He continued, "Over the past five years we saw nearly thirty occasions where two or all three jets landed and took off within 48 hours of each other at the same or adjacent airports. On average they were together about once per quarter. Some of these coincidences coincided with Congressional testimony or meetings with senior government officials."

Dylan continued, "We then had local FBI agents pose as IRS agents to go to the Fixed Base Operator to get the manifest of the people on the flights and we were able to confirm Bryce Carrington and Reginald Clark were on those flights and in one case Watson. We will go back and look for information on Holden, sir. Some of the flights were international so we went to Customs and Border Protection at DHS and were able to review the entry and exit of the individuals and confirm the use of the specific jets."

Lester said, "Excellent job Dylan, we look forward to your update with regard to Holden. Nina can you give us an update on the financial information on the case."

Nina Craig stood and did not move to the front of the room, "Sir, we are dealing with three multi-billion-dollar international public companies. Each of these companies has tens of subsidiaries, and thousands of sub-contractors many of which are located offshore. We have not seen any irregularities but that does not mean it is not there. All their financials are audited but again that does not mean a great deal. With companies this big there are a million places to hide slush funds. With regard to the three executives we reviewed their tax returns and they are all independently wealthy, but their returns appear to be in order, and all were prepared by respected firms."

"Thanks, Nina. Good job. Jordan can you brief us on the price-fixing analysis."

Jordan moved to the front and put up her PowerPoint. Jordan Vasquez was a late-twenties woman with a huge smile and almost waist length reddish blonde hair. "We looked at the pricing of several common products of the three companies. This included Gasoline, Diesel, Natural Gas, Jet Fuel, and Heating Oil. Since these companies are international, we looked at historic prices in multiple markets, the United States, Canada, Japan, and the European Union. We also looked upstream to see if the acquisition of mineral rights or leases changed.

Rod interrupted, "Excuse me what do you mean by upstream?"

"Excellent question sir. The oil and gas business is generally thought of in three broad sectors; upstream, midstream and downstream. Upstream consists of exploration, drilling, and pumping from established wells. Midstream is the transportation from the well to the refinery and includes trucks, pipelines, rail, and ships. Finally, downstream is the processing of crude oil and gas into finished products. This sector also includes the commercial distribution of finished products."

Jordan moved to the next slide in her deck, "As we can see here gasoline prices tend to be adjusted seasonally for two factors. We see peak prices from the refineries when they switch from primarily gasoline production to heating oil and we also see price changes in anticipation of higher demand due to holiday travel not only in the US but overseas as well." She went on to the next slide which drilled into a day level pricing chart. "When we look at the price adjustments by the three companies and their competitors in nearly every instance globally the three companies adjusted their prices within hours of each other while competitors took three to five days to adjust their prices in response to the move."

Rod asked, "Does this demonstrate anti-competitive price-fixing?"

"I don't believe this information alone could prove that, but it is much more than circumstantial evidence."

Jordan continued, "When we look at leases and acquisition of mineral rights, we can see a pattern in various fields where prices were pushed lower, and one of the three companies made an acquisition. We are going to have local agents make some inquiries into specific acquisitions to see if there was an influence to push the price lower."

Rod then asked, "Melissa from an antitrust perspective do we have a case?"

Melissa replied, "Sir, we are building one, but I don't believe we have enough evidence at this time to go to a Grand Jury to get an indictment. We need a smoking gun."

Rod stood and moved to the front of the room, "Everyone, your teams have all done an excellent job with this investigation. I believe we are beginning to uncover a conspiracy to control the oil and gas business both here and internationally. As I mentioned before, I want you to add Jacob Holden to the investigation and we will secure the required warrants later today. Lester do you need anything to get wiretaps on the cell and office phones for the execs?

"I think I have all that I need, I will call you later today to confirm."

"Alright everyone, keep up the good work, and expect to meet again in a week to give us an update." Rod left the room with Lester right behind.

Lester said, "I think you are right, and this could be huge. I'll keep you updated." As they approached the elevator bank Lester's security detail appeared.

"Thanks, and again your team is doing a great job. I'll brief Meredith and I assume you will update the director."

"Of course." Lester entered the elevator with his detail, downstairs they headed back for the short walk to the FBI building. Before crossing Pennsylvania Avenue, Lester turned around and looked at the inscription above the door, 'The Place of Justice is a Hallowed Place' and he thought how appropriate for this investigation. The quote attributed to Francis Bacon about 1600 spoke to justice interpreting the law and not writing the law. They were implementing the law. Then he thought if this plays out there is going to be a shit storm of politics because these guys were in everyone's pocket.

Chapter 29   November 2015, New York City

Bob McCall knocked on Todd Peterson's office door and entered. As CFO at Paragon, it was his job to keep the finances of their global operation running smoothly. This meant managing funds for each office in separate numbered accounts based in the Caymans. The offices would draw funds for operations and payroll and if extraordinary funds were needed for an operation or a bribe then a secure email requesting the amount and use of the funds was sent to headquarters.

Todd looked up from a pile of papers and said, "what's up Bob?"

"Our Lagos, Nigeria office did not pull their normal weekly funds from the account for the past two days. Have you had any communications with them?"

Todd thought for a moment, "No, not since we had them run the op on the minister and they confirmed it went as planned."

"Well, something is not right. Suggest you look into it."

"Good point Bob. I will check it out. Thanks for the update."

Todd thought about the procedure they had put

in place when an office went offline, it had only happened once, years in the past. Todd decided not to send anyone from headquarters because they would stand out like a fly on a wedding cake. The best solution was to send Nick Keller.

Todd trusted Nick, he was an Arab, so moderately dark skin but spent most of his years in London, so he spoke 'proper' English which would fit in well in Nigeria, a former English colony. Keller was now based in their Abu Dhabi office in the United Arab Emirates.

Nick received the secure email from Todd with instructions to fly ASAP to their office in Lagos and investigate. Details including staff photos and bios were in the attachments. One of the many things Nick liked about the job was the unlimited budget. He booked a first-class ticket from Abu Dhabi to Lagos. The best way to get there was to fly Etihad direct about an eight-hour flight. He arrived at about 8 p.m. and went to the InterContinental Hotel. He planned to check out the office the next morning.

After a light breakfast, he grabbed a taxi and went to the office about 30 minutes away. The street was full of ramshackle buildings many of which looked like a strong wind would blow them over. Hundreds of people were walking on the street since the sidewalk was blocked by parked cars and there was a constant throng of taxis and a few cars narrowly missing the people. The office was on the fourth floor of a better than average but still rundown building. He found an open-air coffee shop across the street where he could watch to see if anyone entered the building that looked like the photos he had memorized.

After an hour not seeing anyone, he crossed the busy street and entered the building. He was surprised to find the lift working and took it to the fourth floor. The office door was locked, so Nick took his lock-pick from his rear pocket and thirty seconds later was in the office. The office was completely empty except for the furniture. He looked around but there was nothing.

The CIA office received an alert that someone had tripped the motion detector and entered Global Research's office. They had a high def video of the person entering and looking about the office. The second hidden camera recorded him leaving the office space 15 minutes later.

Nick sent a secure email to Todd advising that the office was totally empty and no sign of anyone. Todd replied with his thanks and said to return to the UAE.

The CIA had DHS reviewed the Lagos customs tapes to find this new person's entry into the country on the premise that he was a potential terrorist. Now that he was flagged, it was easy to tag him leaving the country on a flight to Abu Dhabi. The Lagos CIA office advised their office in the UAE, and they were there when his flight landed. They didn't pick him up but watched to find out where his office was.

****

Most patent applications were not published for 18 months following their filing and therefore were unavailable for the public to review. Paragon had inserted a virus type of software in the system at USPTO so it could receive a patent as soon as it was filed and entered into the system. Paragon no longer had to pay a patent examiner to watch for patents, technology certainly had its benefits.

Todd Peterson was reading the analysis of the Powell patent filing and realized he had an actionable event. He called Harriet Campos in Washington to get an update on Sandy Powell.

"Hi Todd, how are things in the big apple?"

"Good, I was looking to get an update on Sandy Powell. It appears his patent has some merit."

Harriet said, "Well, no real events to report, we have been watching him 24/7 as well as his girlfriend Morgan Dutton. Powell seems to be living with her. We have been tracking their cell phones' locations. For the most part, they stay in downtown DC. With a few trips to Reston and a rural property in Great Falls. From what we can see he is continuing his academic research on hydrogen gas production. Is there anything you want us to do with him?"

Todd reflected, "No, we are good. Continue the surveillance and I will reach out if there is a change."

Todd sent a secure email to Watson, Carrington, and Clark briefing them on the Powell case and patent and requested their recommendation on the next steps. The next day he received Carrington's recommendation that they acquire the rights to the patent for $250,000 and assign the rights to one of their offshore shell companies. Watson and Clark concurred with the approach.

Todd emailed Harriet and asked her to have one of her agents to make an offer.

Chapter 30   November 2015, Georgetown, DC

S andy had prepared an incredible filet of salmon with a mayonnaise and Old Bay dressing. He also had sides of asparagus with hollandaise sauce and new potatoes for Morgan and Vicky. They were all enjoying the get together over several bottles of the buttery Cakebread Chardonnay.

Sandy excused himself to go to the bathroom and went upstairs. Vicky immediately asked Morgan, "so how is it going?"

"I have never been so happy," Morgan beamed. "It just feels so right and comfortable. He is definitely the one..." she trailed off, a dreamy look on her face.

"You are so lucky. I would die for that. So, what's next?"

"We are just enjoying being together and trying to figure it out as we go. Sandy is continuing his research on his grandfather's discovery. He has the farm in Great Falls, and we have my place. I think he will go back to teaching next semester, but we have to see where things are at, he doesn't need the money at this point."

Sandy was returning from upstairs, "So have you girls got it all figured out?"

Morgan tossed her curly hair, smiled, "Sure do, we are doing the dishes since you were the awesome chef you always are."

"Great, I have an idea, if you can knock off early on Friday, let's fly out to St. Louis and see my mother. I am long overdue, and she is dying to meet you. There is a direct flight out of National at 2:40 on Friday and we can be back on Sunday afternoon."

"Great idea, I would love to meet her and learn more about your secret past."

Vicky chimed in, "Well off to meet the mother, do you think she will pass muster?"

"Are you kidding, my mother will love her more than Copper does."

"That is not possible, that dog absolutely adores her," Vicky said.

"Oh, I know, he hardly pays any attention to me anymore. Well, unless I am going for a drive. Then he loves me."

Morgan thought for a moment, "so what are we going to do with Copper while we are gone?"

"No worries, one of my former student's loves to sit him when I travel. I will drop him off Friday morning and we can collect him when we get back or I'll get him on Monday morning."

Friday noontime they grabbed a cab and fifteen minutes later they were checking their bags and off to catch their flight. About 3 hours later they picked up a rental car and were off to Sandy's Mom's house about 20 minutes from Lambert Field. As they pulled up, the house was a beautiful old brick Tudor with a huge oak tree in front. Sandy said, "this is the Kirkwood neighborhood and the house backs up to the Greenbriar Country Club."

"What a beautiful house and a nice established neighborhood."

They grabbed their bags and Sandy's Mom Barbara opened the front door as they approached up the brick walkway. Barbara was about 5'6", with blue eyes like Sandy, a big perfect smile and short brown hair with gray highlights. "Sandy and Morgan, I am so happy you came for a visit."

"Hi, Mom, let me introduce you to Morgan Dutton my better half."

"Morgan, so wonderful to finally meet you. Sandy has told me a little and you are even more beautiful than he described. Please come in and make yourselves at home. I was just going to get some crackers and cheese and Sandy can fix some drinks. We have some unusually warm weather so we can sit out on the deck."

Sandy and Morgan dropped their bags in the entryway and Barbara took their coats to the hall closet. The front hallway led straight back to the kitchen. A formal dining room was on the right and a formal sitting room was on the left. The rear of the house had been refurbished recently to be one large open space with a family room and fireplace on the left, a large kitchen with white black veined marble countertops and mahogany cabinets and an island. The far end of the kitchen had a small round table for casual eating.

As Sandy headed into the family room, he asked, "Morgan, Mom what would you girls like to drink?"

I will have a scotch on the rocks if that is what you're having," said Morgan.

His mom replied, "I'll have a glass of Woodford Bourbon on the rocks if you please."

Morgan stood at the island while Barbara prepared a decorative platter with crackers and various cheeses. Sandy returned with a tray that held the drinks along with the bottles of scotch and bourbon respectively. He set it down on the island and handed Morgan her glass of scotch and the glass of bourbon to his mother. He grinned at them as he saw the look on their faces and a mutual glance at each other.

"What?" He said trying to sound innocent. "I'm

preparing for refills – makes it easier."

Then he grabbed the platter of cheeses and cocked his head toward the backyard.

His mother shook her head and laughed, and they followed her out the French doors to the deck.

The lawn sloped away towards the golf course providing a beautiful view of the fairway and part of the lake. Morgan remarked as they sat down, "What a beautiful view of the course."

Barbara was just beaming, "Oh yes except we had to replace the glass with impact-resistant windows a number of years ago. It didn't use to be a problem but with the new clubs more than a few players overdrive the dogleg and our house gets hit nearly every day. So, tell me about yourself and how you two met and, well just everything."

After about an hour Barbara said, "Sandy, I have some steaks in the frig. Would you be so kind as to fire up the grill while Morgan and I pull together the sides?"

"Happy to Mom." Sandy picked up the cheese platter and headed into the kitchen followed by the women. The conversation was light and delightful as they prepared the meal and, since the weather was still cooperating, decided to eat outside. After dessert, they retired to the family room for sambuca with roasted coffee beans and quiet jazz in the background.

On Saturday, Sandy toured Morgan around the area where he grew up and went to high school. Saturday evening, they went to 'The Hill' the famous Italian neighborhood in St. Louis. Charlie Gitto's presented a two-story building in a semi-residential neighborhood, very different from the hustle and bustle of Georgetown. The dining was elegant, and the food, they all agreed, was stunning.

Sunday morning Sandy and Morgan made a bacon and asparagus quiche combined with Jarlsberg cheese which added a light nutty flavor to the dish. Adding toasted Italian bread, they bought last night on 'The Hill" completed the brunch. Still, surprisingly warm they enjoyed breakfast on the deck. While Sandy was inside attending to some guy project for his Mom, Morgan, and Barbara chatted.

"Sandy makes me so happy. I always feel safe and protected with him. He completes me."

Barbara just grinned, "I cannot ever remember him this happy. When he was married before it never felt like a fit. He is over the top in love with you and I would love to have you as a part of the family when you are ready."

"Oh, I am already there, I am just enjoying each

moment and when he is ready, I will be there for him. Thank you so much for making me feel so welcome."

"I think it is you that completes him. You are a perfect match and I know because I was so lucky to have mine. If you ever have a doubt, call me immediately, I am there for both of you."

The trip back to the airport and back to DC was quiet. A bit tired, and enjoying some one on one time with Morgan, Sandy decided to pick up Copper Monday morning.

By Monday evening, based on the thoroughly enjoyable trip to St. Louis, they agreed they should go to Ithaca for Thanksgiving so Sandy could meet Morgan's family. Little did they know how eventful that trip would be...

Chapter 31   November 2015, Washington, DC

Harriet Campos at the Paragon Washington office got the update Friday afternoon that Powell had flown to St. Louis. Karen had followed Sandy and Morgan's cab to National. Several hours later they had located his cell phone in St. Louis. The assumption was they were going to see his mother and there was no need to fly a team to St. Louis to watch him.

Harriet sent a text to Jason Roberts to stop by her office first thing Monday morning. Jason knocked on her door at 8 a.m. "Jason good to see you, how have you been?"

"Great, keeping busy with the assignment on the guy at the Department of Energy. How can I help?"

"We have an inventor we have been watching and the decision has been made to make him an offer of $250,000 for the rights to the patent he just filed. I sent you his background through secure email and I would suggest you set up a meeting for tomorrow morning at a coffee shop he frequents in Georgetown. You are our best sales guy so convince him it is a great offer and he should accept it. We are not in a rush, but you know how we like to deliver for our clients."

"No problem I will make him an offer he can't

refuse," Jason said in his best Godfather imitation.

****

Sandy was cleaning up the breakfast dishes when his cell phone pinged that he had a text. He snatched it off the island expecting it to be from Morgan, but it was an unknown DC number.

Meet me for coffee on Grace Street at 10 something to discuss – Jason

Sandy had already planned to go to Grace Street for their incredible roasted coffee and continue reading on hydrogen gas production. He thought I should do my thesis on hydrogen after all this work. He sent a quick text to Morgan.

Meeting an unknown Jason for coffee on Grace Street – film at 11 LY S

Ok – let me know – Love YOU Too MD

Sandy went out the front door of the townhouse with Copper and glanced at the black Escalade parked about a block away to the west. They turned east and then headed down to M street. Then they crossed M and continued south on Wisconsin Ave crossing the bridge over the Chesapeake and Ohio canal then down half a block and turned right on Grace Street. Grace Street was a combination of new and old brick brownstones turned into high-end office space, restaurants, and some condo lofts. Since it also was kind of the alley behind the shops on M Street there were multiple overhead doors to docks for those buildings.

Sandy and Copper headed up the stairs and entered the coffee shop. The fragrance of the freshly roasted beans and the pulled espresso almost assaulted him as they walked back to the espresso bar. "Good morning Chip," Sandy said to the barista.

"Sandy... my man. You and Copper are looking great. The usual?"

"Yes, please and I will get a roll to share with Copper."

Several minutes later his triple shot latte and sweet roll were ready, and they headed to a quiet corner in the back. Many days they would sit in the small courtyard behind the coffee shop, but it was a bit chilly today. He sat against the wall facing out towards the pastries. They were intentionally early. So, he quietly sipped his latte and wondered who this Jason guy was and what he wanted.

About five minutes to ten Jason walked over to the table where Sandy was seated. "Hi Sandy, I am Jason. Very nice to meet you." Jason was five eight, brown hair and eyes and slender, clearly not an athlete.

Sandy stood and gave him a full-on man handshake and noticed the slight winch when he squeezed a bit more than necessary. "Nice to meet you, have a seat. You don't look familiar. Do I know you?"

"No, thanks for taking the time to meet me. I will cut to the chase. I represent a client that would like to purchase the exclusive rights to your recent patent."

"Ok, that is interesting. Especially since it hasn't even been issued yet."

"They believe it has real merit and we are prepared to offer you $250,000 for you assigning all rights to their company."

"What if the patent doesn't get issued because of prior art or if the invention doesn't work?"

Looking Sandy straight in the eye, "No problem, you get to keep the money and they will assume all cost and liability to perfect the patent and the technology."

Sandy thought a moment, "Who's the company?"

"I can't say at this time, but obviously that would all be shared when the contract is executed."

"Ok, well this is interesting. I'll have to think about this and get back to you. Can I reach you at the number you sent the text from?"

Jason smiled and looked at Copper who had moved so he was between Sandy and Jason. "Yes, that is my cell. Beautiful dog."

"Thanks. Yes, he is and very protective. I will get back to you next week. It is an intriguing offer."

Jason and Sandy stood up, and Jason almost reluctantly reached out his hand. They shook and Sandy didn't put the full squeeze on since he had already established who was on top. "I look forward to your call. Have a great day."

Sandy and Copper went back to the house where Sandy texted Morgan.

Jason has a client that wants to acquire the patent for $250K

Headed to Reston and the farm C U tonight LY S

Morgan texted back.

Say what!!! Drive safe look forward to discussing tonight LY M

Sandy drove out 66 and took the connector to the Dulles Toll Road. Several minutes later he pulled into one of the many parking garages surrounding the Town Center. He left Copper in the car and went to Jake Nicholson's office on the fourth floor. After catching up with Jake. He took a box with the original transformers and the three new modified ones and went back to the car.

Twenty minutes later they were at the farm.

Sandy went into the house and got food and water for Copper and then went to the barn with his box of transformers. Opening the cabinet, he went down to the basement and set everything up on the worktable. As always, he started with the old transformer. He ran it for a minute, and it was producing copious amounts of gas. Then he tried each of the new transformers and they also produced huge amounts of gas. The answer was clear. The combination of chemicals plus the harmonics of the transformer power split the water molecule into oxygen and hydrogen.

Back at the townhouse, Sandy prepared sautéed chicken thighs which he sliced into strips and presented over a simple romaine Caesar salad. "I tried out the new transformers that Jake had modified, and they worked perfectly. We have a new way to produce hydrogen very cheaply."

Morgan was so happy, "Sandy, this is amazing! You solved it. So, you are the resident expert on hydrogen gas production, what does this mean?"

"Well, first, I didn't exactly solve it! It was a combination of my grandfather's investigation and notes along with Jake's modification of the transformers. But, to your question, it changes everything within ten years."

Morgan nodded and Sandy continued.

"Imagine we no longer use fossil fuels to power everything from cars and trucks to generating electricity across the world. Assuming we can create small hydrogen plants everywhere from gas stations to cities and at power plants, so you no longer must transport the fuel. You produce it where you need it. The conversion of hydrogen gas into electricity produces water. So, at an electric utility, you capture most of the water, recycle and produce more electricity. This means even in a desert you don't need a lot of water. Vastly less carbon in the atmosphere, the whole global warming thing is no longer an issue."

Morgan shook her head, clearly impressed by what she was hearing.

Sandy laughed and kept going. "One gallon of water would produce 1,200 gallons of hydrogen gas. In the past, it has taken more energy to produce hydrogen than the energy created by burning the gas but my calculations show that this production method is insanely efficient because of the harmonics it results in a lot of energy for very little input. This will change the world."

"Wow, you are a genius, one of the many things I love about you. Tell me about your meeting this morning."

"Well, it was kind of strange. First, I get this text

out of the blue from this Jason guy suggesting a meeting at the coffee shop on Grace Street. How did he know I get coffee on Grace Street? Then we meet and basically, he said he has a client that would offer me $250,000 for the rights to the patent regardless if it is issued or the technology works."

Morgan thought for a moment, "How did he know about the patent?"

"I didn't ask, and he didn't say. I guess his client saw it on the web or the USPTO web site.

Morgan said, "Well patent applications are not generally public for 18 months after they are filed. There are lots of exceptions and the rules are complex but on average patents are not published for a year. The 18-month rule applies where the priority date is the same as the filing date. Bottom line there is no way they should know about your patent unless you shared it with someone, and they shared it with this company."

Sandy frowned. "I haven't shared anything about the patent with anyone not even Jackson. So, it had to come from some other source. Any chance someone got it from you."

"No, I am very careful with all my work to keep it very confidential and keep the files secure. They had to have gotten it from the USPTO."

Sandy pondered, "I didn't feel like the guy was trustworthy and Copper was great. He sat there between us and he was not his usual jovial self, so I guess he had the same impression."

Hearing his name, Copper looked up expectantly, his tail brushing the floor rapidly.

Morgan laughed. "I think he feels deserving of a treat since he was so great." And she reached into the dog biscuit canister on the counter, as Copper lifted his head and snarfed it down.

Sandy grinned then quickly looked serious again. "So, what do we do with the offer, however they discovered the patent?"

"Well, what do you think the discovery is worth, say in ten years?"

"Billions or more. Like I said it changes the world."

Morgan looked him straight in the eye, smiled and said, "Well we don't need the money, my thought is we simply say no. Not for a million dollars."

"I totally agree. I'll let him know next week."

Sandy didn't mention that he thought they were being watched not wanting to alarm Morgan, but it did weigh heavy on his mind.

Chapter 32   November 2015, Washington, DC

Diana Scott reached out to Rod Holloway and Lester Hodges to provide them with a brief update on the Valdez case. They met in Rod's office at the Department of Justice.

"Obviously," Diana, began, "what I am sharing is very sensitive, so I did not want to just put it in an email. We are still working on the people in the Lagos office. We know that Bob Jones heads the office. We have not turned them over to the Lagos police, but they believe they are already under arrest. Jones has yet to provide us with his password. We are still trying to break him."

Rod and Lester nodded as Diana continued, "As you know we captured all the documents and computers in their office. We sent the computers to Ft. Meade. We also set up cameras and motion sensors. Last week we caught Nick Keller breaking into the office. We were able to find him entering the country the day before on the customs tapes at the airport and the day after the break-in we were able to watch him get on a flight to Abu Dhabi in the United Arab Emirates. We put a team on him and have located his home and office. He works for a company called UAE Research Limited and we suspect that it is linked to the Nigerian company through a parent company which Todd operates."

"Excellent work," said Rod. "What are the next steps?"

"Well since we are in the UAE we have to be a bit more careful than in Nigeria. I have asked the NSA to try to get anything we can on both Keller and the company. I had one of our technicians attach monitors on the office phone and internet lines, so we are starting to assemble data, but it appears the important stuff is all encrypted. This creates a challenge for NSA, but they are working on it. I hope we have more information next week."

Diana thought for a moment then added, "Oh, and I did reach out to Treasury and they are working the terrorist angle to get transaction data on the numbered account in the Caymans. Nothing yet, but I have not heard we hit a roadblock so hopefully more next week."

Lester suggested, "is there anything you need us to help with at this point?"

"No, I think we are doing all we can. Thanks. Have a great Thanksgiving and hopefully the whole team will have more after the holiday."

Chapter 33   November 2015, Georgetown, DC

Sandy, Morgan, and Copper all loaded up in Sandy's car and were off before noon Wednesday for their trip to Ithaca. Morgan was really looking forward to introducing her folks to Sandy as well as seeing them herself since it had been months since she took a trip up north.

They headed out of town, with a million other people, on the GW, crossed the Potomac on 495 and picked up 270 to Frederick, Maryland. In Frederick, they took Route 15 north passing Thurmont, near Camp David, and then on north passing Gettysburg.

As they were passing the Gettysburg exits, Morgan asked Sandy, "Have you ever been?" pointing at the signs.

Sandy nodded. "Yes. A very moving experience with my parents. You?" he asked Morgan.

She smiled. "Yes – the same exact type of experience with my parents. It's interesting though," she continued, "living in D.C. now. Many people fail to realize that Gettysburg is as far north of Washington, DC as it is."

"And," Sandy nodded and added, "that more men died in the three days of the battle of Gettysburg than in the entire Vietnam war. In many ways, the Battle of Gettysburg was the turning point in the civil war where General George Meade's army defeated General Robert E. Lee's Confederate troops."

Morgan nodded and said, "Well far or not, we're really lucky to be living in a place that is so full of history – even if it is a bit of a drive."

Sandy nodded and they resolved to take advantage of the historical treasures of the area when they got back.

"Maybe a once a month outing to a historical venue or museum..." And they both fell into a contented silence.

The divided four-lane highway was relatively quiet despite being a long holiday weekend and they rolled north now listening to tunes and just relaxing. Sandy noticed a white Lexus sedan following about half a mile back. He pulled off in Dillsburg at the Wendy's to grab a quick bite for everyone including Copper. He noticed that the white Lexus had also taken the left-hand turn and was parked at the adjacent gas station.

When they pulled out of Wendy's parking lot and turned left on 15 the Lexus followed a short way back. They took Google maps suggestion and took Hwy 581 east through Harrisburg crossing over the wide Susquehanna river and then turning north on Interstate 83 to connect with Interstate 81. The Lexus remained a reasonable distance back. Just after the split where 83 continued east to Allentown and they headed north on 81, Sandy turned off at the Love's Truckstop and pulled up to a gas pump.

Morgan looked surprised, "We have plenty of gas. Why did you stop?"

"I think we have someone following us, so I wanted to see what they do. Don't look around but there is a white Lexus parked over on the side of the gas station. I will bet my pension it will stay there until we leave. Do you need a pit stop?"

"Good idea. And I'll take Copper for one when I get back. Why do you think they're following us?"

"My guess it has something to do with the strange offer on Tuesday."

Sandy topped off the gas and when Morgan returned, she took Copper on a leash to do his business. Shortly after leaving the gas station, the Lexus resumed following them.

Sandy asked Morgan to look up Rudy Zimmerman's number on his cell phone and call his mobile. Morgan hit dial and put the phone on speakerphone.

Rudy answered the call, "Sandy you old washed up SEAL what are you up to these days?"

"Hey Rudy, just the happiest guy on the planet."

Rudy shouted back, "Well that must mean you have finally met a gal that will put up with your crazy stunts."

"Yup that's right, you nailed it and she is sitting right here next to me. Need a huge favor."

Zimmer replied, "What do you need me to walk you down the aisle mate?"

"Not yet," Sandy grinned, "but I can picture you in pink and all flowers."

Zimmer laughed. "So, what is it that gives me the pleasure of this call?"

Sandy's smile turned into a slight frown. "Well, I'll make a long story short. I am on 81 just north of Harrisburg and I have a car following me. I wonder if you could have someone pull them over, so I know who they are and maybe get a bit of distance."

"No problem always happy to help." Then Zimmer said, "What do you owe some loan shark some money or something?"

"Nothing like that. I think they are trying to pressure me on an invention I just came up with."

"Cool, I can see you as a creator. Give me about 10 minutes to find out who is in that sector and I'll ask them to call you on your cell directly. Then you can give them the details."

"Thanks, Rudy. I owe you one!"

"No problem man! Can't wait to see you at the team get together in April. Keep the wheels down and call if you need anything else."

Sandy nodded and said, "See you in April and again thanks so much." Then the call disconnected.

Morgan asked, "So who is Rudy?"

"Rudy was part of my SEAL team. We saved each other's lives multiple times and now he is a Pennsylvania State Trooper."

"Good friend to have. Your team is really tight."

"After what we went through together, we would literally lay down our lives for each other. It is a special bond."

About five minutes later the phone rang. "Hi, this is Sandy Powell."

"Officer Francis here," a pleasant female voice came from the speaker, "I just got a call from Zimmer and he said you could use my help. I guess you go back aways."

"We sure do, and I appreciate your help. I have a white Lexus that has been following us since Washington. We are just passing exit 100 on 81 north and the car is about half a mile behind us."

"Ok, it will take me about 15 minutes to catch up

to you. I will give you a call when I get close."

"Thanks so much, talk to you soon."

About fifteen minutes later Sandy's phone rang again. "Hi, this is Sandy"

"Hi, Officer Francis again. I'm about a mile back. Could you speed up to about 80 and we will see if the Lexus picks up the pace? Then I have a good reason to pull them over."

"No problem, almost at 80 now."

"Great, did they speed up?"

"Yes, just like you suggested."

"Ok, I'll pull them over, get a picture of the driver, registration and the license and send them to you as a text. I imagine after I get all done with them, they should be tied up for at least 30 minutes. Of course, if they have wants or warrants it could be days," she said with a chuckle.

A few minutes later they received a text from Francis saying she had them.

Sandy reduced his speed back to a comfortable 65 and they continued north to New York. There was a good deal of traffic, but it was not bad considering the holiday weekend. And, while cloudy, the roads were dry and thankfully no snow or slush. They received a text from Officer Francis. The text included a picture of Karen Young's driver's license, registration, license plate and a photo of her behind the wheel. Francis had included there were no wants or warrants and she hoped the information was helpful. Morgan texted back a thank you.

Sandy said, "We will have to try to check her out when we get home."

"For sure, you really think she was following us?"

"I am pretty sure, but it could have been a coincidence," he said to reassure Morgan while all the while he thought to himself, "But I'm sure."

At Whitney Point, they finally left I-81 and took Route 79 west for 30 miles to Ithaca. Morgan took over navigation from Google maps and directed them across town on Stewart Ave below the Cornell Campus to Cayuga Heights and her parents' home.

The house was a Frank Lloyd Wright Usonian style of architecture. Single story with long thin lines, the roof was only gently sloped forming a low peak. It was built from long thin concrete blocks that were staggered in and out between courses creating long parallel lines. The windows on the side facing the street were only 18 inches high and just under the eaves. Every ten feet along the wall were pencil-thin pairs of windows from the ground to the eaves encased with stained mahogany trim.

A short wall in front of the house created an enclosed patio and they used the same style of block to blend with the house. Everything worked together to extenuate the feeling of length, thinness, and lightness. The house was stunning. In keeping with this architectural style, the front door was off to the right of the house under a flat porch roof. Morgan led the way with Sandy and Copper right behind. She pressed the doorbell next to the dark red front door and a moment later her mom, Betty, opened the door with her dad, Clint, closely behind.

Morgan gave her parents hugs then said, "Folks, I want you to meet Sandy and Copper."

Sandy moved to shake Betty's hand when she said, "Oh no Mister, I want a serious hug," with an ear to ear smile. Like Morgan, Betty was tall and thin, but she had significantly more reddish hair in a short cut, with bright green eyes.

Clint rescued Sandy from the lingering hug and shook hands.

"So glad you both could join us for Thanksgiving. It's nice for the family to get together for the holiday. Please come in."

The front entry was a simple wall opposite the door that was open on the left, with a closet to the right. Walking around the wall Sandy was stunned by a wall of glass facing the back lawn.

His jaw dropped, "WOW that is amazing and you even see some of Cayuga Lake from this vantage point. Did you have this house built?"

"Yes, many years ago one of my clients was a professor in the Architecture School and he wanted to build a house inspired in part by the Frank Lloyd Wright modernist approach. We had this property and it all just kind of worked out. We love it."

Sandy nodded appreciatively as Clint continued, "We have added a large garage off to the right but basically changed very few things about the house."

It felt like touring a museum, every detail was stunning. A transom above the windows was fashioned in stained glass that played with the light from the backyard. The floor to ceiling windows had a latticework of tall thin and square frames of black steel holding both clear and opaque pieces of glass. Everything was framed in rich mahogany.

"I am going to let Copper out if you think he will stay in the yard?" Morgan asked.

"He'll be fine, I'm sure he will sniff everything, but a good run around will do him well after the long ride. He'll come back as soon as we call him."

Morgan opened the door to the deck overlooking the backyard and Copper was off and down the stairs like an arrow from a bow.

Betty suggested, "Let's relax for a minute and catch up, would anyone like a drink?"

"Well, it's after five o'clock so I will have a scotch on the rocks, thanks," Clint replied.

"Sounds great, me too," Sandy said, feeling himself relax in this new, but important, environment.

Betty and Morgan headed off to the kitchen while Sandy and Clint caught up on work and recent events. The women returned shortly with drinks and a plate of veggies. The sunset was amazing and Copper, as always settled at Morgan's feet. Sandy felt very much at home and they made him feel very welcome.

The next morning after enjoying Betty's cinnamon monkey bread, Sandy and Morgan drove over to the Cornell Campus for a nice long run. Everything was quiet with all the students at home for Thanksgiving break. Sandy marveled at the 'Old Stone Row' the original campus buildings built in the 1860s. The buildings were a French Second Empire design with arched windows of limestone and colored slate Mansard roofs. At the northwest end of the arts quad sat the modern and amazing Johnson Art Museum designed by I.M. Pei, best known for his glass pyramid entrance to the Louvre in Paris.

When they got back to the house, everyone fluttered around the kitchen preparing for Thanksgiving dinner. Clint remarked how nice it was not being an active veterinarian since invariably some cow would have a difficult delivery half-way through Thanksgiving dinner or some other emergency would arise requiring his service.

On Friday Morgan gave Sandy a tour of the area. Driving up the west side of Cayuga Lake she took him to the overlook for Taughannock Falls, the highest waterfalls east of the Rockies. The 215-foot falls cascaded from a deep gorge into a massive amphitheater surrounded by soaring cliffs of sedimentary rock. She also took him to Buttermilk Falls where the creek gently flowed over ageless layers of sandstone and shale. Since the day was unusually warm and sunny for November, Sandy suggested, if her parents liked steak, they could pick up some nice thick ones and they would fix dinner for her folks. She loved the idea.

Friday night Sandy and Morgan hummed around the kitchen pulling together a wonderful dinner with Sandy bustling back and forth to the grill, while Clint and Betty sat at the island, watched and chatted.

By Saturday mid-morning the two said goodbye to Morgan's parents. Sandy thanked them profusely for the lovely time.

"Not at all, dear," Betty smiled and reached out to give him another big hug. "It was our pleasure."

Once again, Clint reached out with his hand, saying with a sincere smile, "And don't be a stranger. We'd love to have you come back." And he gave his daughter a knowing look and a wink.

Morgan grinned and gave her dad a slight nod, as if to say "You get it..."

Then, took Copper's leash and headed to the car. The trip back was uneventful with not a lot of traffic since it was only Saturday.

"I wish we could have stayed another full day," Sandy said to Morgan, as they were driving along 81. "But the traffic tomorrow will be horrendous."

Morgan nodded in agreement. "And," she added, "we have a full week coming up - including your new task of checking out Karen Young."

Chapter 34   November 2015, Lagos, Nigeria

After days of interrogating the people from the Global Research office, the CIA team had little more than when they started. It was clear that Bob Jones was the only person who had contact up the chain of command and yet he seemed to only know the mysterious 'Todd' and insisted he had never met the man or knew where he was based. Funds flowed through the numbered account. While the staff had shared their passwords there was no useful data on those machines, all they had were research notes on various oil companies.

They did have Harry Atkinson's confession to pay and supply the arsenic to Faruq Eze and he had quickly thrown Jones under the bus saying that Jones had directed him to make the arrangement. So, they could put them both into the Lagos legal system. The challenge was they did not want anyone to know they had them, so Atkinson could sit at the safe house until they were ready.

Bob Jones, the leader of the office was the key. He was the only one getting the critical information and emails. Danjuma and Ismail had tried to break him for days and it was not working. They decided to use the container again. In their experience, 99% of the time one day was all it took. The next morning, they handcuffed him behind his back, put on a blindfold and put him in the back of a windowless van. As far as Jones knew, they were Lagos police.

They drove him over to the Tin Can Island and put him in the same container used on Atkinson. Ismail said to Danjuma as they were dragging Jones into the container, "You know this thing is really starting to stink in here from the dead bodies. We really need to air it out."

"Yeah, you're probably right but Jones here won't care when it is all over." They removed the blindfold so Jones could see for a few minutes where he was but left the handcuffs on.

Jones started to scream, "You can't leave me here to die! You just can't!"

Ismail replied, "we can, and we will. Goodbye Mr. Jones." They slammed the door closed and padlocked the container. They could hear Jones sobbing inside. They drove back to the safe house.

As before, they returned in the evening with the folding chairs and sat Bob Jones in a chair facing the headlights. He began talking very rapidly.

"Slow down Mr. Jones, we are going to take you back to the police station and get all your information. If there any gaps or unanswered questions we will just bring you back here for a longer stay. Are we clear Jones?" asked Danjuma.

Jones nodded, whimpering.

Ismail remarked as they dragged him from the container, "he soiled himself, God he really stinks, we better hose him down when we get back before we start to question him."

"Yeah, you're right. He really reeks." They pushed him into the back of the van and put on the blindfold. They literally hosed him down in the garage and then dragged him into an interview room in his wet clothes. They sat him in a metal chair and handcuffed him to a desk.

Ismail started the interview, "Let me be perfectly clear. We don't care about you. If you give us the wrong answers you are going back for an even longer visit at our version of Club Med. Who do you report to?"

"I told you before, his name is Todd and I think he is in New York, based on his accent. Can I have some water please."

"We will get to the water in a while."

"So, you have talked to Todd. What is his phone number?"

"As I told you, I don't know, I never call him. If I need to talk, I send a secure message and he calls me back."

Ismail continued the interrogation, "Which gets us to the next question, what is the password for your computer and the secure email and any other passwords we may need."

Bob Jones thought for a moment, "I have a non-disclosure agreement I don't believe I can share that information with you."

Danjuma looked at him and smiled, "Did you hear that Ismail? He has a non-disclosure agreement. Well, that changes everything. Clearly, the company will be upset if he tells us."

He started to yell at Jones, "DO YOU THINK THE COMPANY WILL CARE WHEN THEY FIND YOUR BODY AT CLUB MED!!!!!!"

Both stood up and started to unshackle Jones.

"What are you doing?" Jones asked.

"We are taking you back to Club Med you idiot. Clearly, we would not want you to violate your non-disclosure agreement. Stand up."

"No wait, I'll give you the passwords."

Ismail slid a pad of paper and a pen in front of Jones. "Start writing and make sure you get them right. Any screw-ups and we will give you pain like you can't even imagine and then take you to the container."

"I'll get them right. Can I have some water,

please?"

Danjuma left the room and returned with a bottle of water. He set it on the table but didn't give it to Jones. "When you finish, you can have the water. Make sure you write carefully."

As soon as they had the list of usernames and passwords Danjuma left the room. The computers had been flown over to Joint Base Andrews and been driven the 30 odd miles to NSA at Fort Meade, Maryland. The staff computers had been unlocked and all the data copied off to other drives. There was nothing but research notes.

As soon as the technicians at NSA had the passwords, they unlocked the Self-Encrypting drive and copied all the data to several spare drives that they controlled. Then they began unlocking the encrypted emails and there was a treasure trove of data. They sent word to Lagos that they were into the computers and the passwords were correct.

Now they needed the last bit of crucial information. Danjuma held the bottle of water. It was clear that Jones was dehydrated. He had dry skin, was breathing rapidly and his eyes were sunken. "We need one more thing, Mr. Jones," Danjuma said Jones' name with a mocking tone, "We need the details and passwords for the bank accounts. Please write them down."

Jones just stared at the bottle of water. He took up the pen and wrote down the information on the numbered bank accounts in the Caymans. Danjuma sent a secure email to Diana Scott at CIA headquarters in Langley, Virginia. As soon as Diana had the passwords and other details, she began diving into the bank accounts to see the transaction details.

For now, they were done with Jones. They gave him the water, took him out of the interrogation room, and handed him over to a guard so he could shower and change into fresh prison garb. All in all, a good day for the good guys.

Chapter 35 November 2015, Georgetown, DC

Back home on Saturday night, Sandy and Morgan relaxed and watched a movie. Sunday morning, they slept in and, since it was a cold and sleety day, they relaxed and watched football enjoying traditional football snacks of pizza and wings.

Monday morning Sandy sent a text to Jason.

Let's meet on Grace Street at 10 just let me know what day works for you

Tomorrow is good, see you then Jason

He spent the rest of the day finding out what he could about Karen Young. He knew from her driver's license that she was 5'5", brown hair, brown eyes and weighed 135. In her driver's license photo, she had short brown hair but that was three years ago. From the photo taken by Officer Francis, he knew she had kept the cut but added blond highlights. She lived in Falls Church, Virginia in the Pimmit Hills area. Sandy knew the area because a few of his former students lived there.

The community was developed shortly after World War II and was mostly single-story bungalows on nice shaded lots. Although in the past few years they were being bought up, torn down and replaced with mini-McMansions since the metro was close by and it was an easy commute to downtown and next to the thriving Tysons Corners high rise office buildings.

Sandy learned more from Young's Facebook page. She went to high school in Jefferson, Maryland. Jefferson was a rural part of the state between Frederick and Harpers Ferry. She went to the University of Maryland. She also had two children about 7 and 10 years old and was married to Fred Young.

After paying for a record search, Sandy learned that Young had worked for the CIA but now worked for OI Research. This aligned with the car's registration which was owned by OI Research. The only thing he could discover about OI is that it had an 'A+' rating from the Better Business Bureau and they were in Tysons Corner. He had their address on the registration. OI had no customer reviews, no apparent web site, a dead end. All in all, nothing exceptional except she was following him.

Tuesday morning Sandy and Copper returned to Grace Street and he was lucky to get the same table in the back. As expected, Jason arrived a few minutes early, they shook hands and Jason sat across from Sandy.

"Thanks for coming and I'm glad we can get this wrapped up. I thought about it and decided I am not interested in selling the rights to my patent and invention.

Jason looked troubled, "I am very sorry to hear that. My client does not accept no for an answer. Perhaps I can suggest he increase the offer."

Sandy looked him in the eye, "I would not be interested at a million dollars or even ten million dollars. You should understand that if this proves out, as I believe it will, it will revolutionize the whole world. I won't get into details, but bottom-line I am not going to sell."

"Ok but let me warn you this will not end well for you if you fail to sell."

Sandy got an even more stern look, "Is that a threat!"

"No, simply a promise." Jason stood, turned and walked away.

****

Jason called Harriet and delivered the news, "He is not interested in selling at any price."

"Ok, I will pass the news up the line. Thanks, and I guess for now go back to your guy at the Energy Department. I will let you know if we need anything further. Again thanks."

Harriet sent a secure email to Todd in New York that the answer is no.

THE PINNACLE CLUB

****

In New York, Todd Peterson was thinking things weren't going well lately. First, the Lagos office looked like everyone just left. He had to send someone from NY to find a new office and hire new staff to keep things running down there. Then he got the news that Powell said no to the offer of $250,000 to buy the rights. Now the most difficult thing he knew was coming. He needed to meet with the Pinnacle Club to update them on these events. With very few exceptions he never met with the CEOs, but this was one of those times. He put a call into Bryce Carrington's office requesting a callback.

Later that afternoon his cell phone rang, "Hi, this is Todd Peterson."

"Todd this is Bryce. What's up? It must be important for you to call."

"Thanks for calling back. We have several developments that have just come up and I think we need a face to face meeting of the club and myself."

"All right, but this doesn't sound good. I will call the others and figure out a place and time where we all can meet and let you know. I assume your schedule is flexible to fit into our availability."

"Of course, sir. Just let me know where and when and I will be there."

Bryce called his admin in his office. "Cindy, I need to know my availability later this week when I can get away for the whole day. Look to see what can get moved around on my calendar."

Cindy returned a few minutes later, "Mr. Carrington I can clear your calendar without too much trouble for Thursday, Friday or Saturday."

"Thanks, Cindy. Please call the crew and make sure the jet is available on those days."

Bryce used his cell phone to make a conference call to Reggie Clark and HW. "Gentlemen sorry to interrupt your day but Todd has asked that we meet with him, if possible, this week. Can you check your schedules and get back to me? I am free Thursday, Friday or Saturday." Both agreed to get back to him in fifteen minutes. They agreed on dinner in Miami on Friday night at Barbuto Milos.

Bryce called Cindy, "Cindy book the jet for Friday afternoon, tell them we are going to Miami, I need to be downtown no later than 6 p.m. and make a reservation for a private dining room at Barbuto Milos and obviously car service."

Chapter 36   November 2015, Washington, DC

Rod Holloway held another briefing on the Valdez Investigation. He opened the meeting by saying, "I believe we have made substantial progress and I look forward to each of your updates. Lester, please let's begin."

They stayed in the same format as the previous briefing. Lester Hodges asked Tiffany Flores for an update. Tiffany presented a bio on Jacob Holden the previous CEO at TXO who assumed Chairmanship of Texas Oil and Gas in the spring.

Diana Scott from the CIA had a lot of new information. "First, we were able to break Bob Jones the leader of the Global Research office in Lagos. As a result, we got full access to his computer and secure emails. These files and emails clearly show a connection to a higher authority, a person named Todd. This correspondence covers the past five years and shows a clear pattern of working to either obstruct or influence the oil and gas industry in Nigeria. It names several oil and gas companies based in Nigeria that have either lost contracts or other companies that have gained contracts at what would appear to be very lucrative arrangements. Our CIA office in Nigeria is trying to dig deeper into the companies that have benefitted to determine if they are related to the three companies identified in the Valdez investigation."

She paused and looked at the attentive and serious faces of those in the room, then continued, "The people who worked for Global Research continue to be detained by our CIA office but believe they are being held by the Lagos police. We will have to transfer them soon to the police, but we don't want their whereabouts to be public at this time. It would appear the crimes have only been committed by Bob Jones and Harry Atkinson. The other staff members appear to only be researchers. In addition, we have also been able to clearly establish that Global Research was directly involved in bribes and murder of officials in the Nigerian government and this direction came from Todd. To date, none of the information goes as high as the president but certainly to some of his direct staff."

Rod Holloway raised his eyebrows and said, "Todd must be getting orders from somewhere…"

Diana continued, nodding at Rod, "Well, we were able to track Nick Keller from his break-in of the Lagos office to his office in Abu Dhabi which appears to be a related company in the middle east. We have wiretaps installed on their phone and internet lines but all information that could expose the links has been encrypted and NSA is still working to break the codes. This office is significantly larger than the Lagos office and we estimate nearly twenty people work in this office. Since we lack evidence of a crime, we have not been able to detain or suggest the arrest to the UAE government. We could grab Keller and see if we can, get him to talk if you recommended that course of action."

"So," Rod said, "no evidence? No money transfers..."

Diana looked at him and said, "We also got access to the numbered account in the Caymans and can see the incoming and outgoing wire transfers. The outgoing transfers were all to Global Research's account in Nigeria. We have also collected the past five years' records from that account and are researching those transactions. Now that we know the numbered account that fed money into the Lagos/Cayman account we will attempt to get access to that account. So that is where we are at as of today. Any questions?"

"Excellent update and please pass along our thanks to your team. I would suggest picking up Keller and see what you can learn but of course, that should come from your Director and it's their call. Next up?"

Lester said, "Amber what have you learned?"

Amber took over at the front of the room, "when

we included Jacob Holden in our analysis, we could see a pattern of calls about once per quarter between the three CEOs over the past five years."

Dylan Harrison was up next and like Amber when they added Holden to the flight information, they could see overlap at least quarterly. With the FBI interviews of the FBOs, they had the manifest for most of the flights showing the executives in close proximity to each other. They had updated the international information from CBP which showed that international travel was aligned multiple times.

Nina Craig said there was no new information on the accounting review. Jordan Vasquez also had no new information.

Lester now introduced the newest member of the team. "I would like to introduce Patti Allen. She is managing the wiretaps on the executive phones. I think she has some really great news."

"Hi everyone. We have been monitoring the executive phones and this morning had a breakthrough. This morning there was a call from Bryce Carrington's cell to a Todd Peterson. Peterson said they needed a face to face meeting of the club. Shortly after that call, Carrington called Watson and Clark saying they need to get together. Fifteen minutes later they agreed to meet on Friday evening in Miami. We picked up the call from Carrington's admin making arrangements for his jet and making dinner reservations at Barbuto Milos in Miami for Friday evening at 6 p.m. in a private dining room."

Rod very uncharacteristically pounded his fist on the table and said, "Now we have them! Lester, obviously you need to assemble a team for this. I want pictures of them getting off the planes, pictures entering the restaurant probably through a backdoor, video and full audio of the meeting. Now that we know this mystery guy is Todd Peterson maybe we can figure out who he is."

"I totally agree. I will have the Miami office get on this within the hour and I will get someone working on Todd Peterson as well. Patti, did we get a phone number for Peterson?"

"No, caller id was blocked, and we did not have time to triangulate the location."

Rod stood up, "Again everyone you are all doing outstanding work and let's stay on this. We are getting close."

Chapter 37   November 2015, Houston, TX

Bryce Carrington stepped out of the open door of the Lincoln Town car at the FBO at Hobby Airport and walked the few feet to his Gulfstream G-650 ER. His flight attendant Shirley, a stunning 32-year-old with long wavy brown hair and just enough makeup to turn any eye, was at the foot of the stairs.

"Good afternoon Mr. Carrington, we are ready to depart when you are ready. Will anyone else be joining us today?" She already knew the answer but wanted to make sure plans had not changed.

"Nope, just us thanks so much." He poked his head into the cockpit. "Ed, Carla good to see you, I am ready to go, thanks."

Ed, the Captain turned his head around, "Glad to have you aboard sir, should be smooth most of the way, we may get a few afternoon thunderstorms near Miami. We will do our best to avoid them."

Bryce took his customary seat on the left of the plane, a large leather recliner. Shirley had closed the front door and the twin engines were spooling up. A few minutes later they were taxiing to the end of the runway and were off to Miami. With a top speed of nearly Mach one, they would be on the ground in about an hour and a half.

As soon as they were airborne Shirley came back, "Would you like anything, Mr. Carrington?"

"Thanks, Shirley, I will have some Perrier with lime, and do we have any sushi today."

"Yes sir, I thought you might like some, so I just got some delivered fresh from Takumi. I will bring back an assortment for you.

Bryce opened his laptop and began reading a report from Vietnam on new discoveries in the Nam Con Son Basin located offshore in the south of the country. The reports were very positive, and he wanted to discuss progress with the others tonight. He thought for a moment about what was going on at Paragon that caused this urgent meeting. What seemed a short time later they were on final approach to Miami International.

Carrington's town car pulled up next to the jet and he walked over and entered the open rear door. Thirty minutes later, due to heavy traffic, they drove over the Causeway to South Beach. The car pulled up to the rear entrance of Barbuto Milos. The one-story modern building faced 1st Street, but they used the alley behind to enter through the rear kitchen. The maître d' rushed into the kitchen and escorted Bryce to the private dining room. The room looked like a library and two stewards stood patiently by the wall.

Todd Peterson and Reggie were already at the table and they stood as Bryce entered. "Todd, Reggie good to see you both. I hope your travel was uneventful."

Reggie grinned, "Always good to see you, Bryce, even if I have to fly cross country or around the world to connect."

"Bryce, it has been a while, thank you for putting this meeting together on short notice," as Todd shook hands with Bryce.

A moment later HW entered the room and everyone shared pleasantries. Drinks were ordered, and after a few minutes, Bryce took the lead. Bryce asked the stewards to leave the room and said that they would call them when they were ready.

"So, Todd, what is so urgent and important that we need a face to face?" All the men focused on Todd.

"We have a few developments and with their...shall we say... sensitivity, I wanted to brief you in person. First, the inventor, Sandy Powell, who we discussed via email has rejected our offer of $250,000 to acquire the rights to his patent and his invention. He told our agent he would not even consider $10 million for the invention. He said it will, 'Change the World'. We had our resident scientist look at the patent again and he believes

Powell may be right. His invention could produce copious amounts of hydrogen gas at almost no cost."

Reggie's jaw dropped, "Shit, that could put us out of business. We all know that the only reason hydrogen has not displaced oil as an energy source is the cost to produce it is so high. Yes, we produce a lot of hydrogen from natural gas, but the process and handling are expensive."

Bryce thought a moment, "Reggie is right. So, Todd, what are you recommending?"

"I think we need to eliminate this threat. We can delete the patent as if it was never entered into the USPTO system and, as near as we can determine, he has not shared the idea with anyone except his girlfriend who filed the patent."

HW looked shocked, "We can't just eliminate the guy and his girlfriend. It was bad enough in Nigeria where no one would know. These are Americans. We can't just knock them off."

Reggie replied, "HW... like I told you in Lagos, this is a tough business and the reason we have been, and *still are on top*," he emphasized, "is that we make the tough decisions."

"Well, I for one vote NO to doing any harm to this guy. We need to get him to accept a reasonable offer."

Bryce looked at Todd, "For now just put some pressure on Powell. We can up the offer to $5 million and see if that works. Keep us posted on the status. Anything else?"

"Yes, the office in Lagos is offline. We don't know what happened but all our people in that office have disappeared without a trace. We are working to reopen the office with new staff, but it is strange that they are all gone."

"Do you mean like abducted by aliens gone or what?" asked HW.

"Kind of like that. We had perfectly executed the plan to eliminate Ali Mohammed the Minister of Oil and Gas. The medical examiner said it was food poisoning and a week later our office is empty, and the people are totally missing."

"Do you think someone figured out the plan and grabbed your people," asked HW.

"Reality is we don't know. I don't see how that could have happened but at this point, we simply don't know."

"Any other problems, Todd," asked Bryce.

"No that's it. All of our other projects are running smoothly, and we will figure out this situation in Nigeria."

Reggie looked around and said to Todd, "I have

a great idea. I want you to get in the papers in the next few days. We need some professor to say that all these solar panels because they are black, are going to contribute to global warming."

Bryce sat back and gave a hearty laugh, "That is the best one I have heard in a long time. It's perfect. Run with it."

HW looked kind of stunned, "Do you really think some professor will say that to a newspaper."

"It is easy, you just wave some money under their nose and those liberal professors are just like politicians, they will do anything for research money," Todd said with a chuckle.

Bryce, HW, and Reggie all stood and thanked Todd for the update. He was dismissed and left the room.

After he left Bryce suggested they order dinner and continue the conversation. The food at Barbuto Milos was extraordinary and well worth the trip. They all ordered Mediterranean seafood dishes which the restaurant was world-famous for.

Over dinner, Bryce brought up concerns about how Peterson seemed to be losing control of Paragon. Reggie pointed out several different projects that were running smoothly and overall, they were a good investment. Bryce seemed unconvinced. HW stayed on the sidelines and was continuing to think about how extreme solutions seemed to be taken as a matter of course.

The conversation switched to joint projects. Bryce started the conversation discussing their joint development of several fields in Indonesia and Vietnam. He felt they were in good shape with the joint company to continue pumping in the proven fields and exploration was ahead of schedule.

Reggie brought up developments in Kirkuk, Iraq and how the Paragon paramilitary had repelled several potential attacks to disrupt the wells in that field.

HW asked about how the joint development in Iran was going and was the new company there able to work around the sanctions.

Bryce said it was going well, and the new company was structuring a deal to virtually move the oil through a Russian shell company.

Next, they turned to the timing of the spring price shift. Bryce said, "Listen we have the right guy in the White House and our usual support in Congress and we are looking ahead to the next election in 2012. I think we need to keep prices low and just do an 8 cent per gallon increase before Memorial Day. Memorial Day is the 31st this year so let's roll up prices on the 20th and we can roll them back 4 cents on July 10 and then a full ten cents September 10 through the mid-term election. This will keep the economy in good shape and help the people we need to be elected. If we see things are not going our way, we can adjust."

HW thought a moment, "I like the plan and I can certainly live with those numbers." Reggie nodded his head in agreement

They all had baklava with strong Greek coffee followed by ouzo after the delightful meal. Reggie and HW left separately for the airport. Bryce was staying over at the Fairmont on the beach to see friends in the morning. He had reserved the Fairmont Suite which was the size of a small house. He really enjoyed going out on the balcony and enjoyed the sound of the waves gently rolling in. Tonight, he sat on the balcony, could hear some of the Friday night sounds from South Beach and smell the salt air. He thought life is good... but oh how things can change.

Chapter 38   December 2015, Washington, DC

Lester and the team at the FBI were over the moon happy with all they had collected. They had pictures of all the executives getting on their jets. Pictures getting off in Miami. All had landed at Miami International making it even easier. They had pictures of each of them, including Todd Peterson, entering the rear of the restaurant.

Prior to the meeting in Miami, the FBI had met with the IRS and knew the names of everyone who worked at the restaurant. They knew the maître d', Nick Praxis, was over $100,000 in debt to the IRS. It was rather simple for the FBI to approach him, suggest his IRS problem could go away and get access to the private dining room. They installed four high definition cameras and multiple microphones in the room. They also installed a camera in the rear kitchen, so they got a video of them entering and leaving through the rear.

Lester called Rod on his cell phone and gave him the good news. They agreed to have a joint meeting with the Attorney General and the Director of the FBI hopefully Monday, schedules permitting, to discuss the next steps.

Monday afternoon after moving a few meetings

around the senior group assembled. Meredith Drake, the Attorney General, took the lead for the meeting, "I understand we have put together some solid evidence on these three oil executives. Rod, can you brief us?"

Rod shifted in his chair, "actually I would like Lester to bring us up to speed on the developments from Friday evening, he deserves most of the credit."

Lester began, "This really was a joint effort across a number of agencies that all came together to create a really strong case." He turned on the projector and showed a picture of all three executives, "Harold Watson, Bryce Carrington, and Reginald Clark have conspired to commit murder and have thwarted anti-trust laws to work in collusion to create joint ventures and fix prices. We have pictures, audio, and video evidence." Lester flipped to the video with pieces of the conversation on Friday night that clearly demonstrated the damning evidence they had collected.

Meredith was shocked, "Where did you get this? It is amazing!"

We knew that they had planned a joint dinner on Friday night in Miami. We convinced the maître d' to allow us to install covert cameras and audio equipment in the dining room. We also had agents at various airports photograph their departures and arrivals on Friday."

"Who is the fourth guy in the video?" Meredith asked.

"That is Todd Peterson, we are pulling together information on him and his company as we speak."

Charles Castiglione, Director of the FBI, injected, "We believe this is only the surface of this case and it could go a lot further."

Meredith said, "Ok, what are the next steps?"

Rod suggested, "I think we need to keep digging. Clearly, we have more than enough evidence to take this to a Grand Jury and get indictments, but I totally agree with Charlie and Lester that there is a bunch more we can get. Once we indict and arrest these three guys the whole thing will go underground, and we will have a hard time discovering more. I would like to suggest we spend a few more weeks doing discovery."

"Ok, I agree, dig deep, fast, and by the book. These guys will have the best legal talent in the country so any loose thread they will unzip the pillowcase. Charlie, I think we need to brief the President so he can get in front of this."

"I would recommend we wait the two weeks to see what else gets unearthed. We both know that 1600 is like a bucket full of holes. It will find a way out." said Charlie.

"Your right, ok, let's plan to get together in two weeks and see if we have more. Lester and Ron, please pass on a job well done to the team. This is amazing."

Chapter 39   December 2015, New York City

Todd thought all weekend about the meeting. On one hand, he was pleased that he had shared the bad news with the execs, on the other hand, he was very concerned with HW's reluctance to take strong measures against Powell and that he had influenced Reggie and Bryce. He needed to solve the problem in Nigeria as soon as possible. So, he called two of his best people in New York and had them on a plane on Sunday afternoon.

First thing Monday morning he called Campos in Washington and told her to have her agent meet with Powell and up the offer to $5 million. Harriet called Jason and gave him the updated information on the offer to Powell.

Client has a new offer can you meet tomorrow at 10 on Grace Street

Not really interested but yes will meet tomorrow

Sandy and Jason met as planned. "My client would like to revise his offer to $5 million for the rights to the patent and invention. Same terms as before. If it doesn't work, you get to keep the money."

"What about your threat?"

"I apologize, I was caught up in the moment and

frustrated. My bad."

"Ok, I don't think it will change my mind, but I want to sleep on it and will text you tomorrow."

"I can't ask for more than that, thanks," Jason stood and left the coffee shop. He felt like it might happen, and he updated Harriet.

After Sandy got back to the townhouse, he texted Morgan.

They upped the offer to $5 million let's talk tonight L S

Ok have an awesome day LYM M

LYM????

Love YOU MORE silly

On Monday Sandy had prepared a basic beef broth from scratch using beef bones he picked up at the butcher. He roasted the bones and then cooked them down to make the broth which he let simmer overnight. After getting back from Grace Street he sautéed a pile of onions and combined the broth to make a French onion soup which simmered all afternoon. To this, he added a spinach salad with a zesty tomato dressing and bacon. A nice comfort food dinner on a chilly winter's night. They discussed the offer and agreed they did not want to sell.

Sandy texted Jason.

Sorry not interested at any price, thank you for the generous offer

They will be unhappy to hear this proceed at your own peril

The news went up the chain of command and Todd told Harriet to put the screws on Powell but not to kill him. Harriet contemplated this and decided that Leon would be the best one to crank things up on Powell.

The next morning as Sandy, Morgan, and Copper began their morning run the black Escalade he had seen several times before leaped onto the alley and was heading towards them at a high speed. Sandy pushed Morgan back towards the sidewalk and Copper followed her. The Escalade slid to a stop and the driver lowered the window. He wore a black ski mask so only his eyes showed. He yelled at Sandy, "you should have taken the offer. We will give no quarter." He drove off and turned right at the end of the alley.

Sandy turned, "are you ok?"

"Yes, I am fine just a little shaken and Copper is ok too."

"Let's get in the house and come up with a plan."

"Ok, not sure what you mean about a plan."

Inside sitting at the kitchen table, Sandy looked

like a commander prepared for war. He was quiet and thoughtful. It was a side of Sandy that Morgan had never witnessed and it both scared her and made her feel safer than ever.

"I have had a suspicion for the past month, since we filed the patent, that we were being watched and possibly being tracked. I saw the white Lexus twice in Ithaca but didn't want to alarm you. I have seen that black Escalade several times in the past month. They may have tracking devices in our cars. Today they are so small you would never find them. They could also be tracking our phones and laptops. It is very easy to do. We have to go to ground, while I figure this out."

"What do you mean, go to ground."

"Disappear, we have to disconnect from the web, and I need you to be out of sight for a little bit. My first priority is to keep you safe from harm."

"Sandy, I will be ok, I am a big girl."

"This could get ugly fast and I want to know you are safe while I sort this out. Don't question me on this. I love you and will do whatever it takes to protect you."

"Ok and I love you for that, I always have since we first met. So, what is the plan, Captain?"

"Technically I am a Lieutenant Commander, not yet a Captain," he said with a grin. "I need backup, so I am going to get Jackson here as soon as possible. I trust him completely and we can cover each other. I need you to call Vicky and see if you can stay there for a week or so. I will take Copper to Fairfax."

"NO! I want Copper with me that is final SIR, and I know Vicky will be ok with it and her cat will have to get used to sharing the space. Where are you going to go?"

"I guess tonight I will stay with you and Vicky and then we will play it by ear. Why don't you give Vicky a quick call and see if she is ok with it and that we will be there about lunchtime? Then go pack a bag for at least a week. I am going to call Jackson."

Morgan would be lying to herself if she said she wasn't a bit scared. But she knew Sandy was capable and knew what to do. "Ok, will do." And she bounded upstairs to call Vicky and start packing.

Sandy dialed Jackson even though it was midnight in Australia. "Hey mate sorry to wake you."

A bit groggy, Jackson replied, "No worries, what's up."

"I got some bad shit going down here and I need your help."

A bit more awake now, "Say what, bad shit. You ok mate?"

"Yea for the moment. I need you backing me up. Can you catch a flight tomorrow?"

"Sure."

"Book it, business class, all the way to DC and I will pay you for the ticket. I need you somewhat rested when you get here. I am going to get a burner phone today so I will text and email you my new number. Just let me know when you will arrive in DC. I will meet you at the airport. Probably best to fly into Dulles."

"Slow down mate, I am just getting my pants on and I need to get a pencil and paper. Give me a minute."

Sandy could hear him taking a leak and flushing the toilet, "no worries buddy standing by."

"Ok, I am at the kitchen table. Go ahead."

"Try to catch a flight tomorrow to Washington Dulles airport in business class – I will pay for it when you get here. I am getting a new cell phone and I will send you the new number. Let me know, use the new number, when you will arrive, and I will pick you up at the airport. Pack for a few weeks and make your return ticket a few weeks out. We can always change it when we figure it out." Sandy thought for a moment, "you better bring your gear, this could get heavy and as you know better to be prepared when you walk into a shit storm."

"Ok, I can't pack any weapons, you know it is Australia, not the Wild West of America."

"No worries I have an arsenal. Got to run. See you in a day and a half."

"Cheers mate, keep your head down."

Sandy went upstairs and joined Morgan in the packing. He was thinking through the next steps. When they got downstairs, he said, "we need to empty the frig of anything that might go bad in case we are gone for a few weeks." They poured milk down the drain, put a few items in the freezer and made up a bag of trash that Sandy took out to the bin. He put the bin on the street and took note of the white Lexus parked down the street. This would work well for his developing plan.

Back inside they called for an Uber van and five minutes later they had one outside. Together with Copper, bags, laptops, Copper's food, and bowls, they loaded into the van. It took a couple of trips. Once in the van, they headed for National Airport. Sandy casually watched to see if they had a tail and it looked like they did.

At the airport, they asked to be dropped off at the pickup side. There were always free airport luggage carts to grab, so they grabbed two and loaded everything on to it. Inside the airport, Sandy and Morgan turned off their cell phones. Sandy told Morgan the plan, "we are going to take the walkway over to the parking garage and get another Uber. We can take the Uber to the Walmart Supercenter near Mt. Vernon and pick up some supplies including two new cell phones.

An hour and a half later they were at Vicky's apartment in Alexandria, Virginia about five blocks from the King Street Metro. Vicky helped them cart all the stuff into her roomy two-story two-bedroom apartment. Copper loved the golden-colored Persian cat whose fur almost matched his. Queen Latifah did not share the affection and hissed a few times at Copper who just laid on the floor and watched her longingly. Clearly, he hoped Latifah would come around and want to play. Morgan took him out through the backdoor so he could do his business.

Once everyone was settled in Morgan and Sandy gave Vicky a brief update. Sandy sent Jackson a text with the new numbers. Sandy then said he had to travel out to the farm and would be back about dinner time and not to worry. Morgan thought That's easy for you to say... but put on a brave smile and said, "We will be fine!"

Chapter 40   December 2015, New York City

The FBI New York City Headquarters received orders from Lester Hodges to drill deep into Todd Peterson and his company without letting him know he was under investigation. They had trailed Peterson after his return from Miami and knew where he lived, now to find his office. Cliff Black had been assigned to run the team and he gathered eight of his experienced agents for the task. They were able to watch Peterson leave his apartment building on the Upper West Side of Manhattan and take a taxi down to a low rise building a block east of Times Square on 46th Street. The agent riding shotgun jumped out of the car and followed Peterson into the building and joined him on the elevator. Peterson scanned his key card in the elevator and pressed 5. "Can I help you?" asked Peterson.

The agent looked perplexed, "Sorry no, I am going for a job interview. Is this 140."

"No this is 144."

"Ok thanks, walked in the wrong door and I am already late."

They got to the top floor and Peterson walked off the elevator, turned and said, "Good luck."

The receptionist could be heard saying, "good

morning Mr. Peterson."

The agent took a mental picture of the space beyond the door. A typical office with a receptionist facing the elevator and a sign behind her reading 'Paragon Group'.

Back downstairs and in the car, they called headquarters and reported the location of Peterson's company and its name. This was a big break in the investigation. Now that they had the address and name of the company a whole group of people both in New York and Washington set out on a mission of digital discovery.

Another lucky break occurred when they checked for Paragon job openings. Paragon was hiring for an experienced analyst and a field agent. Two FBI people applied online for jobs that morning. In addition, they called the number listed and asked if they could interview right away. The analyst was able to get an interview that afternoon and the field agent the following day. While everything was fake, their resumes were impeccable and they both started on Wednesday morning.

Having two people inside was huge. Marsha Cohen was an attractive effervescent 5'2" ball of energy which came through in the interview. Paragon's hired her as a hacker but didn't realize she would be hacking Paragon, not other companies.

Billy Vaughn, at 5'11" was slim but had a muscular build, looked like he just walked out the gate at Parris Island, he even had a Marine buzz cut. Vaughn was an experienced FBI field agent with an eidetic memory, like having a living video recorder.

Wednesday morning together with one other guy they went through a mountain of HR stuff. Filling out forms and getting assigned corporate ids and all the usual. Each of the new hires met with their new manager just before lunch and joined their new team for lunch on the company.

Marsha was assigned to gather information on new oil discoveries offshore in North Carolina. Specifically, to find companies that had data on the fields and get into their systems by whatever means and extract and copy that information into the Paragon system. They gave her an Iraqi secure IP to use for the hacking and was told to make certain nothing could be found to lead them back to Paragon.

Billy got assigned to a team watching a new UN diplomat from Saudi. Their mission was to find any dirt possible and document everything. Pictures or videos were the best. They were instructed to catch him at a strip club or drinking so Paragon had leverage on him.

Lester worked with DOJ, and they were able to get the needed warrant for Todd Peterson and The Paragon Group. Even while that was happening, the FBI office in NY and Washington were building files on the company. Through the IRS payroll records, they had a list of every employee that worked for the company for the past ten years. They had details like Social Security numbers and were able to look up current addresses. In addition, they knew when they started and more importantly when they left the company. Another group of analysts was pouring through the Paragon tax filings which told them the big picture of funds flowing in and out of the company. Revenue all appeared to be coming from several foreign companies. This was handed off to another team to dig into those foreign companies.

Marsha had been able to penetrate most of the systems and copy the data to an external drive. Todd's secure emails were copied as well. So far, NSA had not been able to break the code. They suspected that Todd was using public-key cryptography to secure the data. Marsha was able to get the bank and account data for the three New York banks they were using.

Warrants in hand, the banks provided 10 years'

worth of detailed transaction records on the accounts. The analysts now were able to identify the multiple numbered accounts in the Caymans where Paragon was wiring money.

Lester asked Meredith Drake to reach out to the Director-General of the UK's National Crime Agency to get access in the Caymans to the list of numbered accounts they now had information on. Fortunately, they were all at one bank. The case was building, and it was way bigger than they had imagined.

Chapter 41   December 2015, Alexandria, VA

S andy walked from Vicky's apartment toward the King Street metro. A lot was going on, but he felt Morgan would be safe at the apartment. Just before the metro, he ducked into the small coffee shop on the ground floor of the Hilton on King Street. First, he called Gary Sutter, his attorney, thankfully he was in and available.

"Gary, Sandy Powell, I need a big favor."

"Sandy good to hear from you. How are things working out?"

"Good, we filed the patent and I am still figuring out what to do with the farm. I have a group that wants the invention and they are starting to play very rough. I would like you to rent an SUV tomorrow morning and list me as a second driver. I am concerned they may be watching my credit card transactions and I need to move around without them following me."

"Okay, shouldn't you call the police."

"I don't have enough to go to the police and that would likely make things worse."

"Gotcha, no problem. I will get one first thing in the morning and you can pick it up at my office any time after nine.

"Thanks! That's great and make sure you get all the insurance. See you tomorrow."

Sandy's next call was to his local bank in Fairfax. He had been doing business there for years and they had always been terrific. He asked for the branch manager.

"Hello, this is Anita Curtis how can I help you?"

"Hi Anita, this is Sandy Powell, I have several accounts with you, I would like to withdraw $20,000 tomorrow morning in cash. I want to give you a call so you could have it available."

"We can handle that, and I am glad you called in advance since we will have to order it delivered here."

"Yes, I totally understand. Would 10 a.m. give you enough time?"

"That would be more than fine. I assume you want that in $100 bills."

"That is perfect, see you tomorrow and thanks, Anita."

Sandy sipped his venti flat white coffee with an extra shot and thought about all that had transpired over the past few months, as well as the most recent developments. Clearly, a company or someone knew about the patent and very much wanted the technology. They were spending a ton of money to have nearly around the clock surveillance and were not afraid to threaten physical violence to get what they wanted.

He thought, "What's the best next step? These guys were not going to just go away, they would never stop chasing him. By slipping away they were just postponing the inevitable."

He sipped his coffee and put his military training to use. "We must go on the offensive and take it to them not wait for their next response. Step one, find out what we can about the enemy."

There was no need to go to the farm today since he would be out in Fairfax tomorrow. He made a quick call to Morgan on the new phone and she answered on the first ring. "Just wanted to let you know I am on my way back to the apartment. Is there anything you need?"

Morgan could be heard asking Vicky if she needs anything. "Nope, we are good, see you soon."

When Sandy got back, he asked Vicky if he could order some stuff on her Amazon account because he did not want to use his credit cards or Amazon account. Then he went online using Vicky's computer and ordered four GPS tracking devices. He told Vicky he would pay her tomorrow. They had a quiet evening and turned in early. Vicky would be back at work tomorrow and Morgan would have to house sit with Copper.

About nine the next morning Sandy gave Morgan a hug and a kiss goodbye and said he would be out for the day and be back late that night with Jackson. He told her she needs to stay out of sight, for now, use only her new phone and Vicky's computer. Sandy walked over to the King Street metro station and caught a Blue Line train to Rosslyn where he switched and picked up the Orange Line to Vienna. He took the escalator up and walked across the bridge over 66 to the north. He hailed a cab and was on his way to Gary Sutter's office just north of Reston about twenty minutes away.

At Gary's office they exchange pleasantries and Gary reminded him if he needed anything to call him at any hour. He insisted that Sandy be careful and if it got ugly to call the police. Sandy thanked him and with the keys, Sandy jumped in the Chevrolet Tahoe then headed south to his bank in Fairfax. At the bank, Sandy picked up the $20,000 in cash. The two small bundles were less than a half-inch thick each. Back in the car he peeled a thousand dollars from one of the bundles and put the cash in his front pants pocket. The balance of the bundle he put in the glove box and locked it. The other bundle in the compartment between the seats. Not totally safe but better than carrying it all on himself.

Sandy grabbed a bite to eat at his favorite Vietnamese restaurant, on Main Street in Fairfax. He had a Spring Roll and their awesome Seafood Pho, just enough to fill him for the afternoon. After lunch, he went to the Walmart Supercenter in Fairfax and bought three prepaid MasterCard cards and loaded two thousand on one and one thousand on the other two cards. He also bought a new laptop for Morgan. Next, he headed back north to the farm.

Before arriving at the farm, Sandy logged into his surveillance system to check the cameras and motion detectors he had installed a month ago at the farm. Nothing looked amiss and there had been no activity on the motion detectors. Just to be safe he drove past the farm and about a mile down the road there were no vehicles around. He turned around and drove back to the farm. Sandy parked a bit away from the barn because he planned to move some of the machinery out of the barn so he could park the Tahoe inside out of sight. After moving the rake and Ford 8N to an adjacent shed, he backed the Tahoe inside and closed the rolling doors. He walked over to the house and went inside to check that all was well. Nothing appeared to be disturbed so he locked up and went back to the barn.

He entered the basement through the magic

cupboard. All was as he had left it. He grabbed his emergency bags and took them upstairs to the SUV. He went back down and gathered up his firearms and loaded them into the Tahoe.

He rolled open the barn doors and drove the SUV out, closed up and headed to Herndon to grab a bite to eat while he waited for Jackson's flight to arrive from San Francisco in a few hours. Jimmy's Old Town Tavern in Herndon was a fit for what he wanted. He ordered their amazing award-winning wings and the Grilled Salmon salad. Sandy checked in with Morgan and then relaxed and watched some football on the overhead TVs.

Just before 7 p.m. Jackson called and said he had just touched down. Sandy headed for Dulles Airport a few minutes away and parked in the cell phone lot.

The phone rang, "Bloody hell mate, it is freezing cold out, I think I will go home."

"I have a gray Tahoe. What number door are you at, you wimp."

"Number Six mate and hurry up – Oh My God, how can you live here."

Sandy pulled up to door six and jumped out in the mild 35-degree evening air. Jackson rushed over with his three bags, as Sandy opened the tailgate. After a quick hug, they jumped in the SUV and Sandy pulled away from the curb, headed for DC. He gave a quick call to Morgan to let her know they were on their way. Sandy brought Jackson up to speed on all that was going on as they drove down 66 and took Route One down past the Pentagon and National Airport to Alexandria.

Sandy parked in the lot near Vicky's condo and they carried Jackson's bags in. "Hi gals, I would like you to meet my best friend, Jackson. Jackson meet Morgan and Vicky."

Jackson at five-ten with short brown hair and bright brown eyes was built like a soldier coming out of basic training. With his full-on strong Aussie accent, "Hi, so you're the one that captured his heart."

"Yup, that would be me, of course, he actually started it all."

"And you must be the hostess with this great condo."

Vicky grinned and blushed like a high school teenager with a first crush, "You got me there. Please make yourself at home and what can I get you to eat and drink."

"If you have it, love scotch and just some biscuits and cheese. They had pretty good food in the front of the plane."

Copper had given Jackson the once over and was

pleased with the new visitor and settled as always at Morgan's feet. Vicky's Queen Latifah was nowhere to be seen and was still pouting at having this big furry dog inhabiting her house. In her own feline way, she was plotting a way to disgrace this creature.

"Biscuits?" Vicky said with a puzzled look.

Sandy translated, "Crackers here, biscuits down under. Next, we will have to run out and get a jar of Vegemite for his breakfast toast."

Morgan piped in, "What is Vegemite?"

"Oh my, you haven't lived until you've had a Vegemite to start your day. It is a thick dark brown spread made from leftover brewer's yeast with a few special ingredients you put on toast," said Jackson.

Sandy wrinkled his nose, "Takes a bit getting used to. We will have to get a jar at Wegmans."

They sat around the family room and chatted into the night. Vicky finally stood and announced, "Sorry gang I have got to turn in. I have to be off to work in the morning." Then turning to Jackson, she added with a tired smile, "I will get some blankets and towels for you. I wish I had another bed; you'll just have to pull out the bed from the couch."

Jackson smiled back. "No worries! Just appreciative of the place to crash."

Morgan yawned, "I should turn in as well." She and Vicky headed off upstairs to get stuff for Jackson.

Upstairs Vicky whispered, "OH MY GOD, he is a dream."

"Oh yea, talk about a catch. Maybe we each got one. Wouldn't that be cool."

"Let's see how this goes. Australia is a long way away."

"True enough, but still worth checking out."

"I am sure I will be dreaming about him tonight."

Back downstairs, Sandy told Jackson the plan. "Tomorrow we are going to get you rested up and maybe show you some of the sights and then the next day we will take it to them. You know the drill, live the time zone you are in. So, try to get some sleep."

"I like the plan, night mate."

Chapter 42   December 2015, Tysons Corner, VA

Harriet Campos called her team together that had been covering Powell. "So, what is the status?"

"I followed them to National with a pile of luggage," Karen replied.

Verna piped in, "From there they have up and disappeared. We have not seen their cell phones since they went to the airport. Maybe we scared them away."

"Leon, anything?"

"No Mam, I have been watching the townhouse and nothing. I installed a couple of cameras and motion detectors front and back and nothing. My guess they likely skipped town and all we can do is wait till their cell phones come back on."

"Alright, I am going to have our group put them on a watch list. Even if we scared them away, they must be somewhere, and we need to find them. I want all of you to work out a plan to see if they go to any of the places, we have known them to frequent, just in case they are still in town. Let's plan to get together here in three days at the same time as today and see if anything develops." Harriet then called Todd in New York and gave him an update. Todd told Harriet he would have the tech group put them on a watch list.

Chapter 43   December 2015, New York City

The FBI New York office supporting the people in DC were building their case. With Marsha Cohen on the inside, they had a copy of virtually everything on the servers. The email files were encrypted, and NSA had yet to break the code.

They knew the type of research being conducted all of which focused on the oil and gas business or other energy-related fields. Information was amassed from around the globe. It was amazing how much had been gathered and it went back years. They also had reports on hundreds of companies and individuals which included photos that could be used as blackmail, especially of government officials both here in the US and others around the world.

Billy Vaughn was stunned by the bravado of the team watching the UN diplomat from Saudi. Within a few days, they had incredible photos of him, drinking at a topless bar and taking a hooker up to his apartment. They even had a video of him dancing nude about his apartment with the naked hooker. Once they had the goods on the guy, they approached him and pressed him into service to swing deals within Saudi that Paragon wanted. Clear cut extortion.

Lester sent out an email calling the team in for a brief update. The next day at 11 a.m. they assembled in the executive briefing room at DOJ. Diana Scott from the CIA provided a brief on Nigeria. No new developments in the Lagos office. All the individuals remained in custody at the CIA safe house and believe they are in jail. We have not gotten any new information from them. We have had no luck using Treasury and FATF to get access to the Cayman bank accounts.

Amber Dean said there were no new phone calls between the CEOs and Peterson since the meeting in Miami. She also said they were now monitoring Jacob Holden the former CEO and now Chairman of Texas Oil. They had added Holden's phone records, over the past five years, to the analysis and found overlapping calls generally quarterly between the other CEOs.

"With regards to the flights," said Dylan Harrison, "when we added Holden, we saw multiple occurrences where the three could have met. Often, two executives flew to the location of the third's corporate office and likely had a meeting."

Cliff Black video conferenced into the meeting in DC. "We have been very lucky to have Marsha Cohen on the inside at Paragon," He reported. "We have been able to copy virtually their entire database and it is like finding King Solomon's mine. Fortunately, the information is very well organized. We could have a team of fifty work through the files for a year. What we do know is that they have dirt on lots of politicians and corporate executives around the world that could be used as leverage. They have done deep penetration into competitive companies also around the world. With the data we have, we know there are multiple numbered bank accounts in the Caymans. What we still lack is the transaction detail within those accounts."

Lester thought for a moment. All eyes in the room were on him when he sat forward, "Cliff who at headquarters is leading the analysis of the data from NY?"

"Brenda Bates, Sir."

"Thanks, I will reach out to her directly. I want her to see if we can find the two ministers' names in Nigeria in the files and there was another name mentioned in the conversation in Miami. What was his name?"

"Sandy Powell, Sir," said Amber recalling her review of the video and audio tapes from the Miami meeting.

"Right, thanks, Amber. Ms. Scott can you email the information we have on the two Oil ministers in

Nigeria to Ms. Bates. If you have trouble finding her in the system call my admin and she will connect you."

Lester stood, "Ok, everyone great job. It is clear we have a lot and likely more than enough to make arrests and go to the Grand Jury for indictments. I will put pressure on to get the transaction details in those numbered accounts which will tie all of this together. Thank you and keep on this. I will update you when I have more information."

Lester knew they were close, but they needed the information from the numbered accounts in the Caymans and the encrypted emails to have an open and shut case. They also needed to take this to POTUS. Lester sent a brief update to Rod, Meredith Drake, and Charles Castiglione and emphasized the need to get access to the accounts.

Chapter 44   December 2015, Alexandria, VA

The next morning after Jackson's arrival, Morgan copied critical files from her old laptop to the new one Sandy had picked up and was once again able to get online and do some work. Jackson, while tired, got up and refreshed with fresh coffee, did a casual tour of the DC sights with Sandy. Sandy's package arrived from Amazon and they tested the GPS transponders and software on their phones. Sandy fixed a wonderful dinner and Vicky did her best not to flirt with Jackson although the chemistry was obvious. Everyone turned in early because Sandy had an early day planned for himself and Jackson.

Well before dawn, Sandy and Jackson drove off in the Tahoe for Falls Church. They had Karen Young's address from the photo of her driver's license and the license plate for her white Lexus. Driving through the quiet streets of Pimmit Hills they quickly spotted her Lexus parked in the street. Sandy drove around the block and stopped well before her house. Jackson jumped out and casually walked up to the car. He crawled under the car and attached the GPS tracking device with the waterproof magnetic case near the rear bumper.

Sandy and Jackson drove to the 24-hour Coffee Shop in Tysons and waited for the world to wake up. About 7:30 they noticed her GPS started to move and they watched as it drove towards Tysons Corner. They jumped in the Tahoe and arrived just before she did at what Sandy suspected was her office, based on his research and the address on her car's registration. Jackson jumped out when she had parked and walked over to the entrance to the office building arriving at the door just before her and opened the door for her. He followed her to the elevator and rode up with her exiting with her on the fifth floor. He watched her enter an unmarked office and pushed the button to take the elevator back down.

In the parking lot, Jackson climbed back into the Tahoe and updated Sandy. Sandy said, "Let's sit and see if anyone else I think is part of the group shows up." About ten minutes later, Sandy saw Jason Roberts exit his BMW and walk towards the building. "Bingo got another one. He is the guy that made me the offer. We need to tag his car. Why don't you follow him up and confirm it is the same office? We can tag the car later."

Another ten minutes passed, and the black Escalade pulled into a parking spot. While not 100% confident, Sandy was pretty certain it was the same guy that threatened him a few days ago behind the townhouse. Again, Jackson followed him up the elevator and confirmed he went to the same office. Since they were in full view of the office building and it was broad daylight, Sandy drove around the parking lot and parked close to the back of each car so Jackson could slip out and attach the GPS to each car. Now came the waiting.

Sandy suggested, "Hey let's go get some breakfast."

"Sounds great"

Sandy drove over to a favorite diner near the mall in Tysons Corner. Over a delightful breakfast, they discussed the plan. Sandy asked, "Do you think we could mount a camera on a wall near the door to the office to record who comes and goes?"

"Possibly, but it would have to look like something that should be there. Anything but a camera."

"Good point. Let's see if we can find something that could work." Sandy began searching online for a solution. He found a hidden camera that looked like a smoke detector that was actually a hidden high definition recorder. He showed it to Jackson. "What do you think?"

"I think that could work great."

While they were eating breakfast, they noticed that the cars were leaving all about the same time. "Must be the meeting is over. It should be interesting to see where they go. I'll order the camera for overnight delivery."

They relaxed, enjoyed a terrific breakfast of very fresh ingredients and casually watched the cars head for downtown. Thirty minutes later the cars had all come to rest. The black Escalade was parked behind Morgan's townhouse. Jason's BMW was parked near the Department of Energy building on Independence Avenue across the street from the Smithsonian Castle. The building is so massive it spans across L'Enfant Plaza consuming nearly two blocks. Karen Young's car entered a parking garage in downtown and they lost its signal.

"Well it is no surprise that they continue to watch Morgan's townhouse. Clearly, they don't know where we are at this point. Do you think we should kick the hornet's nest?"

"My advice let's wait till we get the camera up and get more data on who else works there. Plus, we need a plan past kicking the bees. What do we do next besides getting stung?"

"Good point. Glad we have the trackers at a minimum we know where they are, and that they don't know where to look for us." Sandy smiled, "This is going to be fun."

****

The next day they took the smoke detector

camera and went back to the office. Jackson wore jeans, a work shirt, and a light jacket and looked like a maintenance guy. Carrying a ladder in from the parking lot he went up the elevator and installed the smoke detector with a clear view of the office door. He was able to link it to an unprotected guest wireless point for one of the tenants in the building and ten minutes later was loading the ladder into the back of the Tahoe. Climbing into the front seat, "Well can you see the office door?"

"Perfect and we can see what it captures today. Clearly, the best views are when they leave the office and we can see their faces."

"Agreed, glad it is working. So, what do we use as leverage after we kick the proverbial beehive?"

"My only thought is to capture them on tape with a threat and go to the cops. I can't picture how we can threaten them with anything else. You got any ideas?"

"Well mate you are probably right. We could piss them off enough to shoot them, this being the wild west here in the USA." Jackson's eyes twinkled at the thought.

They went back to Vicky's condo and watched the office door over the internet. They kept notes on the comings and goings from the office and now knew that about six people worked in the office. No names but they had recorded the faces. No one seemed to take notice of the smoke detector attached to the wall.

That evening, Sandy fixed a scrumptious chicken marsala over fresh fettuccine. Vicky remarked, "Morgan you are so lucky to have a chef for a boyfriend. So, what about you Jackson, do you cook."

With his curl your toes deep Aussie accent, "Well Luv, I am a fire bloke. I love to cook on the barbie. How about I do prawns on the barbie tomorrow night."

Vicky glowed, "You're on, I can't wait."

Over dinner, they discussed the situation. Morgan summarized things, "First, this is not a military operation. We have good reason to believe a company or a very wealthy individual is behind it because of the offer that was made on behalf of a client. So, while this group in Tyson's made the threats, they are simply middlemen to the client. I think you are on the right track. We need to get them to threaten you and record it. Then we can go to the police and we will have a case against them. If multiple people make the threat then we can extend the case to the company and perhaps, and this is a stretch, extended the case to the company paying the people in Tysons."

"I am so happy you are an attorney." Sandy took another sip of the incredible Australian wine Jackson had picked out on their drive back. "I need to order a tiny camera microphone recorder so we can get these guys on tape. Jackson let's see if we have their home locations on the GPS. I have an idea of how to approach this."

As Sandy went to the laptop to search Amazon, Vicky piped in, "Oh my goodness, you do love shopping on Amazon."

"Of course, they have everything and it's here tomorrow or the next day."

"Ok, Jackson and I have an early start in the morning again, so we better wrap it up for tonight."

Jackson nodded in agreement. "But I'll help clean up a bit first."

Jackson joined Vicky in the kitchen and the two were clearly enjoying each other's company as they cleared the dishes and put things away.

Early the next morning in the dark of night, Sandy and Jackson drove to the locations of the GPS trackers for Jason and the black Escalade. Jason was parked in a lot behind a group of townhouses in a trendy section of downtown Vienna, Virginia. It was impossible to tell which one was Jason's. Next, they then drove to West

Falls Church a few miles away. Following the GPS, they spotted the black Escalade parked in the driveway of a large house on Robinson Place. Jackson wrote down the house number and they turned around and headed back to Vienna.

While Sandy waited in the SUV, Jackson went into Artisan Caffe and Roaster in Vienna and got two Latte's and pastries to go. They drove back to the parking lot near Jason's car and waited, hoping to catch him emerge from his townhouse.

"My God mate this is the best coffee I have had since I got here. You need to mark them on your map as special," Jackson exclaimed as he drank the rich, smooth drink.

"Yea, your right. An amazing cup of joe. Do you know where the expression 'Cup of Joe' came from?"

"No mate but I am certain you will enlighten me." Jackson chuckled.

"Well, there are several theories. I prefer this one, just before World War I, Secretary of the Navy Josephus Daniels commonly known as Joe banned all alcohol from all Navy ships. So, sailors called coffee a cup of Joe since it was the strongest thing they could get. It was also a subtle way to voice dissent to the policy."

"Good one. Had to know you would find a way to

tie the Navy to any good story." They sat together sipped their coffees and waited. About half an hour later they spotted Jason leaving his townhouse and stayed low in their SUV so they wouldn't stand out. Now they knew his address as well.

Arriving back at the apartment, Morgan gave Sandy the package from Amazon. They tested out the tiny camera and it worked as expected. Easy to conceal in a jacket pocket but providing crystal clear audio and video.

While at the apartment, they dove into the property records as well as the reverse telephone directory and were able to get the names they needed. The black Escalade driver was Leon Davies. Digging further they discovered he was a former DC cop. It turned out that Jason was Jason Roberts and based on his LinkedIn account now worked for OI Research in Tysons which lined up with Karen Young's car registration. He was a former salesperson for a flooring company. Reversing their look at OI Research they found half a dozen people with LinkedIn accounts including Harriet Campos who listed herself as CEO. They spent the rest of the day gathering intel via Google, Facebook, and others and learned a lot about the individuals working at the company. They even had Campos home address in McLean.

As soon as Vicky arrived home from work, they

ate an early dinner. Jackson's shrimp on the barbie was awesome with a sweet Asian sauce with a touch of cayenne providing incredible flavor that added just the right amount of heat. Jackson showed them how using two skewers made it so much easier to flip a row of prawns.

After dinner, Sandy and Jackson headed out to kick the bee's nest. Fortunately, all of the people lived fairly close to each other. They thought about the order and decided it was best to go to the people that would react the least first. The first stop was Karen Young's house, it was pretty much dark by now but at least it was not too cold. Sandy walked the half-block back to the house and up to her door and knocked. Karen's husband answered the door and Sandy asked to see Karen. A moment later Karen stood at the door not inviting Sandy in. After a few seconds, she recognized him. "Hi, can I help you?"

"Good evening sorry to bother you, Ms. Young. I just wanted to let you know I am sick of you following me and resent the threats your company is making. Please stop now."

Karen paled, "I am sorry I don't know what you are talking about."

"Ms. Young do you deny following me to Ithaca, NY several weeks ago. Do you deny parking outside our townhouse in Georgetown and so many other places we frequent? Do you deny this!"

"No, it's my job. You should take whatever they offered you, for whatever they want, and they will go away. If you don't, I suspect it will get much worse."

"Is that a threat?"

"No, just my experience. Good night," she closed the door and he could hear the locks being engaged.

Back in the SUV Sandy had a satisfied look on his face as he told Jackson, "Well that went well, not a threat but does go to the company being involved. She is scared now." And he glanced over at his friend, adding quizzically, as they pulled away from the curb, "Are you sure you can drive on the other side of the road?"

"Crikey mate, as long as I remember that I have to be sitting in the middle of the road and you sitting on the shoulder it works. Getting used to it. Glad you don't have a lot of roundabouts that might be a bit dangerous. We're good."

Jason's townhouse was next and again Jackson parked down the street. Sandy walked up to the front door, knocked and was greeted by Jason. "Hi, what are you doing here."

I just wanted to say again that I am not

interested in your offer and I would like OI
Research to leave me alone."

"Well like I told you the other day, my client is
very persistent and does not take NO as an answer.
Things are going to get really ugly for you if you
don't change your mind – BUDDY. And I don't
appreciate you coming to my house."

"Is that a threat?"

"In so many words, you should consider some
really bad consequences to your decision."

"Ok, and as far as coming to your house it
doesn't seem to bother you guys in watching mine.
Leave me alone and go away."

"Sorry your so stubborn to know what is good
for you. You will get what is coming to you. Watch
out and stay away from me."

"You have not seen the last of me." Sandy turned
and walked away in the opposite direction of
Jackson. After a few blocks, he called and told him
where to meet him behind the Whole Foods store.
Back in the SUV, "we got a threat on tape. Now to
Leon's house to really kick the bees."

Arriving in West Falls Church, Sandy rang
Leon's doorbell. A minute or two later he answered
the door in casual clothes.

Without giving a hint that he recognized him,

"Can I help you?"

"Mr. Davies, I just wanted to confront you and ask you to leave us alone. We are not interested in the offer and I don't appreciate you following and threatening us. You need to go somewhere else."

"Listen bud, I don't know what gives you the right to come to my house in the middle of the night and tell me what to do. You need to take whatever offer and just go back to teaching school. If you don't take it this will escalate and get very personal and dangerous to you and your family. We know everything about you, and we will not stop until you give in. Now go away and rethink your decision." Leon slammed the door in Jason's face.

Back in the SUV Sandy grinned, "we got them. Let's go see what their boss says."

Harriet Campos could not believe someone was knocking on her door at nine o'clock at night. She opened the door of her beautiful, clearly expensive, home in McLean and was shocked to see Sandy Powell standing on the front porch.

"Ms. Campos, I am Sandy Powell, which I suspect you already know. I want to inform you that I am sick of your company harassing and threatening me and I am here to ask you to just leave me alone."

"Mr. Powell, I am not sure what makes you think

that, but I can tell you if you don't accept the offer from our client that things will get really bad for you and perhaps your family. Our client is even more stubborn than you are, and they really don't care what happens to people that say no, so just go home make a smart decision and all of this goes away."

"Well, I am sorry to tell you I am not changing my mind and stop the harassment."

"Mr. Powell, your life as you know it is about to take a sharp turn down a dark road. Remember this, you are the one that is causing all the harm you are about to face. Good night," she swiftly closed the door and again he could hear the locks engaged.

Back in the SUV, "well we got what we need, and the bees are going to be flying tonight. Let's head back and see what time they all get together at the office. Bet it is early."

Safely back in Alexandria, they turned in with plans to arise early and watch the office.

Chapter 45   December 2015, Washington, DC

Meredith Drake made an appointment to see the President at the White House in the situation room.

At two o'clock sharp the President entered the situation room, he was tall, thin framed with graying hair and piercing gray eyes. He had a look and feel of someone you could instinctively trust at the same time he commanded attention as a natural leader. He found; Meredith Drake, the Attorney General, Rod Holloway, Assistant Deputy Attorney General, Charles Castiglione, Director of the FBI, and Lester Hodges, Deputy Director of the FBI starting to stand. "Please sit. Meredith what's up, clearly this is important enough to bring Rod, Charlie, and Lester along."

"Yes Sir, it is. We have uncovered a conspiracy involving our three largest oil companies' executives that goes back years that involves murder, price-fixing, bribery and more on a global basis. Lester has led the effort to pull this case together and I would like him to brief you."

"Mr. President, almost by chance we uncovered a plot in Nigeria where the CEOs of Texas Oil, Sunco and American Petroleum ordered the assassination of the Minister for Oil and Gas, Ali

Mohammed. As we drilled into things, we discovered they were working together with a company named Paragon based in New York City to disrupt competitors around the globe. We recorded a meeting they held with the CEO of Paragon in Miami where they confirmed what we learned in Nigeria and discussed price-fixing. We now have several FBI agents working inside Paragon and have copied all of their data. Going back years, we can prove that they have worked closely to disrupt things around the world. In addition, we know they have collected dirt on politicians both here and globally that puts them in a unique position to pressure people on both sides of the aisle."

Meredith edged forward in her seat, "Mr. President, first we wanted to give you a heads up that we are in a position to arrest, Bryce Carrington, Reginald Clark, and Harold Watson. We also will be arresting Jacob Holden the former CEO of Texas Oil. We know you have met with these people and wanted you to be briefed before we take action."

"Wow, this is stunning, and I know each of you would not be bringing this to me if it wasn't solid as a piece of granite. Ok, next steps?"

"Mr. President we could use your help. There are multiple numbered accounts in the Caymans, and we need access to their transaction history to complete putting this all together. We have reached out to the highest levels we can, in the UK, to get this information to no avail. Would you be kind enough to make a brief phone call to Number Ten and request his support?" Meredith slid him a piece of paper with the name of the bank and a list of the accounts they needed access to.

"If you have tried all your resources without success, and I am very confident you have, of course, I will. I will give him a call as soon as we finish this meeting. Anything else?"

"No sir that is it on this matter."

The President nodded. "I'll relay my results to you later today. Thanks, and keep me in the loop. This is going to be huge and will impact all of us. Please give me a detailed written briefing prior to making the arrests. It is sure to be front-page news when it happens." Everyone stood and he said, "I will let you know once we have word on access to the bank records," then he turned and left the room.

****

The President called the Prime Minister and gave him a very brief account without details and requested access to the transaction history for the specific accounts at the bank in Grand Cayman.

The Prime Minister, now a close friend, was happy to oblige.

****

"Mr. Williams, I have a call for you."

"Nigel Williams, here, how can I help?"

"Mr. Williams, you are the President of First National of Grand Cayman?"

"Yes, that is correct."

"Mr. Williams, this is the Prime Minister's office, please hold for Sir Robinson."

"Hello, Mr. Williams I am making an official request that you release all the details for a number of accounts at your establishment to the US FBI immediately. This is a matter of international importance. Do you understand?"

"Yes, Mr. Prime Minister, but our bank secrecy laws."

"Stop right there. You know we have anti-money laundering legislation. You WILL provide full access and support to the FBI immediately. Am I clear?"

"Yes, Mr. Prime Minister, we will help them in every way possible. Thank you, Sir."

Within the hour, three FBI agents were in Nigel Williams office with the list of the accounts and advised him there may be more accounts once they began their investigation. Williams was still in disbelief that he had spoken with the Prime Minister. Williams instructed one of his technical people to download all the data including ownership of the accounts to the FBI's computers. The information was transmitted within hours to FBI headquarters in Washington and a team of five financial experts nose-dived into the records.

After working all night, they met with Lester the next day. One of the analysts looking like he had tripped on coffee for twenty-four hours and sans tie. "Sorry Sir, I did not have time to run home for a suit."

"No worries son, I am much more interested in what you learned than what you look like. Suggestion you should keep a spare suit on the back of your office door."

"Sorry I don't have a spot to hang a suit in my cube."

"Good point I'll have to work on lockers for you guys. So, what have you discovered?"

The team put up a diagram on the screen showing the companies and how they all related to one core company. "As you can see sir, this company, Pinnacle Limited in the Bahamas sends money into this one account in the Caymans owned by Globex Limited. The money in Globex then flows out to corporate accounts of companies all over the world."

"Do you have a company located in Nigeria?"

"Yes sir, right here," as he pointed to it on the screen.

"Great, Ok what about New York?"

"Yes Sir, and they have the largest flow of funds, nearly $15 million per year. There are other accounts in the US in Washington, Los Angles, and Houston. The company name in New York is Paragon Research," said Anna Knight the lead financial analyst on this data.

"Anna, what do you know about the money coming into Pinnacle Limited?"

"Sir, almost all the money comes from three companies and even amounts every quarter. The companies are Warbucks, Tyrel, and Clampett. We don't know anything about these companies."

Lester stood up, "Ok, thank you, Anna and team, great job in a few hours. I am ordering you to all go get some breakfast, send me the expense report, take an hour break and then write a clean, brief summary with all the company names, addresses, and money flow. I want it on my desk by 3 p.m. this afternoon. I don't need to remind you this is classified top secret, need to know. Again, great job and you can expect a call from Nina Craig in an hour who will dig into the three companies feeding the money into Pinnacle Limited. Thanks."

Back in his office, his admin had Nina Craig on the line. "Nina, I need you to call Anna Knight in an hour and get what information she has on the three companies funneling money into Paragon Limited. I need by tomorrow morning all the detail you can muster on these companies, financials, and importantly who owns them. They could be shells so it could take some digging. Assemble your team and order pizza or Chinese for tonight it could be a late one. I will have Suzie clear my calendar at 10 for your briefing."

Later that afternoon he had the brief from Anna. The scope was truly global with companies primarily in oil-producing areas around the world including Russia and China. The next morning, he sat with Nina and received her brief.

"You were right, they were all shells. Piercing the corporate veil was not difficult each company is ultimately owned by Texas Oil and Gas, Sunco and American Petroleum respectively. They push money into Pinnacle on a quarterly basis and have been doing as far back as we have records. It amounts to tens of millions per year."

"Excellent work, thank your team. Ok, take your time but assemble a thoughtful report and become prepared to present this to a Grand Jury at some time in the next few weeks.

Lester assembled a conference call with the executives at DOJ and FBI and shared his thoughts on the next steps. Meredith agreed to brief the President.

Chapter 46   December 2015, Alexandria, VA

About 7 a.m. Sandy and Jackson saw the OI staff cars leaving their homes and head for the office. Then they began watching the view from the camera in Tysons. At 7:15 the OI Research bees were assembling in the office. "Yup, just like we thought we gave them an early start to their day."

Sandy let Morgan enjoy her coffee and watch a bit of the morning news. Still, in her PJs and a robe, she watched the recording from last night's encounters with OI people. "This is great and is clear enough to go to court and request at a minimum a restraining order and possible arrest on grounds of the threats they made. I'll call a friend from college that deals with divorce cases with a lot of experience in getting restraining orders against unruly spouses and confirm my thoughts."

About lunchtime Morgan was all dressed wearing a nice pantsuit, "I am going to meet Marlene Pope for lunch and review the videos with her from last night. You guys have a fun afternoon and I will see you later."

Sandy smiled, "sounds good we will come up with an idea for dinner so we may be out shopping when you get back. Have fun, love you."

Morgan called for a cab and was off to meet Marlene at Poogens for lunch. An institution in DC on 15th Street near the VA headquarters was a bit pricy but ohhhhhh so good. Their Low-Country cuisine was to be savored and she knew Marlene loved the place. "Mar, so good to see you, it has been forever, how are you?"

"Great, and I see you are doing well, striking out on your own and I hear you are very busy."

Morgan grinned, "Yes tons of work and I have finally found my guy. So, I am the happiest gal on the planet and how are you and Mark doing?"

"We are great, the kids are now three and five and oh my word it is a handful. They are like bottled energy."

They sat and ordered. Morgan got the She Crab Soup and Marlene got the Shrimp and Grits. They also ordered a plate of Fried Green Tomatoes to share. Morgan shared the video with Marlene and they both agreed they had enough to go to court for a restraining order against the individuals and the company. In addition, they could meet with the Fairfax police regarding having people arrested. The lunch was awesome, and Marlene agreed to take the case forward with Morgan. She would try to get on a Judge's docket this week.

When they left the house, Morgan had forgotten a file for one of her most important clients. Since she was downtown, she thought she should run in and grab it before heading back to Vicky's place. It would only take a few minutes and she would be in an out. She hailed a cab and was off to Georgetown and her townhouse.

She didn't even try to have the cab wait knowing they would be gone anyway. She unlocked the front door, disabled the alarm and headed for the stairs to her office.

Leon was in his Escalade behind the townhouse when the alarm on his cell phone went off indicating that someone had tripped the motion detector on the front door. He pulled up the video and saw that Sandy's girlfriend had just entered the house. This was his lucky day. He quickly jumped out of the car and ran to the back gate. In one minute, he had unlocked both backdoor locks and was inside. He knew the alarm would be disabled with her inside. He carefully sneaked into the kitchen and could hear her upstairs. He moved over near the staircase and waited. After about five minutes he could hear her moving again and starting down the stairs.

Morgan had the file she needed and was headed down the stairs when she was on the first floor someone grabbed her from behind and put one gloved hand over her mouth and the other around her waist. The file went flying and the next thing she knew she was sprawled face down on the floor and her arms were being wrenched behind her back. She felt plastic being wrapped around her wrist and heard the sound of zip ties being pulled tight. She started to scream, "let me go!"

"Listen, lady, you are not going anywhere, so, shut up and you won't get hurt."

The next thing she knew zip ties were being put around her ankles and the man chuckled, "Stay put I'll be right back. Not like you are going anywhere." She heard him head upstairs and he was back in a minute. When he returned, he stuffed a hand towel in her mouth, put a pillowcase over her head and rolled her up in a sheet. He picked her up in both arms and carried her out the backdoor. No one was around as he carried her the short distance to his monster car. He not so gently tossed her in the back seat and rolled her onto the floor.

Morgan couldn't believe what was going on. She clearly was being abducted but had no idea by who. She suspected it had to be one of the people from the company trying to pressure Sandy to sign over the patent. She slowly worked the washcloth out of her mouth. "Mister let me go and I will not press charges."

"Lady, like I said shut your mouth and if all goes well you can go home to your boyfriend tonight. No harm no foul. So just be quiet."

She felt the car moving but had no idea where and being disoriented with the pillowcase blocking her view was beginning to feel almost seasick.

Leon called the office, "Harriet you won't believe it. I caught Powell's girlfriend. I have her in the back of the car and I am headed to a safe place to make an exchange for him signing over the patent. I will text you the address in a few minutes. You better send two guys to back me up. You may want to come to witness the signing."

After ten minutes Morgan felt the car pull over and stop. She imagined he was sending the text.

Nearly an hour later of fast, slow and start and stop driving she could hear the crunch of the tires on gravel. She was amazed she hadn't tossed her lunch. After a bit more driving on rough roads, they finally came to a stop. She heard and felt her car door open and he lifted her out of the well in front of the rear seat and then carried her up some stairs and set her down. She heard him jingle some keys and unlock a door. Then he picked her up again and laid her on what she imagined was a couch. Even thru the sheet, she felt the cold from the room.

"Where is your cell phone?"

"What?"

"I need to call your boyfriend to come pick you up blondie."

"It's in my purse, I hope you brought it."

"Yup it's in the back of the car. Be right back."

A few minutes later he was back, even though she could not see him she knew he was glaring at her.

"What's the number to unlock the phone?"

"1 1 1 1"

"That's creative, well lucky me his number is the only one stored in your contacts." She heard him dial. "Mister Powell, this is Leon, remember we met last night. Well, it seems I have your blond girlfriend here and if you want her back in one piece you better come pen in hand. Drive to Poolesville, Maryland and call this phone when you get there. Come alone, and don't involve the police if you want a good outcome." He hung up the phone and turned on the heat in the cabin.

Chapter 47   December 2015, Washington, DC

Meredith Drake had advised the President that the operation would begin tomorrow afternoon. Being global it would roll out across the planet and take nearly a full 24 hours from start to finish.

Lester Hodges assembled a small operations team and they had spent the last two days carefully planning the global arrests. Since the international portion of the plan required coordination with local or national police it had to be carefully orchestrated. A major concern were leaks that the arrests were coming so on the international front they only advised their partners it was a global conspiracy and provided no details.

When Marsha Cohen took her lunch break, she met with the team preparing to raid the Paragon office in New York. They attached a throat microphone under the neck of her beige turtleneck and a tiny wireless earpiece. She added her standard-issue shoulder holster, handcuffs and had her FBI badge tucked in an inside pocket of her navy-blue jacket.

Back at her desk, she worked on her assigned project for the afternoon. At 2:57 she whispered into her microphone, "I am a go for Peterson's office." She stood up and walked back to Todd's office. His admin looked up and said, "Can I help you?"

At the same time, an FBI technician in the basement was cutting the data feed to the Paragon office.

"No, I'm good. I need to see Mr. Peterson about a matter of importance," she opened his door before the admin could react and walked into his office. Pulling her gun and badge at the same time from under her jacket, "Mr. Todd Peterson, I am with the FBI and you are under arrest. Raise your hands and do not touch anything." Peterson stood and stepped back from his desk, leaving his laptop on.

The team of six FBI agents were waiting in the elevator one floor below the office. Hearing her say "Mr. Peterson" they hit the control to go up to the Paragon office lobby. At the same time, another team of six entered the back of the office through the emergency exit. The team leader with a bullhorn announced to the entire office. "We are with the FBI and you will put your hands on your head, interlace your fingers and remain at your desk until further notice." The FBI agents moved swiftly through the office to secure the premises.

At 3 p.m. Eastern time, raids were

simultaneously launched in the Bahamas, Cayman Islands, New York City, Westchester, Houston, Los Angles and Washington, DC. Hodges knew the key was to get Paragon's home office in New York City and more specifically Todd Peterson.

Lester had decided and Charlie and Meredith concurred that they would not arrest the CEOs in one of those classic FBI pre-dawn raids with a SWAT team entering their homes.

In Westchester, New York at 3 p.m., three FBI agents dressed in business suits went to the top floor of Texas Oil and Gas and walked into Harold Watson's executive suite. They pulled their badges out of their suit jackets and told HW's secretary they were from the FBI and asked her to roll back from her desk and not to touch anything. They then opened HW's office door and while one watched the admin the other two confronted HW at his desk. They told him he was under arrest. We don't want to make a scene so please stand and walk with us. We will not handcuff you now. They escorted him down to the basement parking garage to the awaiting FBI SUVs both HW and his admin were placed in separate cars. One agent remained in the office to make sure nothing was touched.

A similar scene occurred at 2 p.m. central time at the American Petroleum office of Bryce Carrington. In Los Angeles, the FBI detained

Reginald Clark while he was holding an early lunch meeting high above the LA skyline in a very swanky restaurant. Jacob Holden, the Chairman of TXO, was arrested in his mansion in Scarsdale that backed on to the beautiful Fenway Golf Course and a small lake.

Raids occurred at the Globex office in the Caymans, Pinnacle Limited in the Bahamas and the Warbucks, Tyrel and Clampett offices all of which were located in various cities in the United States. Paragon subsidiary offices from Abu Dhabi to Jakarta were each raided shortly after opening their office for the day in their local time zones. As in New York, communications lines were cut just prior to each raid so they could not inform other locations of what was happening.

****

Harriet Campos had received the call from Leon Davies that he had secured Powell's girlfriend and received the text from him on the location for the meeting with Powell. She called Ivan Hammond and Karen Young and told them were to meet Leon outside Poolesville. She was starting to assemble the agreement for Powell to execute when the FBI entered the office. She was arrested and her staff was told to remain in their seats. Campos was handcuffed and led out of the building and driven downtown. The notorious DC traffic was full on by

3:15 and they crawled down 66 toward the city. So many people lived in DC yet worked in the suburbs, like Tysons, that traffic was bad in both directions.

Sitting with her hands uncomfortably handcuffed behind her back Campos was thinking I have to give them something to get out of this mess. She decided the best course of action would be to throw Davies under the bus. While he did a good job the arrogant former DC detective was not her favorite. They arrived at the FBI headquarters building and parked underground. She was led to the elevators and then to a small interview room upstairs. Finally, two agents entered the room. They removed the handcuffs and then re-cuffed her to a ring on the table.

"Ms. Campos you are under arrest for a number of charges related to your operation of OI research, a subsidiary of Paragon Research in New York. That office has been closed and Todd Peterson is also under arrest. We suggest that you cooperate fully, and this may assist you in your case."

Campos sat as dignified as possible and looked at the agents, "Happy to help clear up any misunderstandings. I want to let you know that one of my staff, against my orders, has kidnapped a person we were observing and is now holding her as a hostage, at this moment, in Maryland."

One of the agents stood and exited the room. Outside he picked up a telephone and called Lester Hodges office. He advised Suzie of what he had just learned and suggested that Mr. Hodges might want to take a minute to meet with Campos.

A few minutes later Lester entered the interview room, "Ms. Campos, my name is Lester Hodges and I am the Deputy Director of the FBI. I understand you are alleging that one of your staff is holding a person as a hostage. Is that correct?"

"Yes sir, it is," Campos said looking up at him standing in the doorway. "I am happy to provide the details that I have so you may resolve this situation. If you would give me my phone, I can provide you with the address where I believe he is holding her."

One of the agents removed her phone from her purse, "Give me the PIN code and I will check your messages."

"1955"

With the phone unlocked he went to her messages and saw the directions.

In Poolesville take Budd Rd South to the end, continue south on Hughes Rd to the end turn left on Hunting Quarter Rd to the first driveway on right – south to the end by the river – my cabin

Lester said, "Thank you, any other details you

would like to add."

"Yes, his name is Leon Davies and two other people will be joining him. Ivan Hammond and Karen Young."

Lester left the room and went back to his office and contacted the elite Hostage Rescue Team (HRT) stationed at Quantico, Virginia. The team of six on standby was suited up and assembled in the ready room within the hour they were briefed and the decision was made that they would fly to Maryland in the Bell 407 chopper that was standing by on the adjacent flight deck. The 407 was substantially quieter than the Bell 412, which was similar to the twin-rotor design of the Huey helicopter. The straight-line distance was only 45 miles and they should be on the ground in about an hour.

Chapter 48   December 2015, Alexandria, VA

Sandy was shocked. He couldn't believe they had captured Morgan. It was his worst nightmare, he just stared at the phone.

"What's up, mate?"

"Leon, the guy with the Escalade has taken Morgan hostage."

"Shit! Do we know where?"

"He said to go to Poolesville, Maryland and call him when I get there. Of course, he also said not to call the police and come alone."

"Well that's not going to happen, we better get on our gear and roll. I'll change and be ready to go in five minutes."

"Agreed," Sandy rushed upstairs and changed into black tactical pants and a black turtleneck. His gear was in the back of the SUV he would have to assemble it when they got there. In a few minutes, he was back downstairs as Jackson was also ready to go. "Jackson why don't you jump in the back seat, all the gear is in the back. You can assemble things while I drive." In the back, Jackson turned on the GPS app and they could see that the Escalade was parked a few miles south of Poolesville.

They were a bit ahead of rush hour and rolled up Route 1 to 66 and headed west to the connector to the Dulles Toll Road and jumped on 495 north. Traffic was a little backed up crossing the American Legion Bridge. You would think five lanes in each direction should be enough, but this was DC and as far as traffic goes nothing was ever enough. They continued in Maryland on 495 to the split for 270 headed for Rockville/Frederick. Sandy thought it was not that long ago that he and Morgan were headed this same way driving up to Ithaca. On the other hand, it seemed a lifetime ago.

In Rockville, they exited 270 and took Route 28 west towards Poolesville. What twenty years ago had been mostly rural had filled in with developments on both sides of 28. Forty-five minutes later they were in the middle of Poolesville. Sandy pulled off on a side street near a vacant park and jumped out of the SUV.

Opening the rear door, he removed his coat and put on a black tactical vest. Then he began loading his pants and vest with needed supplies. He put one gun in his holster on his right hip and put the other 9mm Glock in his pants behind his vest. Jackson told him both were loaded with a shell in the chamber, safety on. Next, he strapped a Beretta Nano to his right ankle. Spare clips for the Glock were in his vest pockets. He thought, I hope I don't have to use these, but better safe than sorry. Jackson was also loaded up.

They both had tiny earpieces and throat mikes which they tested to make sure they were working. It was dusk but not yet dark. As they stood outside the Tahoe. Jackson remarked what Sandy was also thinking, "We need to wait a little bit till it's dark to make the call. We will need the element of surprise with this guy and who knows how many others."

"Totally agree, let's give it half an hour. How about we roll over to the McDonalds and grab a coffee in the drive-thru while we wait?" Jackson opened the app on his phone, "looks like Ms. Young is also at the same location as Davies. We may have more company we can't see. I am sure glad you have those night vision googles. We'll likely need them."

Half an hour later parked in the McDonalds lot Sandy called Davies. "Hi, I'm in Poolesville, what's next."

"Took you long enough. Ok, I am going to send you a text with directions. You should be here in 10 or 15 minutes. Drive safe there are lots of deer."

Sandy's phone pinged indicating he had the text. He looked at the instructions, "Ok got the text I'll be there in a few."

****

The FBI helicopter flew northwest to Leesburg, Virginia and crossed the Potomac near White's Ferry and then flew south low over the Potomac. With the wind out of the east, it helped mask the noise of the chopper. The FBI Hostage Rescue Team landed about a mile north from the location based on the directions in the text. Fortunately, this area near the Potomac river had a number of sod farms so they had a flat clear open landing area.

All the agents were equipped with night vision goggles, wireless earpieces, and microphones. Each agent carried a Heckler & Koch HK416 – 5.56mm carbine and wore a Glock 22. The FBI team jumped out of the helicopter while the rotors began to spin down and began jogging in the direction of the camp.

****

About a mile before the location of the cars, Sandy turned off the headlights. They had checked at the McDonalds to make certain the inside lights would not come on when they opened the doors. Half a mile before the location of the cars, Sandy stopped, and Jackson jumped out and started jogging down the road. Sandy gave him a five-minute head start and then turned on the lights and rolled slowly down the road towards the cabin. As he neared the cabin, he could hear Jackson say, "hold up mate I got one on the porch, give me a moment to take him out."

Sandy heard Jackson shout out, "Excuse me, sir, I am a bit lost and twisted my ankle can you help me?" Then he heard a bit of a scuffle over his earpiece. "Sandy he is out of the picture roll on in, I'll go to the rear entrance."

"Roger that." Sandy pulled into the driveway and turned the Tahoe around, so it was pointed out the driveway in case he needed a quick getaway. He walked up the steps and knocked on the door, standing to the side in case someone shot at him through the door. Karen Young opened the door and Sandy walked in with his Glock in his hand pointed down at his side.

He heard Jackson in his ear whisper, "I have you covered through the window in the rear." Sandy nodded his head slightly.

"Ok cowboy put the gun down and no one gets hurt," said Davies.

"Morgan are you ok?"

He heard her through the pillowcase, "Yup just taking a nap."

Sandy looked at Young, "cut her loose."

Karen reached into her large leather handbag and Sandy saw the glint of a pistol handle start to emerge. He shot the pistol from her hand, and it went flying across the room. Out of the corner of his eye, he saw Davies reach inside his jacket, he yelled, "Davies gun!"

Jackson broke the window glass and shot Davies in the thigh. Just as Sandy was drawing a bead on him.

Davies screamed out as his gun emerged and shot wildly into the ceiling, then fell to the floor, writhing in pain. Sandy was about to move forward to kick the gun away when three FBI agents in assault gear burst through the front door behind him.

"Everyone stays put - don't move. Sir, drop the weapon." Sandy dropped the Glock as an agent moved forward and kicked Davies gun away.

Sandy could hear Jackson over his earpiece say, "Yes Sir, my hands are empty and in the air."

Sandy said to the agent behind him, "Sir I have another weapon in my back under my vest and another in my right ankle holster. My name is Sandy Powell, my girlfriend is the one who was kidnapped, she is on the couch. My friend Jackson Hawkins is outside in the rear."

"Turn around please." Spenser Graves was a former SEAL that went through training with Sandy, "Powell, you, old water dog should have known you would wash up in more trouble!"

"Spenser! Figures you would become an FBI agent. I haven't seen you in years. Let's get this buttoned up."

The military training never far away and recognizing Powell's senior rank, Spencer said, "Yes Commander, ok, we will sort all this out in a minute." The agent then said over his throat mike, "secure the outside and I need a medic and transport for two injured civilians inside." Davies was very pale, breathing rapidly but not a lot of blood loss. One of the agents was wrapping gauze around Davies' leg. Sandy had seen much worse from a gunshot.

The other agent got a kitchen towel for the scratch on Young's wrist from having the pistol shot away.

Spencer pulled a multitool from a pocket in his pants, removed the pillowcase from Morgan's head and cut the zip ties on her wrists and ankles. Spencer then removed the guns from Sandy and placed them on the floor.

Morgan flexed her hands and shook her hair loose. Looking wide-eyed at Sandy, "Am I glad to see you." She stood up and walked over and gave him a huge hug and a long lingering kiss.

Graves smiled and said, "Well I think we are

sorting out who's who."

Jackson and Ivan Hammond walked in the front door followed by two agents. "Sir, this is the individual who shot through the rear window just before we arrived. He says his name is Jackson Hawkins. The other individual was tied up adjacent to the house."

"Thank you, that all checks out. Please go outside and put a flare by the driveway we have ambulances on the way for the two injured civilians. You two will stay with them until agents arrive to relieve you at the hospital, they are under arrest." Looking at Powell, "looks like you had things kind of under control when we arrived. Sorry, we weren't here quicker."

"No worries, very glad you are here. Can we go now, or do you need us for a debrief?"

"I want you to drive to headquarters in DC with Agent Cohen and your two companions. You can debrief the team there."

"Thank you again and very happy to help. Hey, you got to make the get together this spring and we should do lunch one of these days to catch up."

Cohen smiled and nodded affirmative. "I'll give you a call...through normal channels if that's alright?"

Sandy grinned, a bit sheepishly. "I'd prefer and I

look forward to that."

It was a little over an hour's drive back to DC and they parked in the garage under the FBI headquarters. Morgan held Sandy's hand all the way and the car was quiet on the way into the city. At headquarters, they were each placed in separate rooms while an agent debriefed them on the events over the past few weeks. After a few hours, they all were back together in a conference room.

"Hello, I am Lester Hodges and I am the Deputy Director of the FBI, please remain seated. I understand you have had a trying few weeks and I want to personally thank you for all that you have been through. I cannot go into details, but rest assured the people that were causing your problems have been arrested. You should be safe now. We will have an agent meet with you tomorrow to pick up your recordings and we will also send a technician out to make certain there are no viruses on your phones and computers. We will reach out to you at some point in the future if we need you to testify to the Grand Jury or in a trial. If you have any concerns whatsoever, please feel free to contact me directly. Have a good evening." He placed his business card on the table in front of Sandy.

Chapter 49   December 2015, Westchester, NY

HW had fully cooperated with the FBI. After the initial set of charges which included conspiracy to commit murder in Nigeria was explained to him, he held nothing back. He was released on bail and returned to his office the next day. He decided he had millions of dollars saved over the years in his retirement plan and was now sick of the corporate world and would retire. He went into his office to pack up his personal things. He emerged from his office with two large FedEx boxes. "Leslie, please send these by bonded courier to Sandy Powell. His address is on the Post-it." A short time later Watson walked out of Texas Oil, a company he had been with for decades, and walked into retirement. At least that was the plan.

****

Sandy, Morgan, Jackson, and Vicky were all back together at Morgan's condo in Alexandria. Copper was excited that everyone was back and circled around and around Morgan's legs. Since it was late, they ordered Chinese and told stories about the crazy day.

Jackson thought for a moment, "I have a great idea. Why don't you all come to Sydney for New

Year's Eve? It is an awesome time, middle of summer so you won't need anything but shorts, a top, swimmers and thongs. Come for a week or a fortnight and I can show you about."

Sandy's eyes rolled "Thong!! Sorry buddy but the girls may wear a thong, but it won't work for me."

"Ahhh, what do you call them, oh yea flip flops, mate."

"Gotcha, ok great idea! Morgan, Vicky can you get away?"

"My white knight, this is really simple. I am not leaving your side. I am stuck to you like glue and I think we should go," Morgan replied.

"I will check with my boss in the morning, but I'm all in."

Sandy grinned, "No worries, I will cover the cost of the trip for all of us."

As they were getting ready to turn in, Vicky whispered in Jackson's ear and the next thing Sandy and Morgan noticed, Vicky was leading Jackson upstairs. Morgan's eyes twinkled, "surprised they lasted this long, bet they sleep in tomorrow."

Then she turned and looked up into Sandy's eyes, "Off to bed Sir Knight, I need some personal comforting..."

Sandy just grinned and let Morgan take the lead up the stairs.

A note about the author

Drew Thorn is the penname for Andrew Tarbox.

Andrew was proud and very lucky to grow up on a dairy farm in upstate New York a few miles from Vermont. The hard work and play helped shape his character. He attended Tamarac High School which was small enough that everyone knew each other and remain close even to this day. He went on to join Alpha Gamma Rho and graduate from Cornell University.

His professional life is marked by transformation. He began in the farm equipment business and migrated in the early 80s to the nascent personal computer industry. Next, he learned about smart cards, a credit card-sized plastic card with a computer chip to store information.

He transitioned this expertise to manage the global migration from magnetic stripe to smart card technology at MasterCard.

In the late nineties, he left MasterCard to start a dot com company in Palo Alto to use smart cards for frequent shopper programs. The ubiquity of smart cards led him to join Booz Allen Hamilton where he assisted multiple government agencies in the US and Australia to utilize smart cards.

He has been fortunate to have traveled across the globe visiting 6 continents and having lived in multiple cities in the US and Australia.

Transitioning again, today he is loving the freedom of writing novels where the only limits are what you can imagine. Today he lives with his family in Ozarks of Missouri enjoying the calm of Midwest life.

Made in the USA
Middletown, DE
08 September 2020

18643407R00213